"Brianna, you and I . . ." Caesare searched for the right words. "We haven't much in common. Nothing permanent can ever come of this feeling between us. But there's no denying it's there. I knew it the moment we met. You did, too."

She nodded.

"I want you, Brianna. I want to make love to you. But with no promises."

"So we would have just an affair."

"Just an affair," he repeated as he pulled her slowly into his arms.

Against her will she melted against him, warmth and hunger growing, spreading as he kissed her.

"I can't, Caesare, I can't."

BRITTANY YOUNG

decided to write romances when she found herself living one. She describes her courtship as being as dramatic as our love stories, and her husband as the quintessential Silhouette hero. Her interests include drawing, music, photography, and history. An accomplished linquist, she can say "I love you" in perfectly accented French, Spanish, and Greek.

Dear Reader:

In the three years since Silhouette Books began publishing with Silhouette Romances we've seen many new developments: American settings and heroines, stronger, more independent characters, longer, more sensual stories and some exciting new authors who have appeared on the scene.

It was during this first year that many of you discovered new favorites including Dixie Browning, Nora Roberts, Brooke Hastings and many others. These authors have continued to write new and exciting stories, whether they are for Silhouette Romance, Silhouette Special Edition, Silhouette Desire or for Silhouette Intimate Moments.

Now you have an opportunity to buy those first books by some of your favorite authors. This month, be sure to look for the "Springtime is Romance time" display wherever you buy books.

Karen Solem
Editor-in-Chief
Silhouette Books

BRITTANY YOUNG
A Separate Happiness

Silhouette Romance

Published by Silhouette Books New York

America's Publisher of Contemporary Romance

Silhouette Books by Brittany Young

Arranged Marriage (ROM #165)
A Separate Happiness (ROM #297)

SILHOUETTE BOOKS, a Division of Simon & Schuster, In
1230 Avenue of the Americas, New York, N.Y. 10020

ISBN: 0-671-57297-0

First Silhouette Books printing May, 1984

10 9 8 7 6 5 4 3 2 1

Map by Ray Lundgren

America's Publisher of Contemporary Romance

Printed in the U.S.A.

To My Husband,
My inspiration.

A Separate Happiness

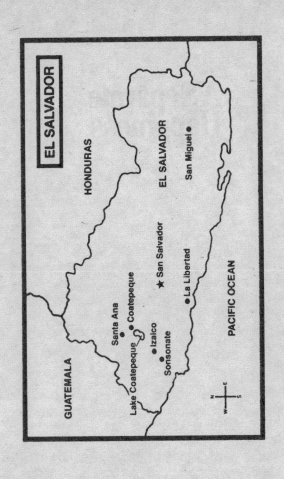

Chapter One

There was nothing behind his fanatical murderous eyes but a calculating cold-bloodedness that froze the writer where she sat. On the inside, she was quaking, but the hand that pushed her raven hair away from her face was as steady as a surgeon's. Showing the man fear would only amuse him and could be fatal—and no magazine interview was worth her life.

The Middle Eastern terrorist boldly assessed her physical charms, but she knew he despised her. She was merely a necessary means to an end. A way of getting his message across to millions of readers the world over.

A ringing telephone somewhere in the enormous *Newsview* magazine office interrupted Brianna Kendall's concentration as she put the finishing touches on her article. It was early Sunday morning. She was at her desk, getting her article ready for publication before heading out to her brother David's home for the Fourth of July weekend—and a party. She hadn't seen David, his wife, Annie, or their eight-year-old daughter, Jenny, in months, and she had missed them. Her work had kept her traveling a lot lately.

The Kendall family had been a close-knit one before her parents' deaths ten years earlier, when she was only fourteen. She was still close to her brother. He had always been a point of stability in her hectic world. But they led such different lives that it was difficult sometimes to keep in touch. He was older than she. A very gentle man. He looked so much like their father. Her lovely eyes filled with tears, expressing a pain she still felt after all those years.

Most people assumed that her parents died together, but the tragic fact was that her father had died in an automobile accident and her poor mother hadn't been able to cope with losing him. Their love for one another had been so overwhelming that she died within two months of her husband.

That kind of love terrified Brianna. It meant losing control of your own life, and after what had happened to her mother, it was something she was determined never to do. The only person in the world she could count on was herself. She had her career, and that was everything to her. It was all she needed.

She wiped at her eyes with the back of her hand, cleared her throat and tried to get her mind back on her work.

It took almost half an hour more to proofread the article, but when she finished, she flicked her fingernail against the pages in quiet satisfaction. It was an interview with a Middle Eastern terrorist, and it was good. She had found the man horrible, and it was obvious in her presentation. Some people didn't approve of journalists weaving their personal opinions into their work, but Brianna disagreed. And her editor supported her. But then Max James always supported her, no matter what. Her opinions were labeled as just that—her opinions. But she had gone to the trouble of tracking the man down, at no little risk to herself. She sat across a table from him and looked into his crazed eyes, and what she found there was chilling. Her readers would never have the luxury of that kind of confrontation, and she gave them a blow-by-blow description of how she had felt and what she had thought.

She paper clipped the pages together and put them in the out box on her desk for the messenger to take to Max. Then she pulled her purse out of the bottom desk drawer and got to her feet. Just then, a man, rather on the short side next to her slim five feet seven inches, came running in, a panicked look on his angular face. "Are you a writer here or one of the cleaning women?"

Her violet eyes sparkled with laughter at the outrageous question. "Today a writer, tomorrow a cleaning woman. Fate is ever fickle," she philosophized.

The man put his hand theatrically over his heart and looked heavenward. "A writer. Great!" He grabbed her hand and dragged her along behind him until she dug her heels into the carpeting, frightened and a little angered by his manner, nearly giving him whiplash with her sudden resistance.

"Just a minute!" She pulled her hand out of his and flexed her squashed fingers, frowning at him. "What do you think you're doing?"

"Saving my job."

"By breaking my hand. You'll have to explain that one."

He scratched his balding head agitatedly. "All right. All right. I work in the television studios in the south wing of this monstrosity of a building on a program called 'Talking Facts.' Ever heard of it?"

"Everyone has. I watch it every Sunday morning that I can."

"Great. Then you know the format. We have three guest panelists and a moderator, all with respectable credentials in journalism, questioning a guest who is currently in the news."

Her frown relaxed. "I know all that. But what does it have to do with me?"

"Everything! One of our guest panelists is ill, and I can't find his backup anywhere. And we only have"—he looked at his watch, and his light brown eyes grew round with horror—"three minutes before the cameras turn on!"

"Ah," she nodded, understanding perfectly now. "And you need another guest panelist, and I'm the only journalist around."

He tilted his head pleadingly to one side. "So, what do you say?"

"Well," she answered wryly, "I'd prefer being wanted because of my writing credentials rather than because I'm *not* a cleaning lady, but I'll do it, anyway." She looked down at her slim-fitting jeans and 1800s-style blouse with the slightly puffed shoulders and sleeves. "I don't think I'm dressed quite right for your program, though."

He looked her up and down appreciatively. "Lady, with a face like yours, no one is going to notice what you have on. Besides" —he lightened the compliment, obviously embarrassed—"you'll be behind a table. No one will see you from the waist down. And the blouse is fine."

Grabbing her hand, he dragged her along behind him—this time encountering no resistance. "Have you ever been on television before?"

"Once," she said, panting. "On the 'Skipper Ryle Show' when I was five. Does that count?"

He laughed. "Hell, you're probably a household name by now!"

She grinned, too. "Who's your guest?"

"A writer from El Salvador by the name of Caesare de Alvarado. Ever heard of him?"

"Of course. I've even read some of his books. They helped me with background for my articles on the political tensions in his country." She grew thoughtful—or as thoughtful as it was possible to be while running at breakneck speed. "Isn't he also a large landowner there?"

"Yes. He's a very, very rich man." Her excitable friend led her through a steel door on which there was a red light flashing and into a cavernous room with thick black electrical cords running every which way along the highly waxed floor. Toward the back of the room was the news-show set, surrounded by hot bright lights and cameras. Four people were seated on it. A makeup woman came running out, but the little man waved her away. "No time!" He unceremoniously pushed Brianna into the vacant seat and attached a small microphone to her blouse. As he leaned over her, his face inches from hers, Brianna asked curiously, "What exactly is your job title, anyway?"

"Director."

Surprise showed on her lovely face. "Aren't you a bit hysterical for a director?"

"Have you ever met one before?"

"You're my first."

"Well, honey, we're all hysterical, believe me. Particularly when people don't show up." He took a pen and a piece of paper from his shirt pocket. "What's your name?"

"Brianna Kendall."

He looked at her in surprise. "*You* are Brianna Kendall? I thought she was older."

"*She* is getting older by the second."

He grinned appreciatively. "You're a nice girl."

"Nice woman," she corrected.

With a short laugh, he handed the paper with her name on it to the moderator. She found all the activity distracting and exciting, and it was a moment before she noticed the dark man sitting directly across from her. But when she did, she couldn't take her eyes off him. His chiseled features were expressionless except for a touch of cynicism around his tawny eyes and well-shaped mouth.

He moved his head slightly, and his eyes met and held hers. She probably should have looked away. That was the normal

American reaction when one got caught staring. But she didn't want to. She wanted to see beyond those tawny eyes and get a glimpse of the inner man.

When the director left and the moderator leaned toward her, patting her hand, she jumped. "Don't be nervous," he encouraged. "You'll do just fine. Follow the other panelists' lead in the questioning and don't be afraid to improvise."

She returned his smile and took a deep, much-needed breath. As the program's music began, she again glanced toward the Salvadoran. He was watching the moderator, and she took the opportunity to study him. His rich, dark hair was on the short side and brushed casually away from his face. It had an attractive tendency to curl at the ends. His face was a strong one, his features well defined. She liked the crease in his chin. It was the face of a man, not a boy, in his middle thirties, full of character.

He wore a double-breasted dark blue pin-striped suit on his lean, well-muscled frame with panache, as though he never bothered much about his appearance but just had a natural ability to choose the right things.

The moderator began speaking, and Brianna lowered her head to block the Salvadoran from her sight so she could concentrate on what was being said.

"What exactly has been your role in the

civil war that is tearing your country apart?"

Brianna looked back up at the Salvadoran for his answer.

"I have no direct role, if that is what you are trying to get me to say. But I have tried to bring a measure of understanding to the people of the United States and Europe through my writing and by appearing on programs such as this. And I have successfully raised money for the areas hardest hit by the fighting."

"Are you, *señor*, on the side of the government or the rebels?"

A corner of his shapely mouth lifted, causing the groove in his cheek to deepen. "Personally, I think both sides are going about things in the wrong way. I am on the side of my people."

Other questions followed—and then it was Brianna's turn. She was completely wrapped up in the questioning. "I was called in at the last minute, *señor*," she explained formally, "so I am not as well prepared as my colleagues."

He inclined his dark head and watched her, his expression enigmatic.

"How much land would you say you own in your country?"

The Salvadoran saw instantly where she was heading. "A substantial amount."

"I see." She tapped her pencil on the table top thoughtfully. "Isn't ownership of most of the land by a few wealthy individuals one of the major reasons for the civil war?"

"That, Miss Kendall, is a most simplistic way of putting it, but yes, it is a problem."

"Then shouldn't you be doing something about that injustice rather than asking for funds from countries that could use a little help themselves?"

He leaned back in his chair, resting his elbows on its arms and steepling his fingers under his chin. A spark of humor flashed behind his eyes. "And how do you know I haven't done exactly that?"

"Have you?"

"That"—he paused for a moment—"is none of your business."

She refused to be put off by his dismissing tone. "A few months ago, *señor,* I interviewed El Salvador's ambassador to the United States for *Newsview* magazine."

"I read the interview, Miss Kendall."

"Then you know he doesn't think very highly of your attempts to get the government and the rebels to sit down together to discuss an end to the violence and the need for compromises in government."

A corner of his mouth lifted again. "I knew that *before* reading your interview, Miss Kendall. I also know that the reason he doesn't appreciate my efforts is because he doesn't believe in compromise. It should be obvious to any thinking person that without compromise on both sides, there will never be peace."

Brianna had to admit she was enjoying the confrontation. Caesare (pronounced CHE-sa-ray) de Alvarado was a worthy opponent. She felt a certain respect for him. But she wasn't finished yet. "I also understand, *señor*, that you have great wealth. How much of that do you share with your country's poor?"

"And how much have you given your country's needy lately, Miss Kendall?"

She was caught off guard by the way he turned the question around. "I pay my taxes."

He leaned back casually in his chair, his eyes on her. "As do I, Miss Kendall. As do I."

"And that's all the time we have for this program," the moderator broke in, sounding unutterably relieved that time had run out. "Please join us again next Sunday morning when we will be speaking to someone else in the news."

The music began once more, and everyone, including Brianna, removed their microphones. The director came running out and slapped her heartily on the back. "Splendid job! Splendid! What are you doing next Sunday?"

"Sleeping late," she informed him dryly, feeling the sudden drain of tension from her body as she got to her feet. It was probably a good thing she hadn't had much time to think about being on television.

The director then walked over to where Caesare stood and talked quietly with him for a moment. Brianna started to leave but hesitated. She wasn't sure why. When she turned back, her eyes found those of the Salvadoran over the director's head.

With their eyes still locked, he excused himself and moved to her side. For a long moment, they said nothing, and yet they were communicating. It was the strangest feeling. . . .

"I am going to be in New York for twenty-four more hours," he told her, breaking the silence. His eyes roamed over her lovely face. "I would like to see you." His perfect English was only slightly accented and very attractive.

"I'd like to see you, too." The words came out without any hesitation, surprising her. But only for a second. She meant it. There was something that drew her to him. And not only his physical appearance. He was a man who had no doubts about himself. He knew exactly who he was and what he was about, with apologies to no one. She knew that from reading his books. She knew also that he was wonderfully intelligent but could communicate to the common man without talking down to him.

Yet something deep within warned her away, told her to keep her distance. "But

I'm afraid I'm already committed to going to my brother's home upstate to spend the holiday."

"Cancel it." His tone was matter-of-fact, as though he were used to having women cancel prior engagements to accommodate him.

"No." She was equally matter-of-fact. Breaking commitments wasn't her style.

He inclined his dark head and started to turn away, but she caught his arm, unable to let him go. "He's having a dinner party tonight. I'd like you to come as my guest."

He looked down at the hand on his arm, which Brianna instantly removed, then at her. There was something in his eyes that made her heart beat faster. "I should like that."

"Do you have your own car here, or should we take mine?" she asked, feeling remarkably as she had at the age of fifteen when she'd had her first real date.

"I'll have to take my plane so I can leave for El Salvador first thing tomorrow."

"And I'll need my car to get back to the city after the holiday. I guess I'll meet you there." She got out some paper and began explaining exactly where he was to go from the small airport where he would be landing, but even as she wrote, he reached out and took the pen from between her fingers. She looked up at him quizzically, and his tawny eyes warmed her.

"If I come, I shall find you. Have no doubt."

Her eyes followed him as he walked away from her. It was only when the door closed behind him that she blinked and came back to her surroundings. The others were beginning to drift away, and she followed them out to the underground garage where her sports car was parked. She sat thoughtfully behind the steering wheel for several minutes before finally putting it into gear. She was glad she had invited him to her brother's. For the first time in a long time, she found herself genuinely looking forward to an evening in a man's company.

But first things first. If she was going to get there on time, she'd better get on with her errands.

Chapter Two

Dusk was already beginning to fall when she turned on to the long drive that led to David and Annie's house. The sunroof on her car was open, and the warm air gently lifted her hair as she parked in front of the ivy-covered Tudor manor.

Lightheartedly, she pulled her suitcase and typewriter out of the car, then walked up the front steps and through the open front door, setting her luggage at the foot of the dark wood stairs that led to the second story. "Hello!" she called out. "Anybody home?"

Footsteps sounded over her head, and then Annie's smiling face appeared over the balcony railing. "Brianna, hi! We're up here getting dressed. You'd better do the same. The guests are due any minute."

She gathered her luggage and started up. "I invited someone. Hope you don't mind."

Annie finished clipping on her earring as she watched Brianna. "I don't mind at all. A man, I hope?"

She reached the top of the stairs and gave her sister-in-law an affectionate hug. "Oh, he's a man, all right. There's a chance he won't show up, though. Is David getting dressed?"

Annie was still watching her closely. "Umhm. He's in the bedroom. But don't change the subject. I want to hear more about this mysterious guest." Annie followed Brianna into the bedroom she used when she visited.

"He isn't mysterious. And I just met him myself this morning."

"What's his name?"

Brianna opened her suitcase on the bed and began unpacking. "Caesare de Alvarado."

"Spanish?"

"Salvadoran. He's a writer."

"And single, I take it?"

Brianna glanced over her shoulder. "You know, Annie, I didn't think to ask. I didn't even notice if he was wearing a wedding band. But I don't think he's married." She remembered those eyes. "Something tells me that he's probably been involved with lots of women, but never seriously."

Annie wasn't sure she liked the sound of that. But she didn't have time right then to go into it any further. A small chamber group could be heard tuning their instruments somewhere in the big house. "We're going to talk about this later, you realize," she told an amused Brianna. "But right now I have to make sure the caterers have everything set up."

"And I have to shower and change." Brianna pulled a gaily wrapped box out of her suitcase. "Is Jenny here?"

"She's spending the night at one of her friends' houses. Won't be back until tomorrow."

"I'll just put this on her bed, then. It's a dress."

"She'll be thrilled. She always loves what you pick out for her." Annie hesitated in the doorway. "Is there anything you want to talk about, Bri?"

Brianna shooed her out the door. "Go take care of your party and stop trying to mother me. You're much too young for the job."

After Annie had gone, Brianna stripped the clothes from her body and hopped into the shower, enjoying the biting sting of water. She washed and rinsed her hair, then toweled herself off until her skin was pink and blew dry her hair, brushing it until it fell past her shoulders in a silky raven wave from a side part.

Padding across the thick carpeting to the closet, she pulled out a full-length dress and slid into it. A critical examination in the mirror told her it was perfect. Black silk held up by two slender shoulder straps and fitting snugly to her waist, then flaring into a wide skirt that reached to the floor. She picked up a wide gold belt and clasped it at her slender waist, then put on a long, full petticoat to fluff the skirt out attractively.

All she needed was a little makeup and she was ready to go. Her eyes looked mysterious in the light, the violet very much in evidence against the backdrop of her raven hair and dress. Her skin still retained its honey summer glow even though she had little time for sunbathing. Her lips were attractively tinted in a rose color. She wore just enough lipstick to heighten their color.

She was nervous about that night, but it was a nice kind of nervous. An anticipation of the unknown. She put her hand against her fluttery stomach and took a deep breath. For all she knew, he wouldn't even show up. But oh, she hoped he would.

By the time she was finally ready, the house was filling with guests. As she started down the staircase, holding her dress up gracefully with one hand, her eyes unconsciously searched the male faces below for the Salvadoran, but there was no sign of him. Her heart sank a little.

But at least there was one friendly, familiar face waiting for her at the bottom of the steps—David, his eyes sparkling with pride at the sight of her. "Are you sure we sprang from the same parents?"

An engaging smile touched her mouth as they hugged. "As if you weren't the best-looking man in the room."

He looked down at himself and lifted the lapels of his tuxedo with his thumbs. "I *do* look dashing, don't I?"

"Well, at least you have a healthy ego."

David laughed and held out his arm for her. "Shall we?"

"Let's."

It was strange, really. She and David looked so different. His hair was blond and curly, his eyes a beautiful hazel. They both had the long, dark lashes and eyebrows of their father. And they had identical dimples near the left corners of their mouths. But, all told, Annie looked more like David than she did.

He walked her through the throng of people, introducing her to those she hadn't already met. But there was someone there she *had* already met. His name was Mark Andrews. He worked in her brother's law firm, and she had dated him a long time before for a very short while. He had a terrible temper and uncontrollable fits of jealousy for no reason. He still held a grudge because of her decision not to see him again—a fact she didn't find surprising. That's the kind of man he was. He turned his icy eyes on her, and an involuntary chill ran down her spine. He was one man she didn't trust at all.

A distinguished-looking older man walked up to her and took her hand in his, mercifully blocking Mark from her line of vision. "Miss Kendall, I'm a great admirer of your work. I'd be honored if you'd have this dance with me."

She gratefully stepped into his arms, and he swung her skillfully onto the dance floor. But even as she moved to the music, her eyes traveled over the room, hoping still for some glimpse of that one particular dark head towering above the others. He simply wasn't there.

She danced with several more partners, but her heart wasn't in it anymore. Turning down the next man who asked, she captured a glass of white wine from a passing waiter and stood to one side, watching the people, her thoughts a hundred miles away. . . .

"Brianna?" Annie gently shook her shoulder. "Brianna? What on earth has you so mesmerized?"

She started, coming back to the party

with a bump. "I must have been day-dreaming."

Annie looked at her more closely and raised an expressive brow. "Well, it must have been *some* daydream. You should see the color in your cheeks."

Brianna loved Annie like a sister, but sometimes she found her exasperating. "Are you enjoying your party?"

Annie wasn't going to be put off. "Don't change the subject. Were you thinking of the Salvadoran? Is he here yet?"

"He's not here, and stop prying."

"I wasn't prying," she defended.

The dimple near Brianna's mouth flashed momentarily. "You were prying."

Annie wrinkled her nose. "All right, I admit it. I can't help myself. So where is he?"

"You're incorrigible!"

"That's why I'm so lovable."

Brianna laughed and shook her dark head. "Don't you have to mingle or something."

"Or something. I can take a hint." She started to walk away but turned back. "You realize, of course, that this means I'll be haunting your room tonight after the guests leave, don't you?"

"How long have you had this secret desire to be a detective?"

"Since you developed such mysterious friendships. Talk to you later."

When Annie had gone, Brianna, still smiling to herself, walked out the large living room doors into the back yard. It was a sprawling place, covering several acres. And as usual, Annie's flowers were spectacular. There were several couples outside, walking arm in arm, their heads together, talking. She walked to an old oak tree with a bench beneath it, sat down, and leaned back, crossing her legs as she sipped her wine and watched. No one could really see her, in the shadows as she was. It was relaxing and quiet. Out here she could give her thoughts free rein. She was really disappointed that Caesare hadn't come. More disappointed than she could have imagined. He was interesting, and she had wanted to spend some time with him.

She started when someone sat next to her. "Well, well," drawled a distressingly familiar voice, "if it isn't the oh-so-charming journalist herself."

She stared at him for a tense moment, suddenly feeling horribly isolated under the big tree. "What do you want, Mark?"

"Why, darling, I just wanted to talk to you. To see how life is treating you."

"Life is treating me just fine—which is more than you ever did. Now, if you'll excuse me . . ." She started to rise, but Mark's hand shot out and pulled her back down on the bench.

"What's the hurry, beautiful?"

She looked down at the wrist he was gripping and got angry. "Take your hand off me at once."

He released her. "Whatever you say."

She rubbed her wrist and glared at him. "I don't know how you even have the gall to approach me."

"Is there someone else?"

She was amazed. "I hardly think that's any of your business!"

His narrowed eyes raked over her. "You're wrong, Bri. Couldn't be more so. Everything you do has always concerned me, and it always will. Everything."

She looked around for potential help, but it seemed as though everyone had gone back inside. "I'm getting out of here." She got to her feet again, but he pulled her back down with such violence that her wine-glass crashed to the ground.

"Nobody walks out on me the way you did."

Now she was frightened. She knew how rough Mark could get when he'd been drinking. "Mark," she said evenly, without pleading, "let go of me."

"You made a fool out of me in front of everyone when you stopped seeing me."

"You made a fool out of yourself. Grow up and place the blame where it belongs for a change."

He still had a grip on one of her arms. His other hand grabbed the back of her head and pulled her face toward his.

She tried to push him away with her free hand, but he was a very strong man. "Mark, please," she sobbed. "Let go. Don't do this!"

Suddenly, he was wrenched away from her as though he were nothing more than a rag doll. She looked up and into the furious eyes of Caesare de Alvarado. "Are you all right?"

She nodded dumbly, unable to take her eyes off him. The Salvadoran's eyes remained steadily on her for a long moment, as though making sure she spoke the truth, then turned his attention to a still-shocked Mark. Caesare was gripping the lapels of Mark's tuxedo. "I believe the lady asked you to leave her alone."

Mark wasn't a small man, but he was considerably shorter than Caesare. "This is between Brianna and me."

"You mean it *was* between Brianna and you. Now it is between you and *me*." He released Mark's lapels and smoothed them out. There was something menacing in the simple gesture. "I suggest that you not approach her again."

Mark backed away from him, straightening out his jacket himself. "Or what?"

The Salvadoran eyed him coolly. "I do not make threats, *señor*. But if you come within ten yards of her, your curiosity will be satisfied. Have no doubt about that."

Mark looked from Brianna, still on the bench, to Caesare, hatred sparking from his eyes. "You've both made a big mistake here." He walked back across the lawn to the house with as much dignity as he could muster after such a humiliating confrontation.

Caesare's eyes followed him the entire distance and only turned to Brianna when Mark had disappeared from sight. His eyes lingered on her face. "Your taste in friends leaves something to be desired."

Brianna made a sound that was half a sob of relief and half laughter. But it faded under the intensity of his gaze. She felt flustered. "Thank you. I don't know what would have happened if you hadn't come out when you did."

"I have a pretty good idea. If I were you, I'd avoid him."

Brianna rose abruptly, without her usual grace, and her shoe slipped on some shards of glass, propelling her into his powerful arms. The sheer unoriginality of the situation was mortifying, and she immediately pushed herself away from him to stand on her own, unable to meet his eyes. But her heart was singing.

Caesare's eyes rested on her downcast face. "I almost didn't come."

She raised her eyes to his. "Why did you?"

He reached out and cupped her chin, softly rubbing her smooth cheek with his thumb. It was an exquisitely sensuous gesture, and her eyes slowly closed as a gentle warmth grew within her. "I don't know," he told her quietly.

She opened her eyes, and there passed between them a long, probing look, as though both were seeking answers to unasked questions.

He lowered his head and kissed first one corner of her mouth and then the other. It was the strangest thing—she was very aware of the steady beating of her heart. She could feel it. She could hear it.

His mouth lazily captured hers in gentle discovery. He didn't try to pull her into his arms but held her face in his hands. Their bodies never touched, and yet she trembled.

Slowly, Caesare raised his head and gazed down at her. There was a look of resignation in his eyes—as though something he had feared would happen had. Brianna reached up to touch the crease in his chin, but he caught her hand in his and brought it to his mouth. Then, abruptly, he dropped it and walked away from her.

It was a moment before she realized he was leaving, but when she did, she ran after him, one hand holding her long silk skirt away from the dew-dampened grass. "Caesare, wait! Please!"

He swore softly in Spanish and stopped.

Brianna only just missed crashing head-long into his back. As he turned, she stood there, catching her breath. Her eyes were hurt. "What did I do wrong? Why did you turn away from me like that?"

A small muscle in his jaw worked. What could he say to her? he wondered. That he didn't dare risk getting involved with her because everything in his life was so uncertain? "Because," he finally told her, "my coming here was a mistake."

A confused frown creased her lovely forehead. "Mistake? What do you mean?"

"I don't have to explain myself to you," he informed her with quiet authority. But at the shadow that passed over her face, he found himself relenting and put his hands firmly on her slender shoulders. "Brianna, because of what is happening in my country, I live a life you could never understand. I have become a man you could never understand. I would end up hurting you."

Brianna straightened her shoulders and stepped away from him. "I wasn't aware that you gave one kiss such importance." Her pride had come to the fore, and she was embarrassed at having chased him.

He placed a finger under her chin and raised her face to his. "You and I both know that what just happened between us was a hell of a lot more than just a kiss. And if you don't, you're naive, a fool or both."

"Well, now that I've had my character read so accurately, why don't we just say good-bye?" She pulled her chin from his hand and tilted it defiantly.

He looked at her for a last long moment, then, with an inclination of his dark head, walked away from her and disappeared into the house.

She let out an unsteady breath and wrapped her arms around herself as she stared blankly into the star-filled night. What had happened to her? She barely knew that man, so why should his rejection matter so much?

With a shake of her head, she started back toward the house to face the guests . . . and the ever-inquisitive Annie.

Caesare arrived at the small airport ten miles north of the Kendall house. The pilot came screeching up in another car moments later, looking bewildered. "I left the hotel as soon as I got your call, señor. You wish to leave now?"

"Now."

The little man asked no more questions. He had never seen his boss in such a black mood, and he had been with him for over ten years.

As soon as the small jet had taken off, Caesare unbuckled himself and sat behind a desk toward the rear of the cabin, pen in hand. But he found himself staring out the window at the disappearing lights below, growing smaller as the jet climbed.

"Damn you, Brianna Kendall," he told the night with quiet force. "Why have you come into my life? Why now?"

Chapter Three

Months later, her dark hair wound elegantly into a French twist and her slender figure
encased in a white wool suit, Brianna
walked into the board room of *Newsview*
magazine with several other journalists to
meet with the editors about assignments
and strategy. The editors themselves had
already been in conference for over two
hours, so they knew what they had to tell
the writers.

When everyone was seated, the senior
editor, Max, looked over his notes and addressed the others in the room. "We have a
good idea where we want to send the major-
ity of you. "Finch," he addressed an older
correspondent seated next to Brianna,

"you'll be going to France to cover the elections. Walton, you'll be going to Italy to follow the recent upsurge in Red Brigade activities. In addition, there's a story in El Salvador we want covered. A meeting between the heads of the Central American nations. It's a one-day event, with a formal reception the night before to which the press is invited. We don't really expect to get much news out of this, but someone should be there. I have a standing offer from a Salvadoran acquaintance of mine to house anyone from the magazine at his place and even guide them if they want. I think all of you have heard of him. Caesare de Alvarado."

Brianna stiffened in her seat, but her reaction to the name went unnoticed by the others.

"I've already told him to expect someone." He looked at Brianna. "I'd like you to be the one, Kendall. You've interviewed some of the Central American leaders who've come to the United States, and you seem to have a natural feel for what's going on there. I think seeing the country for yourself will give you an even better perspective on the political situation there, and that will be useful for future pieces. And, of course, you've met de Alvarado."

Brianna was about to reply, but one of the other editors beat her to it. "Max, I was thinking in terms of a man for this assignment. It could be rough. A lot of reporters are getting hurt over there."

"Hey"—Max lifted his hand—"I'm in the business of getting a magazine out with current news. I'm *not* in the business of discrimination. Kendall has been to the Middle East. She got some classic interviews. I think she can produce something better than the usual drivel coming out of Central America, particularly if she has de Alvarado there to steer her in the right direction."

The other editor still didn't like it. "What about Fred Channing?" he asked. "He's done a good job for us over there the last few times."

Max shook his head. "No can do. I have him in Greece right now."

"Can't he be pulled?"

"To cover El Salvador? He'd quit first."

Brianna had had enough of listening to them argue over whether she would or wouldn't go. She wanted to. The assignment was an obvious challenge. If she did an outstanding job, it could boost her career, but there was more to it than that. A lot more. If she were honest with herself, she wanted to see Caesare again. He had been in her thoughts so often and so clearly. Perhaps the assignment was exactly what she needed to exorcise that man from her life for good.

Without further hesitation, she got to her feet. "I volunteer. End of argument, fellows."

Max looked at her in surprise, a wry smile curving his mouth. "Oh, you still here, Kendall?"

"Very funny, Max. When do I leave?"

"Well, since you volunteered—" He made a note on his writing tablet. "How does tomorrow sound? Think you can have your current work cleaned up?"

"No problem."

He quietly contemplated her. He had to admit that he liked her enormously. She was smart and talented and too darned beautiful for her own good. She was also nice and easy to be with. He was the one who had hired her when no one else would, because they couldn't see beyond that face. It was one of the best moves he had ever made. She had brought badly needed fresh ideas to the magazine. She was young enough not to be cynical and yet clever enough not to be taken in by con artists.

He clapped his hands. "Okay, folks. Back to business. Those of you who have your assignments can take off. Clean up any unfinished work this afternoon and pick up your travel arrangements from Mary, as usual. And Kendall," he said gruffly, his eyes on the pad in front of him, "take care of yourself. You know how I hate to break in new writers."

Hours later, she headed home in the blustering winter darkness. Home was a small cottage about an hour out of New York City, set well off any main road on two acres of heavily wooded land. As she pulled up, she was happy to see Annie's station wagon parked in front. That night in particular she felt she could use a friendly face.

Bundled in her heavy winter coat, she grabbed her bag of carry-out Chinese food and ran for the house, head down in the cold wind. Annie was on the couch, a blanket over her legs, reading a book. There was a fire roaring in the fireplace.

Brianna set the food on the hall table and hung her coat in a small closet next to the door. "What are you doing here on a wretched night like this?" she asked, picking up the food and walking to the couch to give her sister-in-law a hug before heading into the kitchen. Annie followed her.

"David's out of town, and Jenny is spending the night at a friend's house again. I got kind of lonely, so I thought I'd come over here for a few hours."

"I'm glad you did. I could use some company myself. And some help packing." She reached into a cupboard for plates. "Do you feel like sharing a little beef kow and won tons with me?"

"Sounds good." Annie got the silverware and napkins. "What do you want to drink?"

"Diet Pepsi, I think." She carried the things into the living room and put them on the coffee table in front of the fire, then sat on the floor. Annie came in with two tall glasses of soda and sat across from her, then served herself some of the food out of the cartons. "Where are you going this time?"

"El Salvador."

Annie's spoon stopped in midair, and she stared at Brianna. "You can't be serious."

"Oh, but I am." Brianna nibbled a crunchy won ton and studied her sister-in-law. "There's going to be a meeting between the heads of the Central American nations."

Annie wrinkled her nose. "There's *always* a meeting going on between them, and they never solve a thing. You have no business going to that place. Do you have any idea what's going on there?"

"A very good idea."

"I don't understand you sometimes, Bri. If I didn't know better, I'd say you were almost glad you're going." She looked at her more closely. "It wouldn't have anything to do with that indescribably attractive Salvadoran you invited to our party last summer, would it?"

A shy smile curved Brianna's mouth. "Why, Annie. What would David think if he heard you say something like that?"

"Listen, sister mine, I may be married, but I'm not dead."

Brianna barely managed to swallow her soda before bursting into laughter. "Oh, Annie"—she sighed as the laughter faded— "I'm glad you came over tonight."

Annie quietly ate as she watched her sister-in-law stare pensively into the fire. "I thought you barely knew him."

Brianna hugged her knees. "Barely? I don't know him at all. And I don't think he's the kind of man anyone ever really gets to know. Perhaps that's what fascinates me about him. If you'd ever read his books or articles, Annie, you'd know that he's a contradiction."

Annie didn't like the sound of that at all. Not at all. But she knew better than to argue.

Brianna was sensitive to her friend's feelings and tried to ease her worries. "Annie, I'm not going there specifically to see him. If I do a good job on this assignment and come up with some stories from an original point of view, it could give me a big career boost. He's a friend of Max's, which shouldn't surprise anyone. They met years ago at some kind of writers' conference and kept in touch. If this Caesare de Alvarado can lead me to some good material, who am I to turn up my nose?"

"Are you sure that's all there is to it?" Annie probed.

An involuntary smile curved Brianna's mouth. "No, it's not all. I'm curious about him. As I said before, he's a contradiction. Contradictions fascinate me."

"Nothing personal, eh?"

"Wellllll, a little personal, perhaps." She still hadn't forgotten that summer night's kiss they'd shared. But the basic reason she was going remained professional. Anything else that came along, she could handle.

Couldn't she?

Chapter Four

The pilot announced that they were flying over El Salvador, preparing to land. It was a marvelously clear day, and as the jet descended, she pressed her face to the window to see below, as though she had never traveled before. It was Caesare's country. And what she saw left her breathless. Countless volcanic peaks reaching into the sky against a lush green background, some of them smoldering in the clear air. Below them, emerald valleys with rivers rushing to the Pacific. And, in some of the more ancient craters, lakes of the most remarkable Prussian blue nestled peacefully.

San Salvador itself was in the center of an enormous valley, gracefully curving between the peaks of two great volcanoes.

The city seemed to hang suspended like a great hammock. She could almost imagine it swinging gently with the occasional earth tremors caused by the volcanoes.

It was still early in the day when she arrived at the Ilopango airport. A khaki-uniformed porter helped her with her luggage, got her passed quickly through Customs, and then took her to the car-rental area.

Once settled behind the wheel of her rented car, she studied a map to find the best route to the Inter-Continental Hotel. She knew exactly what she wanted to do with her free time that day before the reception at the general's home. She wanted to see where Caesare lived. Officially, she wasn't supposed to see him for another two days. But she was there, and she was curious. She didn't even know if he realized *she* was the journalist Max was sending.

It was hard not to admire her surroundings as she drove. Broad-leafed bananas and waving palms fringed the roads—the *busy* roads. The amount of traffic—vehicular and pedestrian—was amazing. She had assumed that the people there would be in a state of siege, venturing out only when necessary. Instead, life seemed to be going on much as usual. After all, San Salvador was to El Salvador what New York was to the United States.

Her hotel was on the outskirts of the city,

located at the very foot of a volcano. She parked in the lot and stepped out of her car, looking straight up at the Volcán de San Salvador. Awesome. Mary had outdone herself this time.

She checked in, and a man in uniform took her and her luggage to her room. As soon as he had gone, she opened the curtains and looked out. She was on the side of the hotel facing the volcano. And she had a balcony! Sliding open a glass door, she stepped out into the springlike air and leaned on the railing, taking deep breaths and reveling in the unexpected beauty she had found here.

She strolled leisurely back to her room, humming softly to herself, feeling light-hearted and happy. Unpacking took only a few minutes; then she showered and slipped into a pair of white jeans and a forest-green V-necked sweater.

Studying the map once more, she found Caesare's home near a place called Sonsonate and planned a roundabout route there so she could sightsee on the way. El Salvador wasn't an evil place. It was captivating and lovely. And it had problems, like all Central American countries.

Taking off in her shiny red car, she headed for the port city of La Libertad. That was where she would pick up the coastal road so she could drive along the ocean.

La Libertad itself was at sea level—over two thousand feet below San Salvador. But the Salvadorans had managed to build a gently sloping road that reached the port city in twenty-four kilometers without once giving her the feeling that around the next curve was the end of the earth. The roads were beautifully paved and maintained.

The little city was nothing more than an open roadstead with a long pier and no particular sights to interest anyone. But just west of town was the Chilama River. She stopped the little car and stretched her legs in the warm ocean air, enjoying the sight of women washing clothes in the narrow rocky river. Small, naked brown children played happily in the rushing water, screaming as children the world over do when they're swimming, while their mothers worked, pounding the brightly colored clothing against the rocks.

Some families appeared to have staked a claim to a particular part of the river. Poles had been erected and a palm-frond roof laid flat on top, giving some of the women a shelter from the hot sun. And all around was brilliant color from the newly washed clothing spread out to dry on flat stones.

Reluctantly, she climbed back into the car. But it was a reluctance short-lived. As she drove along the coastal road, she saw the most unbelievable shining-black beaches, contrasting sharply with the white foaming waves of the Pacific as they forcefully washed up the palm-dotted shore.

At times, the road swept inland to bridge a small river, and she was able to look down on the clusters of huts gathered on the fertile deltas. Little by little, as the country unfolded before her, she began to understand why the people from El Salvador were not merely Salvadoran but fiercely Salvadoran.

As she approached Sonsonate, a knot formed in her stomach, and though she knew it was ridiculous, she couldn't seem to help it. After all, she was only going to see where he lived. Not him.

She saw the turnoff for his home ahead. It was walled in, and there was an enormous gate. She slowed down, trying to see some sign of the house, but it was useless. Feeling ridiculously let down, she picked up speed and rounded a sharp curve. Without any warning whatsoever, an enormous truck of World War II vintage came around from the opposite direction at precisely the same time. Brianna was caught completely off guard. All she had time to do was jerk her steering wheel to the right to avoid a head-on collision, and just like that, the little rental car was quite literally airborne.

She was amazed at the absolute calm that filled her. Her life was over. She knew it unquestionably. And there was nothing she could do but wait.

The front wheels hit the ground first, and the car flipped end over end, finally coming to rest right side up against a tree.

Brianna just sat there, her hands gripping the steering wheel. It was so strange . . . the radio was still playing its cheerful Central American music. She could hear it. She must be all right. The seatbelt had held her in. But it was as though her body were frozen in place.

A furious hammering at her car window brought her out of the daze. A voice asked her in Spanish if she was okay. She could barely think in English at the moment, much less Spanish.

"I'm all right," she finally managed, not recognizing her own shaking voice.

The man struggled with her door, but it was stuck fast. He said something to her in his excited Spanish and took off. For what seemed an eternity, she sat there, waiting, so dazed that it didn't immediately register when someone began prying open the passenger door.

She watched as it was forced open and then found herself looking straight into the tawny eyes of Caesare de Alvarado. Her heart leaped in dismay. "What are you doing here?" she whispered hoarsely.

He looked at her in surprise; then a dark

brow lifted sardonically. He reached across and popped open her seatbelt. "The woman is two thousand miles from home," he said under his breath, "in a car she just managed to smash into a tree not fifty yards from my property, and she wants to know what I am doing here. The truck driver had my guard call me."

"Oh," she mumbled inadequately, feeling like a fool.

"Is anything broken?" He was all business now.

"I don't think so. But my head hurts."

"All right. Brianna, I am going to drag you out of the car by your shoulders. Move as little as possible until I have had a chance to check you over. Do you understand? Simply remain limp."

She obediently did as he asked. Any reserve of energy she had had after the long trip that morning had been sapped by the accident. Remaining limp was about all she could manage.

His strong arm slid under hers and rested across the top of her breasts, giving her a feeling of marvelous security. He pulled her toward him, his other arm pushing against the seat to give him leverage as he dragged her from behind the steering wheel and across the seat until her body was half out of the car. Then one arm went around her back and the other under her knees until he had carefully lowered her to the grass some distance from the car.

He didn't say another word as his hands firmly but gently went over every inch of her aching body. Despite the headache that was raging, she was tinglingly aware of his touch, of his dark head bent low over her, and of the clean scent of his soap.

His eyes seemed purposely to avoid hers as he lifted the raven hair from her forehead. "Miguel!" He shouted.

"I'm coming!" A man she hadn't seen before came crashing down the hill on foot through the long grass and wildly growing shrubbery. He had a first-aid kit in his hand. "I found it!"

Miguel was a Salvadoran, darker than Caesare, and smaller, with a compact build seemingly wired with energy. He handed Caesare the kit and kneeled on the ground beside Brianna. "How is she?"

"She hit her head." Caesare dug through the kit. "There is a cut with some bruising. The seatbelt probably saved her life."

That was too much for Brianna, even in her drained state. "*She* would very much appreciate being talked *to* and not *over*, if that isn't asking too much of you gentlemen."

Miguel chuckled, but Caesare ignored her except for his surprisingly skillful medical ministrations as he cleaned the cut.

"Ouch!" she gasped as he dabbed a stinging liquid onto it before putting on the dressing. Her dark-lashed violet eyes glared at him accusingly.

"It is only what you deserve," he informed her, unyielding as he worked.

"Of all the people who have to come to my rescue, I get a sadist." She winced as he dabbed it one more time for good measure.

Miguel looked curiously from his taut-jawed cousin to the girl on the ground. "I take it the two of you have met?"

Caesare packed things back into the kit. "This is Brianna Kendall," he told him in a monotone.

Miguel's dark brown eyes now sparked with interest as they looked back at the girl, making Brianna wonder exactly what Caesare had said about her, because he had obviously said something.

Caesare helped her into a sitting position, and she got her first look—a distressingly clear look—at the totaled car. A very large sigh escaped her lips. "Now what?"

Miguel looked at it with her. "The truck driver is long gone. He wouldn't have been able to pay for the damage, anyway."

Caesare rose and held out his hand to her. A muscle in his cheek was working, which made her heart sink further. Why on earth hadn't she just waited the two days out instead of traipsing out there like this?

"Can you walk up the hill and to my house?" he asked quietly.

It wasn't easy, but she forced her eyes to meet his. "Yes." She allowed him to help her up but dropped his hand immediately and walked away, following Miguel. She even took several strides away from him before a wave of dizziness started somewhere in her toes and washed completely over her. She stopped and swayed. Her legs buckled.

The Salvadoran had obviously been watching for just such a thing, because he lifted her in his strong arms before she had a chance to hit the ground.

"Miss Independence," he said in gentle resignation as he held her protectively against him and walked.

Feeling near to tears at her predicament, she lowered her head onto his shoulder. "Oh, shut up," she ordered weakly.

She felt rather than saw him smile and drew even nearer to tears when he gave her an encouraging squeeze. "You will be fine, *querida*."

He carried her effortlessly up the steep hill and down a long, winding gravel road to his home. It was an enormous and rambling Spanish-style house set amidst exotic and fragrant flowers and sculpted shrubbery, lovingly tended. Palms lined and shaded the drive.

They went in through a large arched doorway. The two thick carved doors leading into the foyer were both opened wide, allowing the fresh air to flow unhampered through the house.

It was bright and friendly inside. Colorfully patterned Indian rugs covered the rich wooden floors. Woven art mixed with splendid paintings decorated the walls.

A young Salvadoran woman approached. Caesare said something in Spanish, and she rushed down the hall, with Caesare following more slowly behind to a room in one of the wings. That particular wing fronted on a courtyard. They walked down a covered stone terrace lined with arches. The maid opened a door and ran into a room to pull the covers down on a high, antique four-postered bed.

Caesare laid her down and pulled off her sandals, then lifted the sheet to her chin. He straightened and gazed down at her, his remarkable eyes lingering on her lovely face, with its straight nose and dark-lashed violet eyes, now a little glassy from pain. "I will bring you some aspirin," he said suddenly, and was gone.

Brianna watched until he was out of sight, then tightly closed her eyes against the throbbing in her head before opening them again and looking at her surroundings. The windows were enormous and shuttered. The walls were bright white, hung with intricate and bright Indian weavings. The floor was plushly carpeted in white. There was a long dresser and free-standing armoire, both antiques and both beautiful. The room was a large one— nearly as large as her brother's living room. In a corner was a small round table with two chairs covered in brightly patterned red chintz.

The bed she was in wasn't canopied, but there were dark wooden poles running along the top from poster to poster with curtains in the same chintz material as the chairs, caught and tied gracefully at the posters.

She liked it there. For all its elegance, it managed to be friendly.

She heard Caesare at the doorway and watched as he came toward her with aspirin and water. The knot that had been in her stomach earlier returned.

He waited until she had finished taking the medicine before sitting on the edge of the bed. His eyes were unreadable as they met hers. "I take it you're the journalist Max wired me to expect."

She nodded and winced. "Yes."

He rubbed his forehead tiredly and sighed. "It never even occurred to me that he'd send a woman."

She resented his attitude. "You're under no obligation, you know."

"Meaning you'll go back to the States if I turn you away?"

"Meaning I'll find my own way around and get the stories I need."

He raised an expressive brow. "How is your Spanish?"

"I'll hire an interpreter," she informed him.

He shook his dark head. "You would do that, wouldn't you?"

Her gaze was steady, though she wasn't nearly as sure of herself as she appeared.

He rose to his feet and looked down at her. "We will talk in the morning. Right now you need to rest."

"No!" There was a world of distress in her voice as she raised herself on her elbows.

"I beg your pardon?"

"There is a reception in San Salvador tonight. I *must* go. It's one of the reasons I'm here."

"No." He was firm. "That is out of the question. Certainly you are not seriously injured, but you would never make it through an evening like that. You need bed rest for at least a day."

"Caesare." She closed her eyes for a moment against the steady throbbing. "I wasn't asking your permission. I was telling you what I'm going to do tonight. If you'll help me get back to my hotel, I'd appreciate it. If not, I'll get myself back."

A reluctant admiration entered his gaze,

and a corner of his handsome mouth lifted. "Do you ever do anything you are told to do, Brianna Kendall?"

"Of course . . . if I happen to agree."

At that, the Salvadoran tilted his head back and laughed. It was a deep, delicious sound that sent a shiver of pleasure down her spine. His eyes sparkled as they touched her. "Very well, my liberated American. I must attend this evening as well. I will take you."

"That isn't necessary . . ."

His look of impatience silenced her. She was well aware that she had pushed him to the limit of his endurance.

"But thank you," she finished the sentence.

He inclined his head. "Rest now. Then we will drive to your hotel so you can change clothes."

Feeling at peace now that everything was taken care of, she closed her eyes at last and within minutes was in a deep and dreamless sleep.

Caesare returned two hours later, already in his tuxedo. It enhanced rather than hid his powerful build. The front of his crisp white shirt held no hint of the frills most men wore with formal garb. The collar and bow tie were right out of *The Great Gatsby*. It suited his dark, carved looks.

The girl on the bed was still sleeping

soundly. She moved restlessly when he pulled a chair near the bed and sat down, his elbows on the arm rests, his fingers steepled thoughtfully under his chin, watching her. A most delicate and completely adorable snore whispered for a moment in the silence, but was replaced immediately with her light, even breaths. The creases around his eyes deepened at the sound. He knew instinctively that she would be appalled if she knew she snored even a little.

But as he watched her, he grew serious again. What an enigma the woman was. Strong yet vulnerable. Intelligent. And so lovely that she had haunted his thoughts since their first meeting.

There was no way he could turn her loose in El Salvador. Too many things could happen. He would never risk it.

An old woman walking past the room noticed the door ajar and stopped to look in. As she stood there, she saw her grandson lean toward the girl on the bed to look more closely at her, as though by that simple act he would discover all the secrets that made the American different from the other women in his life. At first, she was taken aback. But as she watched, she saw a gentleness in him she had never seen before.

A pleased little smile curved her mouth, and as quietly as she had come, she left.

Reluctantly, Caesare put his hand on

Brianna's shoulder. She opened her eyes and looked sleepily up at him. An enchanting smile touched her mouth, and his heart caught.

Then she realized where she was and that it wasn't a dream. Her smile faded. "You!"

He leaned back in the chair, his aloof mask firmly in place. "Yes. It is nearly eight o'clock. If you wish to attend the reception, we should leave for San Salvador immediately."

She sat up abruptly and groaned when the throbbing began immediately.

"Your head still hurts?"

She flashed him a meaningful look.

"But you are still going." His voice was disapproving.

"It's my job."

The Salvadoran swung her legs over the side of the bed and kneeled in front of her, fastening on her sandals. She found it a disconcertingly intimate gesture. And it was that confusion he saw when he finished and, still kneeling before her, looked into her eyes. "Would the earth stop revolving if you did not cover the story?"

"I told you, it's my job."

He got to his feet and looked down at her. "And that's important to you."

She returned his gaze with a steady one of her own. "It's *every*thing to me."

He reached out with a gentle hand and

traced the line of her jaw. "I see." Then he turned from her and started from the room. "We must go."

She put her hand to her face where his touch had burned a trail and followed him. The only thing she was sure of then was that when she finally left El Salvador, she would be a different woman from the one who arrived there that day.

The drive into San Salvador was a quiet one, with each of them wrapped in their own thoughts. When Caesare pulled in front of her hotel, Brianna got out of the car without his help. She hurried up to her room and did her best to forget that he was in the lobby waiting as she stripped and showered.

She wasn't looking forward to the evening looming ahead but was determined to get through it in as dignified a fashion as possible. During the time she had left in that country, she was going to have to keep an emotional distance from Caesare. It would be difficult, since some of that time would obviously have to be spent with him. But she was sure she could keep things on a business footing.

With a little click of her tongue, she stopped daydreaming and slipped into the teal-blue Grecian gown she had brought for the reception. It was caught with a delicate brooch over one shoulder, leaving the other

shapely shoulder bare, and it flowed gracefully over her slender figure.

She brushed her softly waving hair until
it shone like a raven's wing, letting it fall
from a simple side part to just below her
shoulders. It nicely covered the small bandage on her forehead.

With a final look at herself in the mirror,
she put her hand on the doorknob, ready to
go, but paused and closed her eyes a
moment—whether to gain relief from the
throbbing in her head or to gain strength for
the evening ahead with Caesare, she didn't
know.

But she did feel better for it and with
determination, turned the knob and went
out to the elevator. When she stepped out of
it, Caesare stood with his back to her, about
twenty feet away, reading a newspaper.

Annoyingly, her heartbeat quickened,
and she found herself stopping and staring
at him.

Sensing her presence, he lifted his dark
head and slowly turned. She could feel the
electrical current between them, drawing
them closer and closer to one another
until—

"You are very quick." He stood in front of
her, his eyes warm as they moved over her.
"And very beautiful."

The minute he said the words, she knew
that she had wanted to be beautiful for him

that night. What was happening to her? She felt as though she were losing some of the precious control she had over her life, and it frightened her. Caesare frightened her.

They drove to the general's house. Actually, it was more of a palace than a house, very well lit, with uniformed soldiers in the front. When Caesare pulled up, two of the soldiers met them—one who opened the door for Brianna and one who then parked the car.

She gave an involuntary start when Caesare put his hand warmly in the middle of her back and hoped futilely that he hadn't noticed.

Once through the door, they were greeted by the general and members of his staff. Caesare escorted her to a formal ballroom that held well over two hundred people and a small orchestra playing the kind of music that makes one's body sway to its rhythm. Caesare lifted two glasses of champagne from a passing waiter and handed one to her, raising it in a brief salute, his eyes eloquent, his lips silent.

Still without speaking, he put his hand under her arm and led her toward a circle of men. "The one nearest you," he explained, "is from the United States. The other three are from El Salvador."

She recognized two of them. Caesare introduced everyone and then excused himself and left her alone with them.

She made a heroic effort to keep her mind on what the men were saying, and for the most part she succeeded, but her eyes searched the room for Caesare until they found him dancing with a stunning auburn-haired woman in a rose sheath dress. They moved beautifully, and it was obviously not the first time they had danced together. The longer she watched, the more distracted she became.

Before she fully realized what she was doing, she had walked across the room to the couple and tapped the woman on the shoulder.

She turned and looked at Brianna curiously, an elegantly plucked brow raised in question.

Wondering if she had lost her mind, Brianna said calmly, "I'm cutting in."

The woman's look turned to disbelief. "You are what?" she demanded.

A slow smile curved Caesare's mouth as his tawny eyes rested on his American. "I believe the lady said she was cutting in," he answered for her.

The woman, not knowing what else to do, left the floor. Brianna just stood there, wishing lightning would strike her. What on earth was she doing?

Caesare saved the moment, and her dignity, by stepping in front of her and firmly pulling her into his arms. "Brianna," he said in her ear, "since you were so desperate to dance with me, the least you can do is appear to enjoy it."

Her cheeks flamed. "I'm so sorry." She tried to turn away, but he held her that much tighter. She looked up at him pleadingly. "If I just slink quietly off the dance floor, perhaps no one will notice."

They swayed to the music. "Everyone will notice, *querida*. You are no doubt the first woman they have seen cut in." He put his index finger under her chin and lifted it until she had no choice but to look into his encouraging eyes. "You started this, Brianna Kendall. Now you must play it to its conclusion. Relax."

She wondered if he was referring to the dance or something else, as with an obedient and very tired sigh, she gave in to the temptation of allowing him to pull her closer and rested her head on his solid shoulder. "You must think I'm a complete idiot."

"A completely delightful idiot." He sounded almost affectionate.

"What about that woman?"

"Elena?" He shrugged. "I imagine she finds you somewhat less delightful."

A small laugh escaped. "That wasn't what I meant."

"I know. Now be quiet and dance."

His hand, warm on her back, guided her expertly through the steps, and soon she found herself relaxing and enjoying herself.

Caesare was a marvelous dancer. She felt as though they flowed into each other and danced as one.

When the music ended, he held her in his arms longer than was necessary. What worried Brianna was that she wanted to stay there. Fighting against the desire, she took half a step back, still in the circle of his arms, and looked up at him. His eyes slowly, lingeringly, traveled over her lovely face and came to rest on her softly parted lips. "I want—" he began, only to be interrupted by the general, who appeared suddenly beside them.

He spoke rapidly in Spanish, then turned apologetically to Brianna. "I fear I must take Caesare from you for a time, but I promise to return him shortly."

As she watched him walk out of the ballroom with the general and several other men, her heart still pounded from what she had read in his eyes. Why, she wondered, of all the men in the world from which to choose, did she have to be so attracted to *that* one? Any relationship with him could end only in heartbreak. Caesare himself had told her that.

Determined to push him from her thoughts, she mingled with the other guests, inconspicuously questioning the VIPs. But after a time, the throbbing in her head became worse. The bright lights of the ballroom were taking their toll. She walked through some open doors she had noticed and into a darkened, quiet courtyard.

With a sigh of relief, she lifted her flushed face to the cool breeze and closed her eyes, still as a statue. Only her hair moved as it was gently lifted and her dress as it was molded gracefully to her slender body. The dark man stood in the doorway, watching. Transfixed.

Brianna felt his presence. Slowly, she turned to face him. Caesare moved toward her, his eyes never leaving her face. "She walks in beauty, like the night," he quoted softly, "of cloudless climes and starry skies. And all that's best of dark and bright meet in her aspect and her eyes; Thus mellow'd to that tender light which heaven to gaudy day denies. One shade the more, one ray the less, had half impair'd the nameless grace which waves in every raven tress or softly lightens o'er her face . . ."

He stood before her, his hands cupping her rapt face. "Byron wrote those words for you, whether he knew it or not."

She put her hands over his and unwillingly read the message of desire in his eyes. "Caesare," she said huskily, "no."

"Brianna, you and I," he said, searching for the right words. "We haven't much in common. The worlds we live in are light years apart. Nothing permanent can ever come of this feeling between us. But there's no denying it's there. I knew it from the moment we met. I think you did, too."

She nodded.

"I want you, Brianna. I want to make love to you. But with no commitments. No promises."

"So we would have just an affair."

"Just an affair," he repeated as he pulled her slowly into his arms, kissing first one eyelid and then the other before his mouth finally captured hers. Against her will, she melted against him, her body curving into his. A warmth and hunger grew within her and began to spread as the kiss deepened and her lips parted to receive him. His mouth left hers to trail a moist, warm path down her arched throat to the sensitively pulsating spot at its base. She could feel his desire through the thin material of her dress, and a moan caught in her throat at her own long-suppressed need.

But the sound brought her abruptly back to her senses. "No," she whispered hoarsely, putting her trembling hands on his shoulders and pushing herself away from him until, still in the circle of his arms, she could look into his questioning eyes. "No," she said again. "I can't, Caesare. I can't treat this cavalierly. It's too important a step for me. There has to be more than simply attraction. Do you understand what I'm saying?"

The Salvadoran exhaled a long breath and buried his face in her fragrant hair as he pulled her still-trembling body back into his arms. It seemed to her that he trembled, also. "I know, Brianna, I know," he said, sighing. "I'll take you back to the hotel."

Chapter Five

When Brianna awoke the next morning in her hotel, she rolled onto her back with a tired sigh, her hands behind her head. She had spent the night tossing and turning, unable to get Caesare out of her thoughts or to forget the feelings he aroused. Just remembering the previous evening made her breathing quicken.

Rolling onto her side, she hugged a pillow to her and wrapped her slender legs around it. She had nearly reached a point of no return with him. The passion he aroused was new to her. At twenty-four, she was still a virgin. Not by any conscious choice. It was just the way things had worked out. All of her life she had avoided any real emotional involvement. She had had her share of dates, and certainly she wasn't a complete innocent.

Thank heavens she had stopped things when she had the previous night. She couldn't have picked a worse man for her first true involvement. No matter what feelings he aroused in her, she must keep in the forefront of her mind that he was all wrong for her. The attraction then was purely physical, and she mustn't let it go any further. She remembered her mother, and her determination to cool things between them increased. She would not spend the rest of her life pining for someone she couldn't have. She wouldn't get involved in the first place.

During the long night she had considered simply attending the meeting that morning and going back to New York without taking Caesare up on his offer to Max. But that would be unprofessional. Tempting, of course, but unprofessional.

Her path was clear, and as long as she didn't stray from it, she would be all right. She would treat Caesare with courtesy, use the contacts he provided for her stories, and leave.

With renewed determination, she dressed in a full dirndl skirt patterned with black, red, white and turquoise, and a white sleeveless blouse of cotton voile with spills of ruffles running vertically down the front. Under the skirt she put on a full white slip and around her waist a red belt. It wasn't the most businesslike outfit she had, but she knew from past experience that members of the press were rarely treated like professionals. Most of her time would be spent standing and waiting and chasing people for quotable quotes, and she intended to be comfortable. To that end, she fastened on some low-heeled white canvas shoes.

Caesare kept creeping into her thoughts, but she resolutely pushed him away and concentrated on what lay ahead of her that day.

She checked her map for the location of the National Palace and decided it was well within walking distance. Grabbing her purse and note pad, she headed out. It was a glorious day—warm, bright and cloudless.

Crowds were already gathering at the green-colored palace to catch a glimpse of the dignitaries. A small lean-to was set up near the street with the most delicious aromas wafting from beneath the palm-thatched roof.

She made her way through the people and looked inside. Two women were there, cooking a native Salvadoran pastry called *quesadilla*, a sweetish bread made from rice flour, eggs, butter, cheese and milk and cooked as a flat, thin square. She bought two of them along with a cup of cocoa and ate them right then and there.

She didn't know if *quesadilla* was truly the most delicious thing she had ever tasted or if hunger made it so, but she was determined to learn how to cook it before she left the country.

The busy women smiled and nodded as they watched her, pleased to see someone so obviously enjoying their cooking.

After a quick lick of her fingers, Brianna took the press card out of her purse and attached it to her blouse, then made her way through the throng of people to the steps of the palace. Security men were very much in evidence, checking identification. The media people were higher on the steps in a cordoned-off area, and Brianna made her way up to join them. It was amazing how well behaved the crowd was, considering its size. Men on horseback kept them off the street itself.

Occasionally, the crowd would surge onto the steps and push those already there off balance and into the ropes. But the Salvadoran crowd control was effective as the uniformed men guided the people back down.

It wasn't long before cars began pulling up and recognizable people emerged. Nearly all of them stopped for the photographers and for a few questions from the journalists. Brianna took down all the information she got and managed to fire a few questions of her own. But no one was making any startling revelations. No one really wanted to talk seriously about the issues at that point.

Another limousine pulled up. She didn't pay much attention at first, because she was busy writing, but when the crowd began noisily applauding, her pen came to a halt, and her eyes found Caesare de Alvarado. He was devastating in his light suit. For the first time she realized the depth of his popularity with his people.

Miguel and a man whom she didn't recognize got out of the car. Caesare seemed preoccupied as his eyes searched the crowd, but when he didn't find what he was looking for, he started up the steps. Brianna's heart started that steady pounding it seemed to do only when he was near. Unconsciously she stepped back so that he wouldn't see her.

A hand caught her arm and she looked up, startled, into the unfriendly brown eyes of a soldier. He said something to her in Spanish, and all she could do was look at him blankly, until it occurred to her that he wanted to see her press I.D. She reached down to unclip it from her blouse—but it was gone! Her heart sank as her eyes began frantically searching the ground for the fallen card. It wasn't anywhere.

He said something else to her, and again she didn't understand. When he grabbed her purse, she grabbed it back, glaring at him as she did.

Without thinking she dropped to her knees to look for the card among the dozens of pairs of shoes. It could have been under any one of them. But the guard, not understanding her abrupt action, yanked her to her feet and twisted her arm behind her back.

Brianna was operating purely on an instinct for survival. The man was shouting at her in Spanish as he jerked her arm higher behind her back. The people who had been pressed against them now pulled back, not wanting to become involved, giving the struggling pair a clear area.

She tried one of her self-defense techniques on him, jabbing his ribs with the elbow of her free arm, but he just jerked her other arm higher, bringing stinging tears of pain to her eyes. It couldn't be happening! Being put in jail here was tantamount to death.

Just when she thought it was all over, Caesare was there. He said something quietly and effectively to the soldier, who then inclined his head crisply and released her into the Salvadoran's arms. When he walked off, Caesare shook his dark head and looked down at her as she straightened away from him and rubbed her aching arm. He would have to be the one to rescue her—again. She lifted her hands in frustrated resignation. "Don't say it," she told him.

"You mean about your wanting to head into the countryside alone with only an interpreter?"

"That's the one."

He inclined his head. "As you wish." His point had already been effectively made.

Then, to her surprise, he turned and disappeared into the palace. Brianna's eyes followed him. His attitude toward her was different that day. More distant. Cooler. Perhaps she wasn't the only one who had soul searched the previous night.

What a contradiction! She found herself resenting the change in him, knowing full well how unreasonable she was being. It was one thing if *she* decided to act aloof. It was quite another when *he* did.

And what was he doing at that conference? Why on earth hadn't she thought to ask him? He was a writer, not a head of state, or even a politician.

Another limousine pulled up. She pushed him from her mind as she got back to work. But concentration wasn't as easy for her as it usually was. Once again, Caesare was interfering.

The day was every bit as long and tiring as she had known it would be. During the walk back to the hotel, all she could think about was the bubble bath she was going to soak in while she organized in her mind the story she would send Max the next day.

When she entered the hotel, she stopped dead just inside the doors. Caesare stood there, leaning against the front desk, watching her.

Consciously straightening her shoulders, she moved toward him. "I wasn't expecting you."

His handsome face was expressionless. "I told Max I would lead whomever he sent to some worthwhile stories, and I shall keep my word."

"I haven't packed—"

"I took the liberty of having one of the maids do it for you. Your things are already on board my helicopter."

"You took the liberty?" she asked in disbelief. "I prefer doing my own packing, thank you. Some of my papers are very personal."

"And in English, presumably. I don't think you have anything to worry about." He moved away from the desk. "We should be going."

He took her arm and turned her toward the doors. She went along with him, not talking, out to a wide lawn where a helicopter waited, its blade slowly slicing the air.

Annoyance was forgotten in her nervousness at the prospect of her first helicopter ride. But that, too, disappeared as the craft slowly lifted itself straight off the ground and gracefully swooped by the Volcán de San Salvador.

It was a wonderful, exhilarating trip. She only wished it wasn't so dark so she could see something other than twinkling lights below.

The Salvadoran watched her expressive face intently. Talking was impossible because of the loud noise of the helicopter, but then there wasn't much to say, anyway.

The flight was a short one. Only half an hour. Caesare stepped out first, then put his hands at Brianna's slender waist and lifted her to the ground. His touch burned her, and she stepped back from him. He looked into her eyes, but his hands immediately fell to his sides. Wordlessly, he turned and headed for the house. She followed, her emotions in a jumble. Since childhood, she had carefully mapped out her future. She was a very organized person, but lately she seemed to have lost control of the course of her life. It concerned her. Caesare was dangerous to her peace of mind.

A maid met them inside the open front doors. She and the Salvadoran spoke briefly in Spanish; then he spoke with Brianna over his shoulder. "Come. I wish you to meet my grandmother. She is in the salon."

She followed him down the same hall through which he had carried her only the day before, but this time he turned into one of the rooms.

It was a wonderful salon, large and un-cluttered, with a conversation pit half circled by a couch covered in natural colored burlap. A round dark marble coffee table nestled comfortably in the half circle, and other brightly patterned chairs were strategically placed. Several paned doors were set in one wall and were opened to the lighted courtyard beyond.

There were a few people in the room, but her eyes went immediately to a smiling old woman who rose at Brianna's approach and held out her hand. Her lovely white hair was pulled into a casual knot on top of her head as though she had more important things to do than wrestle with it. Her eyes were an amazing blue, with a piercing intelligence that seemed to be concentrated on her newly arrived guest. She took Brianna's hand in both of hers and held it. "So you're Brianna Kendall. Caesare told me to expect you."

Brianna curiously tilted her head to one side. The woman had absolutely no Spanish accent whatsoever.

She guessed what the girl was thinking.

"I see my grandson didn't warn you. I'm as American as you are."

She glanced at Caesare, who was unsmilingly watching his grandmother. "No. He didn't mention it . . . but then we haven't really had many conversations, Señora de Alvarado."

"Oh, please, call me Kate. Everyone does."

She turned to the others in the room, and they rose. "I think you met Miguel yesterday."

He walked over to her, his dark eyes smiling in a friendly fashion. "We did. And again today. How are you feeling?"

She liked him, and it showed in her face. "Much better, thank you. My head just aches a little."

"And this"—Kate motioned to the man Brianna had seen that afternoon getting out of the car with Caesare and Miguel at the palace—"is Antonio Rojas, a neighbor."

He bent low over her hand, a half smile curving his too handsome mouth. It didn't take much for her to figure out that he was very, very impressed with himself and assumed that everyone else was as well. When he kissed her hand, it was all she could do not to draw it back. He was far too slick for her taste.

Antonio sensed her aloofness and took it as a personal challenge. She saw it in his eyes and unconsciously moved away from him and toward Caesare.

The old woman watched as her grandson's eyes rested on the back of the American's dark head with an unfathomable expression in their depths. She would have given a lot to know what was going on in that intricate mind of his.

But the moment was lost when, with a tautening of the muscle in his cheek, he strode away from her to an elegant bar.

Then it was Brianna's turn to watch as he poured himself a drink and looked toward her, a question in his eyes. "White wine, please."

He inclined his head and brought the wine to her. She sat down on the couch and tried to carry on a conversation with the others, but she was distracted by Caesare, who had taken his drink to one of the open doors and now stood thoughtfully staring outside, one broad shoulder leaning against the frame.

Kate gently touched her arm. "Brianna? I was asking how you got into journalism. Working for a magazine like *Newsview* at your age is quite an achievement."

She smiled apologetically. "I'm sorry. I wasn't listening." She sipped her wine thoughtfully as she remembered her childhood. "I knew I loved writing at a very early age. I don't think it ever occurred to me *not* to be a writer. But I think the reason I chose journalism over fiction was because of the people my parents introduced me to over the years. They used to invite their friends to our house for long, leisurely weekends, and it was always those involved in writing the news and interviewing newsmakers who were the most interesting.

"I imagine when you get married and have a family it will make things difficult."

Brianna's dimple appeared near her mouth. "I don't think the career I've mapped out for myself is compatible with a husband and family. I'm quite content with my life the way it is."

Kate raised a skeptical brow. "You sound as though you've been reading the *American Feminist Manifesto*."

At that, laughter bubbled in Brianna. It was a charming sound, and catching. Caesare turned his head and watched her, a half smile curving his mouth. "Seriously, Kate"—Brianna's laughter faded—"the beauty of living in America today is that a woman *can* choose the kind of life she wants to live. And not everyone is cut out to be a wife and mother. It takes a special kind of strength to devote yourself to others, and I've spent too much time alone, looking out for myself."

Miguel frowned at her. "But not to have

children! What kind of old age will you have?"

"I don't think fear of being alone when you're old is a valid reason for having children, do you?" she countered.

Caesare, still standing in the doorway, turned toward the group and leaned his back against the frame as he tossed back the rest of his drink. "So, Miss Kendall, what would you consider a valid reason for having children?"

Her eyes met his. "Love," she finally answered softly. "To love a person so completely that you want to create something precious from the passion of that love."

The muscle in his jaw worked again at her unexpected answer. There was an inexplicable anger in him directed toward her. She felt it across the room and saw it in his eyes but was helpless to look away—until the maid entered and announced dinner.

He broke eye contact abruptly and spoke to his grandmother in Spanish before putting his glass on the bar and striding from the room.

Brianna inhaled deeply, only then realizing she had forgotten to breathe. She looked quizzically at Kate, who shrugged her shoulders sympathetically. "He said he has things to do and has no time for dinner with us."

Her immediate feeling was disappointment, but she battled it, knowing she was being absurd. Caesare's motives were becoming increasingly clear. She hadn't fallen into bed with him the previous night the way he expected, and it was his way of punishing her. She mentally shrugged it off—but deep down it stung.

Miguel moved next to her and tentatively held out his arm. He was such a nice, unassuming man that she couldn't help but relax as she placed her hand on his arm and walked with him into the dining room.

It was a pleasant enough meal, but Caesare's absence was felt by everyone, and it was a relief when it was over and Kate walked her to the door of the room she had slept in after her car accident the day before.

She changed into her pajamas, then sat down at the writing table with a legal pad and tried to organize her thoughts into a story for *Newsview*.

But after an hour she wondered whom she was kidding. Thoughts of Caesare kept intruding. She finally gave up and walked to the doors leading to the courtyard, opening them wide to let in the brisk fresh air. The weather was perfect—comfortably warm during the day and cool enough at night to make climbing into a warm bed a pleasure.

Chewing thoughtfully on the end of her pen, Brianna paced the room in the red football jersey with a big white "12" on the front and back that served as her pajamas. Decidedly unsexy, she thought, unaware of how it emphasized her long, shapely legs and how the material clung loosely to her breasts.

She accidentally dropped the pen and bent to retrieve it, her mind miles away, when Caesare's voice cut across the silence and startled her into straightening a lot faster than she should have. Her eyes crossed to her nose, and she pressed her hand to her forehead when the injury she had all but forgotten protested with a resounding stab.

He stood in the doorway in his tan trousers and short leather jacket, watching her. "Head still hurt?"

"It *was* just fine," she answered dryly.

He moved farther into the room. "Sit down on the bed."

Brianna stared at him, not sure she had heard correctly. "I beg your pardon?"

He pushed her gently backward until she fell onto it. "Do not worry, my liberated little American. I have no intention of seducing you. I merely want to check your forehead."

Bending over her, he removed the bandage he had applied the day before. Brianna was intensely aware of his nearness. She felt the warmth from his body and smelled his subtle aftershave. His firm but tender touch as he inspected the cut was nearly her undoing. "It looks better," he finally told her, straightening. "By next week you won't even know you were hurt."

She got up quickly and moved across the room, hating the way his nearness affected her. Then she sat on the chintz-covered chair near the table, curling her long legs beneath her, feeling suddenly very exposed.

He sat on the edge of the bed and watched her with unsmiling eyes. "I saw your light from the courtyard. What are you doing up so late?"

She motioned toward the legal pad. "Writing my story."

"How is it coming?"

"If you're really interested, not very well. And incidentally, what were you doing at that meeting today?"

"Still on duty, eh?" A corner of his mouth lifted. "Let us simply say that I've had some recent contact with the guerrilla forces and the Salvadoran government wanted my input."

"May I use that in my story?"

"I would prefer that you do not."

She tapped her pen on the table nervously. She knew what she wanted to ask him. It was simply a matter of collecting her courage. When she had, she took a deep breath and looked him right in the eye. "Caesare, why do you dislike me so? I mean, you couldn't even bring yourself to sit down at the same table with me this evening."

He studied her quietly. "You think it is because I dislike you?" He shook his dark head, and the grooves in his cheeks deepened. "Oh, Brianna Kendall, in some ways, you are such a woman—and in others such an unawakened child." He rose from the bed. "Good night, *querida*." As suddenly as he had come, he was gone.

She sat deep in thought, pondering his words. An unawakened child? If by that he meant that she had never experienced the grand passion, he was right. She had yet to meet a man she felt she couldn't live without quite happily.

In the depths of the rambling house, someone began playing the piano. Its rich strains reached her across the courtyard, and she recognized it as one of her favorites —Rachmaninoff's Rhapsody on a Theme from Paganini. Whoever was playing did so exquisitely. She lost herself in the beauty of the music, the darkness of the night, the fragrance of the exotic flowers just outside her doors and the privacy of her thoughts until the music stopped, nearly two hours later.

At last, with a tired sigh, she slid between the cool sheets and drifted into a peaceful sleep.

Chapter Six

She awoke refreshed the next morning after one of the best sleeps she'd had in a long time. With a cheerful whistle, she set her typewriter up on the round table and got to work on her article. Max would be expecting it.

Surprisingly, she flew through it and had it finished within two hours. Then she slipped into some white shorts with pockets in the sides and a "sort of" sweatshirt, bright white, with a marine blue striped yoke in front and back. She pushed the sleeves up her forearms and put her hands in her pockets as she walked out of the room, a spring in her step. It was another beautiful day.

Just off the veranda outside her room was

a stone path leading through the gardens. And what gardens! Exotic flowers, sculpted bushes. The house was a square U shape with the gardens spilling down a not very steep hill to a smooth green lawn. She walked toward the main wing of the house via a short path until she came into the open and found a very large, cool-looking blue pool.

But it wasn't the pool that caught her eye and stopped her. It was the man in it, swimming with powerful strokes back and forth, seeming never to tire. The muscles in Caesare's shoulders rippled and gleamed as he propelled himself along, stopping finally at her feet. Putting his palms on the cement, he pushed himself straight out of the water, then picked up a crisp white towel and draped it across the back of his neck. His black hair was slicked straight back— which she found surprisingly attractive.

Tawny eyes touched violet. "Good morning, Brianna."

She loved the way her name sounded when he said it. A smile touched her mouth. "Hello. Do you always swim this early?"

"Always."

She didn't mean to stare, but she couldn't help it. His broad bronzed shoulders tapered to a flat, muscled stomach and trim hips with long, powerful legs. The short, dark hair on his chest curled into a T, which disappeared beneath the very brief blue swimming trunks. Oh, yes, he was an attractive man.

She lifted her eyes and ran straight into his sardonically amused ones. A hint of a blush touched her cheeks, but she didn't drop her gaze. "I was up early this morning, as well, finishing my article," she continued as though there had been no pause.

He walked away from her toward a breakfast table set on the green lawn. "I heard you typing. Do you want breakfast?"

She followed and sat in one of the comfortable wicker chairs. Juice and coffee were already there. "Thank you."

He poured her and then himself a cup of coffee. "Were you more inspired this morning?"

"A lot more. I think Max will like it."

He relaxed back in his chair and looked at her over the rim of his cup. "Max thinks highly of your work. You apparently have a bright future with *Newsview*." There was a touch of sarcasm in his tone.

"I hope so." She didn't mean to sound defensive, but she couldn't help it. "Speaking of which"—she poured herself a glass of juice—"what are we going to be doing today? I'd like to get a feel for the type of stories we'll be going after."

He hesitated, and she at once grew alert. "The situation has deteriorated considerably since I made my offer to Max . . ."

"Meaning?" If he backed out at such a late date, she wouldn't quite know what to do.

"Meaning I think it would be foolhardy for you to travel into the harder-hit areas."

She rapped the table sharply with her knuckle, not at all pleased. "I *knew* you were going to say that. I bet if I were a man you wouldn't bat an eyelash . . ."

He leaned forward and caught her hand in his, forcing her to look at him. "Your gender has nothing to do with this, Brianna."

She was surprised into a rare silence.

"I meant exactly what I said to you before. This offer was made two years ago. I had no warning that Max was sending someone. If I had, perhaps I could have prevented it. There is a war going on here. I will not risk anyone in my charge—man or woman—becoming involved to the extent of getting injured."

She retrieved her hand and leaned back in her chair. "So why am I here?"

"Two reasons. I knew if I told you that while you were at the hotel you would take off on your own."

"And?"

"And I thought perhaps you could do something different with your writing on El Salvador. People write about wars, and people read about wars, but to those not involved, what does it really mean? You give body counts and someone clicks their tongue and says, 'What a pity.' What is not being told is how the war is affecting individuals. There is the tragedy. There is the story."

She hated to admit it, but he was right. He was absolutely right. Telling a single story would bring home the reality of what was going on there much more effectively than general facts and figures. "Do you have someone in mind?" she asked.

He inclined his dark head. "In a few days, I will take you to a woman who lives not far from here. She is visiting relatives in another part of the country."

"Will she be willing to talk with me?"

"If she thinks that by talking with you she can save even one mother the grief she has suffered over her son, she will talk." His eyes sparked with impotent anger as he ran his hand carelessly through his thick hair. "It is so senseless, Brianna," he said harshly. "So tragically senseless."

In an unselfconscious gesture of comfort, she reached across the table and touched his hand. He looked down at it for a moment, then covered it with his other hand, lifting his eyes to hers. Her mouth parted softly as though she might speak.

"Ssshhhh," he whispered, leaning slowly forward until his mouth was so close she could feel his breath. "You talk far, far too much."

"Good morning!" Brianna blinked as his grandmother's voice cut between them.

Caesare didn't move for a moment, and the warmth of his gaze lingered. "We have both been saved," he remarked sardonically, backing away as his grandmother came into view, walking from the house to the table.

"Am I in time for breakfast?"

Brianna didn't answer. She was still thinking about his remark about having been saved. Saved from a kiss?

At that moment, the sound of an approaching helicopter could be heard. Caesare tossed his napkin on the table and rose, kissing his grandmother's cheek. "I have an early appointment in San Salvador." His eyes lingered on the girl. "You take care of Brianna for me, Kate."

Kate sat down with a smile as Brianna watched him disappear through the living-room doors. "I see the two of you are getting along better this morning."

Brianna's eyes moved reluctantly from the now-empty doorway to the woman next to her. "We get along all right most of the time."

Kate's eyes were skeptical. "When the two of you are in a room together, you could cut the tension with a knife."

She really didn't want to talk about it with Kate or anyone else. So she changed the subject. "I was surprised to learn that

Caesare had an American grandmother. He's so—"

"Latin?"

"Exactly," she said, smiling.

"Well, I *am* something of a black mark on his genetic record."

"Doesn't he like Americans?"

She lifted her hand in casual denial. "Oh, no. On the contrary, he admires them greatly. But American women baffle him. You see, Caesare is Latin through and through, just as my late husband was. To him, women will always have a place in the world—the kitchen, the nursery. American career women are a complete enigma."

"But surely if your blood runs in his veins—"

"Oh," she admitted, "I see signs of it at times. But rarely. He is his grandfather's grandson—his father's son." Her blue eyes twinkled. "I'm sure the two of you have already had your share of differences of opinion."

Brianna hedged. "Let's just say we can find things to disagree about if we're pressed."

"You know," Kate said thoughtfully, "the two of you remind me of my husband and myself. He was exactly like Caesare, believing that women should ask no more out of life than to do their husband's bidding at all times, not talk back and generally fade into the woodwork. And then he met me. I'm an artist, you see, and as you know, artists are notorious for their nonconformity. I was considered something of an oddity even in the United States in my trousers, smoking cigarettes, so you can imagine what Caesare's grandfather thought when he first met me."

Brianna was fascinated. "How did you meet?"

"It's a long story. Are you sure you want to hear it?"

"I have nothing but time on my hands. What happened?"

Kate mentally traveled back through the decades to a time when she was young. "I was in my twenties and slowly gaining recognition for my landscapes. But I wasn't satisfied. I wanted to do something different. So I decided to capture Central America on canvas." She came momentarily back to the present. "I don't know if you've had time to notice, but the scenery here is stunning. I had read about it and was enthralled. So I packed my paints and trousers and ended up here. As a matter of fact, I was painting a volcano very near this house, called Izalco, which was still active at that time, when I spotted a man on horseback. He was a gorgeous creature—the man, not the horse—and I proceeded to capture him on my canvas, as well. He turned out to be the owner of the land I was on and rode over to me, demanding to know what I thought I was doing trespassing. We got into a terrible row over it, ending with his ordering me to pack my things, tent and all, and leave.

Well, as I stormed off, I tripped and twisted my ankle—much to my future husband's fury. He couldn't very well leave me like that, tempting though it must have been at the time, so he ended up lifting me onto his horse and taking me home with him to stay until my ankle got better."

"And you fell madly in love and got married," Brianna finished for her with a romantic sigh. She loved happy endings. There seemed to be so few in the world anymore.

"Well," the older woman conceded, "it was a rocky path, to put it mildly. I thought he was the most arrogant, overbearing man I'd ever met, and quite frankly, he felt the same way about me. But always there was that pull between us. The attraction of opposites. Our marriage was full of heated arguments and more love and passion than I ever dreamed could exist between a man and a woman. He's been gone for many years now, and not a day goes by that I don't think of him and miss him terribly."

Brianna's heart grew heavy as she remembered her own parents. Another example of why you should never let yourself be consumed with love for another person. It seemed there was always someone left behind to suffer. Well, not her. Never her.

She leaned back in her chair and looked around the property. "It's very lovely here. How long has it been in the de Alvarado family?"

"Which time?" Kate asked cryptically.

"What do you mean?"

"I mean it had been in the family for over two hundred years when, shortly after I married Caesare's grandfather, there was an abrupt change in the government of El Salvador. A radical change. The new leadership decided that my husband wasn't running the *finca*—that's what the Salvadorans call a coffee plantation—the way he should. He was giving more and more land away to the people who worked for him so that they could work for themselves and their own families."

Brianna was appalled, because she knew what Kate was going to tell her next. "They took his land away from him?"

Kate breathed a short, unamused laugh. "His land, his home, his money. Everything."

"What did you do?"

Kate sipped her coffee. "Well, we had very few options. Many relatives of the de Alvarados lived here, and the family had to split up. My husband and I had two small children to provide for. I was able to sell my paintings, but my husband had great pride. It destroyed him to take money from me. We ended up living in a very poor section of San Salvador with no indoor plumbing or electricity. Caesare was born there."

She couldn't imagine . . . or could she? Yet another facet.

As soon as Caesare could understand, my husband told him the story of what had happened, over and over again. By the time he was six, it was burned into his mind. He was a determined child, and he kept telling us that one day he would buy it back."

"Where were his parents?"

"Dead. He never knew them, really."

Brianna's soft heart went out to the little tawny-eyed boy who had been Caesare.

"He studied harder than anyone else," Kate continued, "and worked at any odd job he could find, saving enough to put himself through college and start a small business. De Alvarado Exporting is today one of the largest and most profitable businesses in the country."

"I didn't realize that."

"Yes, though it is run for the most part by the employees themselves these days. His first love has always been writing. As soon as he had enough money to buy his land back, he began his true work in earnest."

"So the government allowed him to buy it back?"

She shrugged. "The government had changed again by that time, more than once. It no longer mattered as long as they got their money." Kate eyed the tender expression of her fellow American. "So what do you think of my grandson now?"

A thoughtful smile touched her mouth. "Still confusing, but less so now. I'm used to men who have a lot of little boy left in them. Caesare has left his boyhood behind him completely—if he ever had one."

"And you don't like that?"

Brianna slowly shook her raven head. "Oh, no, I like that very much." Her violet eyes focused on the knowing smile of the other woman, and a shyly embarrassed smile touched her own mouth. "I mean I find it interesting."

"You said what you meant the first time, and we both know it," Kate admonished. "I don't know what it is with the youth of today. You're all so afraid of your feelings. What's wrong with you?"

Brianna lifted a brow. "You mean you weren't?"

She leaned forward and caught one of the girl's hands in hers. "Of course I was. But the difference is that I allowed myself to feel things. To experience things. I didn't run away every time I didn't understand what was happening. I came to realize that you can't plan your life down to the very last detail. People come into your life . . . and people drop out of your life. If you fall in love with someone and you deny yourself the pleasure and joy of experiencing that person because you see no future with him, then your life is in a very sad state, indeed. There are times when you have to live for the moment. Those moments are what memories in old age are made of. Life is so short, dear. Take what it offers." She hit the table with her open palm. "No! Grab it. Be greedy. And if things don't work out, at least you will have had that moment. And that is something never to be regretted."

"Until that person dies or simply leaves you."

Kate's eyes narrowed on her. "Brianna, I'm not going to tell you I wasn't in agony when I lost my husband. I wanted to die, too. But I didn't. And now I'm thankful that I had him for the time I did. I would never dream of erasing all the wonderful times we shared to avoid the pain that came when he was gone. Never. My life would have been nothing without him."

Brianna quietly took in Kate's words, but her mind had already been made up a long time before. That kind of love was not for her. Kate had hoped to put a dent in some of Brianna's armor but wasn't sure she had succeeded. With a little sigh, Kate got to her feet. "Well, think about what I've said. Right now I want to do some painting. Why don't you wander around the house and get to know it?"

"I will, thank you." But Brianna sat there by the pool long after Kate had gone, thinking. She wished she was the kind of person who could really let herself go without considering the consequences. But she wasn't. She never had been.

She thought of Caesare. They were so different, and yet she found herself attracted to him. She didn't want to be. The only thing they had in common was their writing. He was the biggest threat to her emotional well-being that she had ever met. It would be easy to love him and to let him make love to her. And it would be fatal.

With a shake of her head, she rose from the table and wandered into the house. If only she could have the interview that very day and get out of there.

She went through the living room and explored some of the rooms off the foyer. The first one she found was a music room. A concert-sized grand piano dominated the area, its lid up. Curiously, she glanced at the open music. It was the Rachmaninoff piece she had heard the night before. Over a chair near the piano was the jacket Caesare had worn the previous night. She walked over to it and touched the soft leather. Strangely, she wasn't surprised that he had such a remarkable talent. He could do anything . . .

Lifting the jacket in her arms, she inhaled deeply of the clean smell of fine leather.

"*Señorita?*"

Brianna jumped guiltily and looked up to find a maid watching her curiously. With admirable nonchalance, she laid the jacket back on the chair. "Yes?"

"I saw you as I walked past. Is there anything I can get for you?"

"No. No, thank you." Brianna was embarrassed, as though she had been caught doing something wrong.

The woman inclined her head and disappeared. Brianna abruptly left the room and walked into another one. It happened to be Caesare's study. It was also a library. There were books lining one wall; on another wall was a fireplace with a leather couch in front of it. An Indian blanket was draped over the back of the couch. Opposite the fireplace sat an enormous ebony carved desk with papers and files neatly stacked on it. Two chairs had been placed near the desk, and a chessboard was set up between them. It was a wonderful room. Warm and lived in.

Feeling like an intruder, she went back

outside and across the lawn, past the pool and through the gardens. It was a perfect day for exploring outside. The morning had sped by. It was already past two o'clock.

The gardens spilled down a hill, past the house. She followed the path until she came to another expanse of green lawn. About a hundred yards away was an elegant white building with arches in the Spanish style and a pasture next to it. Stables, she guessed, heading toward it.

At the edge of the gardens, she stopped to inhale the perfume of an orchid and became suddenly alert. She had an uneasy feeling that she wasn't alone. Slowly, she straightened and looked around, not wanting to appear alarmed. No one was there.

With a nervous shrug of her shoulders at her nonsense, Brianna ambled on toward a long white fence that disappeared into the distance.

Shading her eyes from the bright sun, she put her foot on the bottom rail and peered into the outlying pasture, looking for horses. But again the feeling that she wasn't alone overcame her. Once more she turned quickly and looked around, but just as before, no one was there.

Feeling fidgety, she turned back to the pasture. A chestnut horse came into view, framed by a slumbering volcano several miles away. A gamboling foal raced around the mare on long, awkward-looking legs. Brianna's heart melted at the sight.

Then she saw a huge black horse stop suddenly, his head upraised. She could imagine his nostrils flaring, even though she couldn't see them, sniffing the wind in her direction. It had to be a stallion. There was a certain arrogance about him. He probably belonged to Caesare, she thought wryly.

A movement some distance down the fence caught her attention. Her heart began pounding at the sight of a tall, dark-skinned man standing there, watching her. So she hadn't been imagining that she was being followed! And he didn't look particularly friendly.

"All right, Brianna," she told herself under her breath. "Stay calm. Don't panic. He might be a worker or something." With studied casualness, she turned away from the fence and headed back across the lawn to the gardens. If he didn't follow, everything would be fine. If he did . . . well, she'd be in trouble.

Somewhere in the back of her mind she heard the sound of a helicopter, but it didn't really register.

Again, as casually as she could manage with her heart pounding the way it was, she glanced over her shoulder. He was following! Adrenalin pumped through her veins.

She was in trouble, and her only hope was to run. She had always been fast, but never more than now as she raced for the cover of the garden.

But as fast as she ran, the man behind her ran faster. She knew he'd catch her if she didn't do something immediately, so when she rounded a curve in the path and realized that he couldn't see her, she plunged off to the side and into some thick bushes. She watched in absolute stillness as the man's feet pounded by without stopping, then painfully drew some air into her burning lungs.

She stayed huddled there, wishing she had worn something besides bright white.

Tense and alert, her breath caught in her throat when she heard him coming back. His worn shoes stopped not three feet away from her. Brianna didn't twitch a muscle.

It seemed like hours before he moved on, but in reality it was only seconds. Still afraid to move, she stayed where she was for a few minutes before inhaling deeply and rushing out of the bushes and back onto the path toward the main section of the house. She ran as though the wind carried her.

Through the living room doors, she raced, praying that Caesare was back. She threw open the door of his study and ran in, slamming it shut behind her, her back pushed up against it. Her breasts heaved with the effort of pulling air into her lungs.

He was there, behind his desk. Brianna had never been so glad to see anyone in her life. Caesare was in front of her immediately, his strong hands on her shaking shoulders, a worried frown creasing his forehead. "Brianna! What is wrong?"

"You're never going to believe this," she gasped, "but I went for a walk, and I noticed this man following me, so I ran, and then I hid, and then when he left, I ran again and made it to the house, and you've no idea how happy I am to see you!" It all came out in a breathless, panting paragraph. She closed her eyes and put her hand over her pounding heart. "Brother, am I out of shape!"

As Caesare looked at her, she saw understanding dawning in his tawny eyes, and amusement replaced the concern.

Brianna was dumfounded. "You could at least *pretend* to be a little worried."

Someone knocked frantically on the door she was leaning against, and Brianna nearly jumped out of her skin. Caesare took her firmly by the shoulders and moved her aside to open the door. A tall, dark man stood there, out of breath, a distressed look on his face.

She couldn't believe her eyes. "That's him! That's the man who was chasing me!"

As soon as he saw her, the man's face registered relief.

Caesare seemed more amused than ever. "Brianna, I'd like you to meet your body-guard, José Mathias."

Her mouth fell open as she looked from one man to the other in amazement, not believing what she had just heard. "You can't be serious," she said in a low voice. "You can *not* be serious."

Caesare said something to the man in Spanish and closed the door when he had gone. Brianna felt like a fool. "You should have told me."

The Salvadoran leaned one shoulder against the wall, folded his arms across his chest and watched her with his mocking eyes. "Yes, I should have."

She glared at him. "Why on earth would you do something like that? That poor man out there nearly frightened me out of a decade of my life—and I don't think I did much for his longevity, either." She paced across the room but returned to stand in front of him, arms akimbo. "I think you owe me an explanation."

Tolerant amusement was replaced by cool annoyance. "I owe you nothing. You are on my property now, and you will do things according to my rules."

His answer momentarily took the wind out of her sails. How did one answer something like that? She raised her hands help-lessly. "I don't know what else to say to you. I'm not some child who needs to be taken care of. For your information, I'm a very competent woman. I can take care of my-self. What is it with you men that makes you think women need to be protected and coddled from the 'evils' of the world?"

"You mean like the way you protected yourself from that man at your brother's party? Or the soldier yesterday? You will pardon me if I find your arguments uncon-vincing," he said dismissively. "You really have no idea what you could get yourself into here, do you? El Salvador may be a beautiful place, but it is *not* a friendly place at the moment. Someone might try to get at you because of me."

"That's ridiculous."

"You know that, and I know that, but not everyone does."

She walked to the desk and sat on its edge, drumming her fingers on its surface. "You mean someone who disagrees with you about something might try to hurt you by hurting me."

"Exactly."

"I still say that's ridiculous."

Caesare's patience, which he considered commendable up to that point, snapped. Stepping abruptly forward, he gripped her shoulders and gave her a little shake. "I have never met a more provoking woman in all my life."

Brianna was startled into silence.

"The facts are as follows: while you are here, you will have protection. If you don't like it, you may leave at any time. In fact, I wish you would."

His words hurt, but she wouldn't have shown him that for the world. "Not until I interview the woman."

The Salvadoran dropped his hands from her shoulders and ran them through his dark hair. "Naturally. I find myself forgetting how ambitious you are."

She wasn't sure she liked hearing herself described with that word. It was all right for a man to be ambitious, but for a woman —well, it sounded a little hard and calculating. She wasn't like that. "So the bottom line is?" she asked after a moment.

"The bottom line is that as long as you are my responsibility, José will continue to follow you whenever you are alone. No amount of arguing by you is going to change that one simple fact."

Well, Brianna knew when she was beaten. A corner of her mouth lifted wryly as she looked up at him. "I'm furious with you, you know."

He looked at her in near wonder. He had never met anyone quite like her before. "Are you also hungry?" he asked suddenly.

"Famished."

"Good." She watched as he walked back to his desk and made some notations in a file, standing as he wrote rather than sitting. He had on a pair of slim-fitting jeans and a vivid blue and white striped cotton shirt with the top three buttons undone and the cuffs rolled halfway up his forearms. That done, he closed the file and walked past her. "Wait here. I shall be right back."

Wondering what was going on, Brianna slid off the desk and walked to the windows, looking out. He was a very difficult man to stay angry with. A warning buzzer sounded in her head, but Caesare returned before she had a chance to analyze it. He had a picnic basket in one hand. She looked at it curiously, but he offered no explanation. "Get some jeans on and then we'll leave."

"For where?" They walked through the living room, outside and down the veranda to her room.

"You'll see. Just get your jeans on."

She did, leaving her "sweatshirt" top on, and met him outside her door once again. Taking her hand in his and swinging it as they walked, he seemed almost cheerful. They took the same path toward the stables that she had taken earlier that day.

Brianna suddenly realized what he had in mind, and her heart plummeted, but she wasn't about to tell him she had never been on a horse in her life. What kind of admission was that from a girl who had grown up in the country?

Inside the stables, two horses were tethered, saddled and waiting. Caesare had obviously called someone. One of the horses was the black stallion. The other was a little mare with great dark, friendly eyes.

Brianna patted her silky nose and tried to look as though she knew what she was doing.

Caesare mounted his horse after strapping on the picnic basket, then looked down at her. "Well?"

She looked up at him and somehow managed a smile. Then she walked to the side of the horse and put her foot in the stirrup.

"One mounts a horse from the left," he told her, a curious look entering his tawny eyes.

"I know that," she lied. "I was just checking things over before getting on." With a lengthy indrawn breath, she walked around to the horse's left, put one foot in the stirrup and swung the other over the saddle. That had been easy enough. She felt inordinately pleased with herself. She settled into the saddle and took the reins loosely in her hands, glancing at Caesare, who continued to watch her. "Ready when you are!" she informed him.

Raising a dark brow, he moved his horse next to hers, took the reins from her hands and adjusted them, then handed them back to her, fitting them through the proper fingers. "Don't make the reins so tight that they drag on the horse's mouth, but hold them firmly enough so that if you need to pull her up short you can do so instantly."

She nodded. "I know that, of course. It's just that I'm used to riding bareback." She couldn't believe what had just come from her mouth.

A corner of the Salvadoran's mouth lifted, but he didn't call her an outright liar as he pulled his reins to one side to turn his horse toward the huge double doors leading out of the stables.

Brianna clicked her tongue at the mare, just the way the men did in all the westerns, but apparently the mare hadn't seen any of them, because she just stood there.

Brianna patted her neck and talked to her. "Okay, girl. Let's go. Come on now, sweetheart. Giddy-up. Click-click." The words were accompanied by a slight bouncing motion in the saddle.

Caesare, already out in the bright sunlight, turned his head to look at her. "Squeeze her gently with your knees."

She was skeptical, but she did it—and to her amazement, the little mare shot forward, causing Brianna to hang on for dear life until she pulled even with the stallion. Then she trotted along nicely. Brianna gave Caesare a long sideways glance. "That's

not how they do it in the old West, you
know. Hopalong Cassidy would turn over in
his grave. Squeeze her gently with your
knees, indeed," she said in mock disgust.

The Salvadoran threw back his dark head
and laughed, but then the laughter faded,
and his eyes came to rest on her again. He
grew contemplative. "Brianna Kendall, for
reasons that I have yet to fully understand
and as infuriating as I sometimes find you,
you delight me."

She felt a warm glow deep within.

Caesare signaled his horse, and the stallion trotted at a faster pace, forcing
Brianna to really concentrate to keep up.
Her seat was precarious, to say the least.
But even at that, the stallion seemed to
need holding in check. He wanted to race.
She could see it in the ripple of muscle
under the shining black coat. In fact, both
the horse and Caesare seemed to be bursting with energy they needed to release.

For just a moment, she dared to let go of
the reins with one hand to touch Caesare's
arm. "I think your horse wants to run."

He looked down at the stallion, and a
corner of his handsome mouth lifted. "He is
used to freedom." His eyes met hers. "We
both are."

She dropped her own gaze. His message
was clear. "Why don't you take him for a
run? We'll just trot along back here."

"You are sure?" He seemed uneasy about leaving her behind.

"I'm not only sure, I'd appreciate it. If *he* calms down, perhaps my horse will, too."

With a slight inclination of his head, the two of them took off. Brianna and her mount stopped in their tracks and watched them, so well matched, so powerful. Brianna's breath caught at the sheer physical beauty of what she saw. The stallion's strides were so long and graceful that he hardly seemed to touch the ground. And Caesare, leaning forward in the saddle, low over the horse's neck, moved with him as one. A stone wall loomed in the distance. She saw Caesare bend lower as they approached it, and her heart pounded at what she was about to see. The horse didn't slow down at all but raced straight for it, vaulting into the air. Caesare's powerful forearms seemed to lift the horse off the ground as they sailed over the obstacle and hit the ground running. "Oh!" she breathed in wonder.

She and the mare trotted toward the wall at a much slower pace. She saw Caesare and the stallion in the distance, heading back toward them. Her mind wandered as a dark cloud spread itself across the sky. It couldn't rain! Not now. She wanted to enjoy the rest of the afternoon.

But while Brianna was thinking about

the weather, the little mare went feminist on her and decided that whatever the stallion could do, she could do better. Completely without warning, she shot forward. The reins fell from Brianna's hands as she made a desperate bid to grab the mare's mane to keep from falling off. No amount of yelling stopped her as she soared into the air and cleared the wall with a foot to spare.

As the Salvadoran watched in horror, the mare landed with such force that Brianna flew off her back and crashed to the ground. The mare kept running, but Brianna lay still and unmoving.

Man and horse raced madly across the pasture toward her just as a light rain began to fall. Caesare leaped off the stallion and kneeled beside her, his jaw clenched, his face suddenly pale. He touched her cheek gently with a trembling hand. "Brianna?"

She hadn't been unconscious. Just winded. And when she opened her eyes and looked at him, a wry smile curved her mouth. "Did I happen to mention that I lied about knowing how to ride?"

Caesare closed his eyes and let out a long breath. "Thank God. If anything had happened to you, I—"

Her smile faded as their eyes met. The rain fell harder, but neither of them noticed. "Would it have mattered to you?"

Caesare pushed the wet hair away from her face, his eyes warm on her. "It would have mattered a great deal."

When his mouth came down on hers this time, it was the most natural feeling in the world. She felt his flesh, warm against hers, through their wet shirts as his body pressed hers into the soft, fragrant grass. She wanted to say no, but as his mouth passionately plundered the sweet depths of hers, her ability to think rationally faded. A delicious warmth grew low in her stomach and spread as his hands found their way beneath her shirt and skillfully caressed her smooth skin. His mouth left hers to blaze a trail down her throat to the V opening of her shirt. Caesare pulled it open far enough so that he could caress the gently rounded swell of her breasts with his mouth.

She inhaled sharply at the flood of passion that surged through her veins. Her fingers tangled in his thick, wet hair and pressed him to her as her back arched toward him.

The Salvadoran pushed one hand flat against the ground, raising himself high enough to look down into her enchantingly flushed face, looking for some sign of doubt about what was happening between them.

Brianna was lost. It had been coming for a long time, and now that it was here, she had neither the strength of will nor the desire to push him away. All of her carefully considered decisions were as air. Nothing mattered but that the two of them were there, then, together.

Her lips were softly parted as she looked up with eyes darkened with desire. She raised an endearingly trembling hand and traced the groove in his cheek, trailing it down his face to the crease in his chin. He caught her hand in his and pressed it to his mouth, lightly touching the soft palm with his tongue, his smoldering eyes searching hers one more time. Seeing no doubts, he lowered his mouth to hers and rolled onto his back, pulling her on top of him. His hands slid down her sides to her hips and stayed there, pulling her tightly against him. His need became hers. For the first time in her life, Brianna was out of control. She wanted him so much it burned within her; the consequences didn't matter. Nothing mattered but the quenching of the fire he had started.

Suddenly, he rolled her off him and stood up. "No!" he said vehemently. Then, when he saw her stricken look, he said more softly, "No."

Brianna, shocked and humiliated, sat up and hugged her knees tightly to her. A solitary tear made its way hotly down her cheek before she caught it with the back of her hand and dashed it away. Painfully, she tried to envelope herself in what little dignity she had left. It took all her courage, but she looked up and directly into his eyes. "Why did you do that? What did I do wrong?"

In a gesture she was becoming familiar with, he ran his hand through his hair and hunkered down in front of her. His voice was gentle. "You didn't do anything wrong. On the contrary. You did everything right. I want you. I want you more than I've ever wanted any woman."

"I don't understand."

He reached out to touch her face, but she pulled away from him. His hand dropped. "I know you don't. And I don't know how to explain it to you other than to say that making love with you is something I dare not do."

"Why?" she asked quietly. She needed to know. It was one of the most important questions she had ever asked.

"Because I know I can never really have you, and once we cross that line, I don't know if I'll be able to give you up. And give you up I must, make no mistake."

While they were talking, her mare had returned from her mad gallop and began grazing near them. Caesare helped Brianna to her feet and then lifted her onto the horse. "Go back to the house."

Brianna's chest was tight with emotion. She didn't want to leave him. A horrible truth was dawning. She had found that one

man in the world put there just for her—
and she couldn't have him. "What about
you?" she asked with a catch in her voice.

"I'll come later. Now go." He slapped the
mare's rump and stood silently in the rain,
watching until they disappeared from
sight. Then he raised his carved face to the
skies and let the drops cool his hot skin.

Chapter Seven

That night was terrible. She tossed and turned the entire time. Caesare occupied every corner of her mind. She couldn't get away from him. And she didn't really want to.

When morning came, she was more tired than she had been when she went to bed, and nothing was settled. She knew she could go back to the magazine without the special-interest story, because while Max wouldn't have been at all pleased if she'd missed that meeting two days earlier, she honestly didn't think he'd hold it against her professionally if she left now without getting any more.

And yet she would have lost respect for

herself. She wasn't a quitter. Her feelings
for Caesare—and she was still unclear
about their depth—were going to have to be
faced and conquered. Every time she
thought about the way she had behaved the
day before, she cringed. She had all but
thrown herself at him. Facing him that day
was going to be difficult.

She skipped breakfast that morning and
wandered around the house, her hands
stuffed in the pockets of her softly pleated
blue skirt. She found her way to his bedroom door and stood in front of it, screwing
up her courage to knock. But she couldn't
and hurriedly turned and walked back to
the main section of the house, slowing
down only when she reached the foyer. The
large doors leading to the house from the
driveway opened, and Caesare walked in. It
was obvious that he had been out all night.
His face, shadowed with beard, looked hol-
low and exhausted.

He saw her suddenly and walked straight
to her, pulling her into his arms and holding her close. She was so surprised that her
arms automatically went around his waist.
And she was frightened. The hold he had on
her wasn't passionate. It was desperate.

"Caesare," she said against his shoulder,
"are you all right? What's wrong?"

With a tired sigh, he released her and
rubbed his forehead. "Nothing is wrong,"

he said quietly. "I just had a long, awful night, and when I saw you standing there so sane and so clean, I wanted to hold you."

Something was definitely wrong, but she had learned enough about him by that time not to push.

"Can I get you some breakfast?" she offered, not knowing what else to say.

His mouth curved into a slow, devastating smile. "I am too tired to eat. All I want to do is get cleaned up and fall into bed." He walked past her and headed for his room. Brianna stared after him until Kate draped her arm around her shoulders.

"Well, good morning. The two of you seem to be getting on even better than yesterday."

The remark embarrassed Brianna, and it showed on her face. "How long were you standing there?"

"Long enough. And if I might make a suggestion, he probably *will* be hungry after he finishes showering. Why don't you take him a little something?"

"But he said—"

"Men are always saying things they don't mean."

"Or meaning things they don't say," suggested Brianna.

Kate smiled at her. She was becoming fond of the girl. "A nice turn of phrase. Now go to the kitchen. Theresa should still be there."

She was. Theresa was a mountain of a woman who obviously enjoyed her work. She beamed and nodded at Brianna's request for Caesare's breakfast and whipped up a marvelous omelet, toast and strong black coffee in no time, then neatly arranged it on a tray and handed it to Brianna. She carried it through the house and to Caesare's room, balancing it on the palm of one hand while knocking lightly on the door with the other.

"Come."

She opened it a little at first and hesitated when she saw him standing there with only a towel wrapped around his waist. But then she realized how ridiculous she was being. "I thought you might change your mind about eating," she said, walking bravely into the room and putting the tray on a table by the bed.

Caesare lay down and put his right forearm over his eyes. "Stop trying to mother me, Brianna."

She leaned over him and lifted his arm so that he had to look at her. "I feel a lot of things when I'm with you, Caesare de Alvarado," she informed him. "Angry, confused, curious . . . but *never* motherly."

His teeth flashed white at her unexpected audacity. "And stop trying to make me laugh. I am too tired."

She put his arm back over his eyes and stood looking down at him until the rise and fall of his broad chest was deep and even; then she tiptoed to the door and opened it, looking back at him for a moment before closing it behind her.

Leaning her back against it, she stood with a thoughtful smile. Facing him hadn't been as bad as she'd feared.

The rest of the day was long and slow. She wasn't used to inactivity but made the best of it by writing about her impressions of the El Salvador she had seen since her arrival. Toward evening, she took her notebook outside and sat at the table by the pool.

"*Buenas noches*, lovely lady," greeted Miguel cheerfully as he walked from the house to join her.

"Miguel." She smiled, happy to see a nice, uncomplicated man for a change. "Is it already time for dinner?"

"We have at least an hour, and we might just be dining alone." He wriggled his expressive eyebrows, causing Brianna to chuckle. "But I promise not to attack until after the main course. Hunger does not a good lover make."

At that she laughed. Really laughed for the first time in days, and it felt good. "Thank you, Miguel. I needed that."

"Is something troubling you?"

"I think some*one* would be a more accurate way of putting it, but it's nothing I want to talk about." She quickly changed the subject. "What have you been doing with yourself? I haven't seen you at all."

"I have been around, working on the *finca*."

"Ah"—she sighed—"so you're one of the magicians who grows this delicious coffee I've been drinking lately."

He seemed pleased by her response. "You like our coffee? Most North Americans find it too strong for their . . . paler . . . tastes. The coffee you people usually get is only ten percent Central American with ninety percent of the weaker South American coffee mixed in to tone it down."

"How much coffee do you export annually?" The reporter in her was coming out.

"Not very much anymore. Caesare has been little by little turning the land over to the people who work it, the way our grandfather tried to do."

Something Caesare had said during her questioning of him on "Talking Facts" returned. That was what he had meant. He *was* doing something for his people. Her attention returned to Miguel. "Where does that leave you?"

He shrugged. "Very busy. I still have our own land to manage and at the same time teach the others how to take care of their newly acquired property so that they can farm it to the best of their capabilities."

"Are they all growing coffee?"

"All of them are growing some coffee. But none of them exclusively. Food is much needed in El Salvador. It seems that most of our crops are for export, and none of them are food. We have a small, poor country with not much arable land. And what arable land we have is needed to grow things we can eat. Caesare is hoping to get other large landowners interested in what he is doing."

Brianna paused. "Miguel—do you know where Caesare was last night?"

His smile faded abruptly. "Yes."

She waited, and when he said nothing further, prompted him. "Well?"

"Why do you wish to know?"

"Yes, Brianna, why do you wish to know?" Caesare asked as he walked out of the house and sat next to them at the table. He looked much more rested than he had that morning.

"I was curious," she explained lamely.

Caesare's tawny eyes were watching her, but he spoke to Miguel. "What do you think. Can she be trusted?"

Miguel looked at her, also. "I think so. She is not stupid."

"Well, thank you for that vote of confidence," Brianna said dryly.

But Caesare was serious. "You must never write about what we will tell you. Is that clear?"

"Very."

He hesitated, then began. "Miguel and I and some other men have set up an aid network for the civilians caught in the middle of the war between the government and the rebels. They have nowhere to turn for medical supplies or food if there is fighting in their area. If they turn to the government, the rebels think they are traitors to the cause. If they turn to the rebels, the government thinks they are traitors to the country. It is a hellish situation for them to be in."

"So you smuggle them food and medical supplies."

"And doctors."

"Where does the money for all this come from?"

"We all contribute. If you could see the people, you would realize how desperate the need is."

"I can imagine. Perhaps I could meet some of these people while I'm here."

Caesare's eyes narrowed on her. "No. There is too much danger. I would never allow it."

She looked at him incredulously. "You would never *allow* it?"

He flashed Miguel a look. "Forbidding this woman to do something is tantamount to waving a red flag before a bull."

Miguel laughed, and she wrinkled her

nose at both of them. "I'm glad to see you enjoying yourselves so much at my expense."

Caesare grew more serious. "Brianna, we have a network of dozens of men and women who get the supplies into the areas that need them. It is not fun. It is not pretty. We do it because it is something that must be done and for no other reason. While you are here, in my care, I will do nothing to jeopardize your safety merely for the sake of that incredibly curious mind of yours. Nor would I jeopardize the safety of those involved by bringing in someone who didn't know what she was doing."

The last part was something she could accept. She didn't want to get anyone hurt, either.

"Where is Kate?" he suddenly asked Miguel.

"In San Salvador for the night," Miguel answered. Then his eyes grew enormous, and he slapped his forehead with the palm of his hand in a universal gesture of *"mama mia!"* and rattled off something in Spanish to Caesare. The only thing Brianna got out of the entire exchange was the name Alicia. And then he ran off.

"It would appear," Caesare explained, "that there will be only the two of us for dinner tonight. Miguel had a date and nearly forgot. As it is, he will be an hour late."

A woman came out of the house with a

tray. On it was a bottle of wine with glasses and a delectable appetizer. Caesare poured a glass for Brianna and himself.

After the woman had gone, he raised his glass to Brianna, and she reciprocated. Their eyes were locked. "To happiness," he toasted.

She drank. "Whose happiness?" she asked.

A corner of his mouth lifted. "Yours. Mine. Separately." He offered one of the hors d'oeuvres. "These," he explained, "are *pupusas*. You will get them only in El Salvador."

She bit into one and lifted her eyes heavenward. "It's delicious. What's in it?"

"Cheese folded into the center of a corn-dough tortilla. It is then flattened and cooked on a griddle."

She looked at him in mild surprise. "That's a very thorough description. If I didn't know better, I'd think you knew how to cook."

"I know how to do a lot of things, my little American. And you," he asked, "do you play chess?"

"Yes."

"Well?"

An engaging grin curved her mouth. "Is that a challenge?"

"If you like." He picked up the wine and glasses, and she got the *pupusas*. Once in his study, they set the things down on a table and took their seats at the chessboard. A fire crackled cheerfully in the fireplace, taking the chill off the night air.

At first, the moves went quickly, but then, as the board setup became more complicated, they slowed to a crawl. Brianna watched Caesare as he contemplated the board. He still looked a little weary to her. She wished she could help him in his work. . . . What he was doing was very worthwhile, but she knew he could be in terrible danger if he were caught by either side, and the knowledge chilled her. She respected him for his work more than any man she had ever met, and yet she wished deep down that he wasn't involved in it.

"You're a very curious man, Caesare de Alvarado," she said, interrupting the peaceful silence.

His lazy smile touched her. "I am a man. What else is there to know?"

"Everything. I want to know everything about you." As soon as the words were out, she realized, as never before, how true they were. "I want to know if you've ever been in love. I want to know if you'll ever marry. I want to know what you think and how you feel. Everything."

His tawny eyes narrowed on her raven beauty. The muscle in his jaw worked. "You are getting into dangerous territory, Brianna. You will get your interview with Señora Conchetta in a few days, then you will leave here and put me, and this country, behind you."

Her violet gaze was unwavering. "I don't know if I'll be able to do that, Caesare."

He reached out to touch her face, his expression softening, and then the telephone on his desk rang. Both remained motionless until Caesare broke the spell and rose to answer it. He listened for a long time and spoke only a few words, his expression grim by the time he hung up. Without looking at her, he said, "Go to bed now. It is late, anyway."

She rose and approached him, suddenly very worried. "What's wrong? Where are you going?"

"Two of our doctors are having a problem getting out of an area." He started to walk out but stopped and turned as though compelled, relenting at the distress in her eyes. Returning, he took her face in his hands and rested his lips against her forehead. "Oh, Brianna," he said harshly, "what are you doing to me?"

Before she could speak, he was gone. She pushed her hair away from her face and leaned against his desk with a sigh. The real question was What was he doing to her? Her well-ordered life was collapsing around her ears, and she didn't know how to stop it.

A glance at her watch told her it was only eleven o'clock. She knew perfectly well she wouldn't be able to sleep until he returned safely, so she picked out a book, an English mystery thriller, puffed up some pillows and laid down on the couch in front of the fire.

Hours passed. Brianna struggled valiantly to concentrate, but she was too tied up in knots.

When Caesare finally returned, she sat up, weak with relief. He looked exhausted as he threw his jacket over a chair and fell onto the couch next to her, putting his arm around her shoulders and resting his head along the back of the sofa. "Why aren't you in bed?" he asked.

"I wasn't tired."

"I wish I could say that," he sighed, resting his cheek on her silky head.

"Perhaps you should go to your room and go straight to bed," she suggested.

"It's too far to walk."

Brianna closed her eyes tightly, for a moment reveling in his nearness. He was safe. He was there. She kissed his cheek tenderly, then put her head back on his shoulder. There was an indescribable peace in sitting there with him like that. She felt rather than saw him smile. "What's so funny?"

"Oh"—he exhaled a long breath—"you are warm and soft, and you smell wonderful. It is three in the morning—a perfect time to make love. And I am too damned tired to do anything about it."

Smiling, she pushed him into a prone position on the couch and covered him with the Indian blanket from the back. "Stop talking and get some sleep," she ordered.

He gazed at her with heavy-lidded eyes. "You'd better watch it, Brianna Kendall," he threatened. "I might get used to having you here, waiting up for me." Then he slowly closed his eyes and slept.

She curled up in the chair next to the couch and watched him sleep. Long dark lashes shadowed his bronzed cheeks, making him seem younger than his years. And vulnerable.

She tilted her head to one side and rested her cheek on her knees as she hugged them. A great peace settled over her. She knew. Without question, she knew that she was in love with this wonderful, contrary man. There would never be anyone to compare with him. But the tragedy was that she could never have him. Not really. He had been right when he said they came from different worlds. She was a living advertisement for the freedom of the American people, particularly American women. His ways were Latin and incompatible with hers. He belonged to his country and his people. How could she possibly compete? There was no room for her in his life, no matter what he felt, and she knew he cared for her. It was something she was going to have to live with for the rest of her life, because she was too weary to fight it any longer. The thing she had feared most in the world had happened.

When Brianna awoke the next morning, it was in her own bed. Someone, probably Caesare, had carried her there.

That day she wasn't going to waste any time. There was a story right here. Not Caesare's, of course. Even if she changed the names, people would be able to figure out who he was. But his grandmother's. It wasn't news. But she was a fascinating woman. Her life had been a full one. And if the magazine didn't want it, she would keep it for herself . . . rather like a written portrait of someone she liked.

She took her note pad beneath an enormous tree on the back lawn and enjoyed the brightly warm weather as she worked, overlooking the pool. Antonio Rojas came strolling out and, much to her dismay, spotted her immediately and headed toward her. With a silent groan of distaste, she started writing frantically on her note pad, hoping he would take the hint and leave her alone.

Needless to say, he didn't. Sensitivity was not one of Antonio's strong points. He simply couldn't believe that any woman could find him other than devastating.

"Hello there!" He sat down next to her.

"Hello," she responded coolly, continuing to write until he playfully took the pen from her fingers and held it high in the air over his head.

"Antonio," she said, sighing, "please give me my pen. I'm not in the mood for your little games today."

"You would be if you gave yourself a chance," he suggested.

"I don't think so."

"Come on. Give me a kiss, and I will give you your pen."

She hated this. "Antonio, let me put this to you as gently as possible. The fact is that you find yourself far more irresistible than I do. Now give me my pen."

He frowned at her like a little boy who had just had his ball taken away, then handed the pen to her sulkily. "There are other women who would jump at the chance to be with me."

"Then I suggest you find them."

But there was no rebuffing the man. "If you are turning your back on me because you think you stand a chance with Caesare, you had better think again. He has no use for you."

She raised an ironic brow. "And you do?"

"I know how to treat a woman like you."

"I'm sure that will be thrilling news for 'women like' me the world over."

He wagged his finger at her. "Ah, you are sarcastic, but that is all right."

It was hard not to be amused by his persistence. "You know, Antonio, you bring out the worst in me. I can't remember the last time I was so intentionally rude to a person—with so little result."

He ignored that. "I am telling you the truth, whether you believe me or not, my pretty one. If you have set your heart on Caesare, it will be broken. He has had many women in his life, but always other things came first. Do you think you will be any different?"

"I have no intention of discussing this with you, Antonio. My feelings are my business." But she already knew only too well that what he said was true.

He shrugged and rose to his feet, looking down at the top of her shining raven head. "So be it. But remember my words. And remember that when he throws you over, I will be around to pick up the pieces."

She stared after him as he walked into the house. What an odious man. But her hard-earned peace of the night before had been shattered beyond repair. Then she had been resigned. Now she hurt. And the pain would only get worse unless she did something and did it quickly. But what?

* * *

At dinner that night, it was just the four of them. Caesare, Kate, Miguel and Brianna. Throughout the meal, Brianna kept her emotional distance from Caesare, not even daring direct eye contact. If she looked at him, she'd be lost.

He watched her with a frown that grew increasingly black as the meal progressed.

She didn't really have a plan of action. Just to get through the hours until she could interview the woman who had lost her son and leave. When dinner was over, she tried to make her escape. But Caesare wasn't having any of it. He knew exactly what she intended and rose at the same time she did. Taking her arm in a firm grip, he spoke to the others but looked only at her. "If you will excuse us, it would appear that we have something to talk about."

With that, he forcibly led her to the study, closing the door behind them firmly. There he let go of her and folded his arms across his chest. "All right, Brianna. What is going on?"

She rubbed her arm—which really didn't hurt—and looked at him as nonchalantly as she could. "I don't know what you mean."

"You know exactly what I mean."

"Just because I'm not falling all over you the way you're used to women doing—"

"Stop being ridiculous. Being civil to someone does not mean you must fall all over them. Something happened to make you change your attitude. I want to know what it was."

Brianna walked away from him, her heart pounding. "You're making this very difficult."

"Making *what* very difficult? Talk to me, woman."

She forced herself to look into his eyes but was helpless to speak.

He took her shoulders in his hands and gave her a gentle shake. "Talk to me," he said again softly.

She couldn't stand being so close to him and backed away. Their eyes were locked. She knew she couldn't lie to him. She didn't want to. "I'm in love with you," she finally blurted. "And it's going to be the one great tragedy of my life. I think I knew it even before I accepted the assignment to come here." She gave a short laugh. "It's probably the reason I accepted the assignment in the first place. But I know that nothing can ever come of it. You're committed to the old ways of your people, and I'm committed to the new ways of mine."

He ran his hand tiredly through his dark hair and walked to the door leading to the courtyard, staring outside. "What you say is true," he finally admitted quietly, turning toward her. "I can offer you nothing beyond today. And that would never be enough for you. Marriage between two such as we is out of the question."

Brianna took a shaky breath and lowered her head. The dreams were gone.

The Salvadoran moved to stand in front of her, cupping her face in both of his hands and gently forcing her to look at him as he wiped away the tears she didn't even know were there. A sad smile twisted one side of his mouth. "We are ill-fated lovers, are we not?" Then, with a sigh, he rested his forehead against hers before abruptly pulling away and leaving the room.

In inexpressible pain, she wrapped her arms around herself and swayed.

Chapter Eight

Time dragged. Caesare stayed away. Days passed, and he didn't come home. He had sent Brianna a message telling her that Señora Conchetta was home and that José would take her to see the woman. She had gone and, as a result, wrote one of the most touching and worthy pieces her magazine had ever published. It had been worth every moment of the wait. And now it was time for her to return to the United States. She had only twenty-four more hours before her plane left.

She met Kate on the lawn for breakfast. Both of them were quieter than usual. Brianna's thoughts were with Caesare, wherever he was. Kate gently touched her hand. "What are you thinking about, girl?

Lately, every time I look at you, your mind is somewhere else. Has my grandson done this to you?"

Unhappy violet eyes turned to the old woman. "Where is he, Kate? It's been days."

"He's at his apartment in San Salvador."

She was so relieved. "I didn't know he had an apartment there."

Kate clicked her tongue. "You two. Do you mind if I make a suggestion?"

"What?"

"Why don't you go to him there before you leave the country? Tell him the things I see in your eyes."

"He knows," she said bitterly. "That's why he's stayed away."

She reached out and touched Brianna's hand. "Child, I know what's going on inside you. Believe me, I was there myself many years ago. If all you have is twenty-four hours, don't let it slip past uselessly. You will regret it, and so will Caesare."

Brianna hedged. She wanted to see him one last time more than anything in the world—but if he'd wanted to see her, he would have come there, wouldn't he?

In her heart, she knew what she had to do. There was no argument. If he refused to see her, then so be it. But she would make the effort. She turned to Kate, her mind made up. "May I borrow your car?"

Kate immediately handed her the keys.

Brianna looked down at her full white cotton skirt and white short-sleeved blouse with button-down pockets over her breasts, trying to see herself through his eyes. "Do I look all right?"

Kate smiled. "I expect he'll think so."

With a lilt in her walk, Brianna headed through the house and outside to the little car. Now all she had to do was drive.

Kate came running out, waving a sheet of paper. "Here!" she panted, leaning in through the open window. "Just on the outside chance you need to know where you're going."

Embarrassed, Brianna took the paper. She was so nervous that she had forgotten she didn't know where he lived.

"Follow the directions—and don't take any side roads. There has been some fighting near San Miguel. Avoid it. That shouldn't be a problem, because the only way you'll end up there is if you take a very, very wrong turn."

Kate stood back and waved as Brianna drove off, a smile in her blue eyes. Well, well, she thought. This just might work out after all.

The drive seemed to take forever, which, of course, it didn't. She made good time until she reached San Salvador, where she was slowed to a crawl by the heavy traffic. Very carefully, she followed the instructions on the sheet of paper Kate had given her and made her way through the city to the outskirts on the other side, then up and up into a charming area with lovely homes.

Brianna finally spotted the tall building in which Caesare lived. She parked and sat quietly for a time, gathering her courage. With a deep breath, she got out of the car and made her way to the big double doors. A security guard let her into the lobby and asked what she wanted—in English, no less. She told him who she wanted to see, and he looked at her apologetically.

"*Señorita*, he left over an hour ago."

She looked at him blankly. Of all the things that had occurred to her, his not being there wasn't one of them.

"Please." He took her by the arm and escorted her to a comfortable chair near a window. "Sit here. I will be right back."

He returned in a moment with a cup of coffee. "I called the *señor's* office and left a message. I feel sure he will be calling back shortly, Miss—"

"Kendall. Brianna Kendall."

He nodded as though something had been confirmed for him. "You will wait, then?"

She sipped the coffee. "For a few minutes."

"Very good." He bowed. "Excuse me, please."

She sat staring out a window, getting increasingly nervous. Her doubts all came rushing back. What kind of idiot was she, chasing a man in such a way? What would he think?

She put the cup and saucer on a small table with a clatter and got quickly to her feet. She had to get out of there. This whole thing had been a mistake. Without bothering to search out the guard, she walked to the car and sat there, her forehead resting against the steering wheel.

The car door was suddenly jerked open, and she found her wet violet eyes staring into tawny ones. For a long, long moment they looked at one another, saying nothing.

"Move over," he finally ordered.

"I beg your pardon?"

"Move to the passenger seat."

She slid over, and he got behind the wheel and drove off. Her heart was singing. He had come! "Where are we going?" she finally thought to ask, though it didn't really matter.

The Salvadoran pulled the car to the side of the road and turned to her, taking her face in his hands and kissing her, tenderly at first and then hungrily, as though he had missed her as much as she had missed him. She responded with complete abandon, aching to be in his arms. Nothing else mattered.

He lifted his face from hers, and his tawny gaze traveled over her face, memorizing every detail. "It took you long enough," he said huskily.

Her lips parted softly. "You mean you knew I would come to you?"

"I hoped."

"And if I hadn't?"

A corner of his handsome mouth lifted. "I would have come to you."

Everything came pouring out as she cherished the sight of him. "Caesare, after the way we parted, I was so confused. What you said kept whirling around in my head, and you didn't come back, and you didn't call. I wanted to talk to you so badly . . ." Her voice had a catch in it that forced the man to take her in his arms again.

"It wasn't easy. But at the time I thought it best."

"I'm only going to be here until tomorrow."

"I know. Spend that time with me, Brianna. All of it."

There was nothing she wanted to do more, and she finally had the courage to do it. He read the answer in her lovely eyes and held her to him once again. He knew they had only a few hours. But for that short time they would belong to each other. It wasn't enough. It wasn't nearly enough. But it was all they had.

Reluctantly, he let her go and put the car back into gear. "Where are we going?" she asked again.

"To lunch in a place so beautiful it must be seen to be believed."

To get there, they passed through fruit country, heavy with pineapples glowing with a hidden orange, papayas as big as watermelons and cantaloupes. They passed through the town of El Congo, unimpressive and dirty, particularly in contrast to the beautifully kept *finca* that straddled the road a few kilometers away, its hedges ablaze with poinsettia and bougainvillaea.

He took her to a place called the Hotel del Lago. Caesare turned in at the gates and parked under a tree.

They were on the Volcán de Santa Ana, a volcano with the highest peak in El Salvador, and the hotel was built on Lake Coatepeque. Brianna admired her surroundings with wide, appreciative eyes as they sat at a white-clothed table on a terrace overlooking the lake. She was fascinated by fishermen so still they seemed painted rather than real, floating on its surface.

"The men are called crabbers," explained Caesare, who was also watching them. "Notice that their boats are made not from hulls but from planks. They are seated on chairs attached to the boats."

"Why are they so still?" She felt as though she should whisper.

"They use no hooks. What the men are dangling are lines baited with meat. The crab grasps the line with his claw. His tug is so gentle that if the water is disturbed from the man's movement, he would probably miss it."

"Doesn't the crab get away when the man pulls him to the surface?"

"Crabs are funny creatures. They are reluctant to release their grip, and if the fisherman does his job patiently and well . . ." He shrugged.

A waiter approached them. Caesare ordered without consulting her, then leaned back in his chair and watched her lovely profile as she stared out over the lake.

"It took a lot of courage for you to come to me."

Her eyes met his. "It would have taken more to stay away."

The waiter returned with two thick, steaming bowls of crab soup. It was delicious, but her mind wasn't on the food.

"Caesare." She hesitated. "Do you think you will ever live in the United States?"

"No. Not in the foreseeable future. My people need me too much. It is important that you understand that, Brianna."

"But later, when the war is over—"

"It could be decades."

Her heart fell. She couldn't help but hope, no matter how futilely. She pushed the soup away. "Caesare, I want you to hold me."

His eyes lingered on her; then, wordlessly, he put some money on the table and walked her to the car. They didn't speak during the drive to his apartment, and once inside, with the door closed behind them, they just looked at each other, not moving. Her heart beat steadily and strongly beneath her breast.

Slowly, inevitably, she moved toward him. The Salvadoran opened his arms and gathered her against him. They stood like that, holding one another. Then, without speaking, he lifted her high into his arms, close to his heart, and carried her down the long hall to the bedroom.

He didn't lay her on the bed, as she might have expected, but set her on her feet near it. Their lips met in a gentle caress, as with consummate skill he unbuttoned her blouse and slid it from her shoulders. His mouth sensuously moved down her neck and over her bare shoulder, sending a wave of passion through her.

Following his lead, she unbuttoned his shirt and ran her hands lightly across his bronzed, muscled chest. His mouth lingeringly caressed her ear and then made its slow way to her softly parted lips as her hands slid around his bare back and held his body closer to hers. She reveled in the feel of his bare skin.

He finished undressing her and himself and lowered her onto the bed, looking into her heavy-lidded eyes. Her soul was laid bare for him to read as he wished, and she didn't care. Brianna was holding nothing back, nor did she want to.

They lay on the bed, facing each other in the semilit room, touching, exploring each other in wonder. His hand slid down her curved waist, over her slender bare hip and thigh, sending a delicious tingling through her.

Caesare cupped her firm bottom and pulled her tightly against him. He groaned at the contact, and there was no mistaking his desire. Brianna's own need flamed in response as their lips met once more in passionate exploration. Brianna gave herself completely.

Caesare pushed her back against the pillows and lifted himself above her.

The telephone next to the bed rang shrilly.

Caesare buried his face in the pillow next to her head with a groan. It rang several times before he recovered enough to roll onto his back and answer. The conversation was similar to the one he had had in the library, and Brianna found her arousal being replaced with worry.

When he hung up, he pulled her into his arms and held her quietly against him for a long time. Then, laying her back against the pillows, he tenderly pushed her raven hair behind her ears, his eyes lingering on her face as though to memorize it for future reference. "I have to leave you, Brianna. I am needed."

Her heart grew heavy. With fear for him and with grief, because she wasn't allowed to have even this night with the man she loved. "Stay with me," she pleaded, hating herself for saying it but unable to stop.

"I want to." He kissed her eyes. "God knows I want to. Letting you go is hard enough as it is."

"I could stay."

A gentle smile touched his lips. "You would be miserable. And you would be in danger." He left the bed, and she watched as he dressed. He had a beautiful body. "I will call you if I am going to be too late getting back. There is a chance I won't see you again before you go."

In pain, she turned her face away from him when he would have stroked her cheek. He paused, then leaned closer and kissed her temple. "Good-by, Brianna."

When he had gone, she lay very still. Almost like a statue. How was it possible to love a man so much? She closed her eyes and hugged a pillow tightly against her.

Somehow she slept. It was dark when she awoke. The phone by the bed was ringing again. Thinking it was Caesare, she answered it quickly. "Hello?"

There was a pause at the other end.

"Brianna? This is Miguel. Is Caesare there?"

"He had to leave a few hours ago."

"Oh. Then he is probably already at San Miguel."

"He didn't say where he was going." Then Kate's words returned to her. "San Miguel? Isn't there fighting going on there?"

"A lot of it. Some of our supplies aren't getting through, and one of our doctors has been arrested."

Her heart plunged. Caesare was in the middle of it, and she was sitting there doing nothing. But not for long. As soon as she hung up, she dressed and headed for Kate's car in the parking lot. She knew which road to take to get to San Miguel, and that was exactly where she was going. She wouldn't get in the way, but she would be there if she was needed.

It was a fifty-kilometer drive. Parts of the road were terribly potholed, and after one particularly bad stretch almost forty kilometers into the trip, a tire blew. She maneuvered the car to the side of the road and immediately got out and opened the trunk. There was no spare tire. Kate had probably used it and forgotten to get it replaced.

For the first time, she really looked around the place where she was stranded. There were no streetlights. It was completely deserted—and completely eerie. She had come too far to return to San Salvador, but it was ten miles to San Miguel. She started walking.

One hour and several blisters into her trek, she realized she had made a mistake. Not a single car had passed in all that time. She sat by the side of the road and took off her sandals, rubbing her aching feet. To paraphrase an old, old song, those shoes weren't made for walking.

With a reluctant sigh, she strapped them back on and continued her journey. What was Caesare going to say when he found out what she had done? Good intentions aside, it was the result that counted.

Something caught her eye in the distance, and she narrowed her gaze. She couldn't tell for sure, but she thought she saw a car's headlights. Now that she was actually confronted with the possibility of someone's driving by, she didn't know whether to hide or flag them down.

She settled for indecision, which meant she neither hid nor flagged them down, but merely kept walking.

The car came toward her, then went past, but screeched to a halt twenty yards away.

She heard something that sounded like a cap gun in the hills, but when she saw Caesare step out of the car, highlighted by the moon, she forgot about it. "Brianna?" he called incredulously.

She swallowed hard, not knowing if she was ready for what was going to be a very big disagreement, and headed reluctantly toward him to face the music. She saw some bright flashes of light in the hills across the road and heard that noise again.

"Brianna!" he yelled suddenly. "Hit the ground!"

But it was as though she had turned to stone. She quite simply couldn't move as the realization dawned on her that what she heard were real guns. She saw Caesare running toward her, and before she knew what had happened, he had knocked her to the ground; then, with his arms around her, he rolled off the road and down a steep hill, where they were stopped by some bushes.

It was only a matter of moments before they heard a loud explosion, and even from where they were, they could see bright flames shooting into the air.

Caesare swore sharply in Spanish.

"What happened?" She clung to him even more tightly.

"My car was just blown up. Are you all right?" he asked in an urgent whisper.

She nodded and felt him let out a relieved breath. But when she would have said more, he clamped a hand over her mouth, gesturing toward the sound of voices some-where above them, laughing loudly. Her whole body stiffened in fear. They must be the men who were shooting at them.

It seemed like hours before they left, but in reality it was minutes. When they could no longer hear the voices, they still remained absolutely motionless.

Finally, Caesare rolled off her and sat up. Anger was in every line of his body. "What in heaven's name are you doing out here?"

She had well and truly landed in the middle of it this time. But there was no running from his anger. "I thought perhaps I could help . . ."

He ran his hand through his dark hair more in frustration than anything else. "What you did was foolish. You could have gotten us both killed."

"I realize that now. I'm sorry."

He was still angry as he helped her up. They walked up the hill, not touching, then stood staring at the smoldering blackened shell of his car. She gasped at the total devastation. She hadn't seen any war going on since she had arrived and, as a result, had taken it less seriously than she should have. This brought it very much home to her.

"How did you get here?" he asked suddenly.

"Car, mostly."

"Where is it?"

"Down the road several miles with a flat tire and no replacement."

He clicked his tongue. "Then we walk."

Though her feet protested, she didn't dare say a word. They headed into the hills, walking for nearly an hour until they came to a small, round house shrouded in darkness. He knocked on the door, and when there was no answer, pushed it open. He lit a match and looked around, finding what he had been seeking in the middle of a rough-hewn wooden table. A lamp. He lit it with a new match, and now they both looked around.

The entire house was only one room. There was a small sink and wood-burning stove off to one side but no running water that she could see. The floor was wooden, with handmade cloth rugs scattered on it, and off to one side was a small, soft-looking bed with a colorful blanket on top and a carved chest at its foot. Everything was spotless, so someone obviously still lived there.

"Where do you suppose they are?" she whispered in the dim light.

"They probably fled from the area when the fighting started. They will return when it is over."

He walked to the chest and opened it. There were spare blankets in it. He pulled one out and tossed it on the bed, then walked back to where Brianna stood and blew out the lantern.

"What are you doing?"

"The last thing we want to do is announce our presence," he told her, taking her by the arm and leading her across the room to the bed. "Lie down."

She did. Then Caesare lay next to her and put the blanket over them. His arm went around her shoulders—reluctantly, she thought—and her cheek rested against his chest. She felt absolutely safe there with him.

A peaceful silence fell over the room.

"Brianna?"

"Ummmmm?"

"If you ever pull a stunt like that again, I will turn you over my knee."

She couldn't help smiling. "Yes, sir."

"Good night."

"Good night."

Both of them drifted into a restless sleep, exhausted as they were. How long they slept, she hadn't any idea, but suddenly she was awakened by a sharp movement next to her. Caesare was sitting straight up in bed, his face covered in perspiration. She could see it in the moonlight beaming through an uncovered window. Sitting up next to him, she cupped his face in her hands. "Are you all right?"

He was shaking. "I am sorry if I awakened you."

"Did you have a nightmare?"

"Just forget about it," he said harshly, and then instantly regretted his sharp tone.

Pulling her into his strong arms, he held her close against him and buried his face in her dark hair. There was desperation in the way he held her.

"Caesare?" She pulled back and looked up at him. "What is it?"

"You." He shook his head. "I don't know what to do with you. And I don't think I'm going to know what to do without you."

A cryptic remark. He got out of bed and gently lowered her back onto the pillows. "Go to sleep now, *querida*."

She looked up at him. "What about you?"

He pushed the dark hair from her face. "Sssshhhh. Do not worry about me. I will come back to bed soon."

Chapter Nine

But he didn't. When she awoke the next morning, she was still alone. Caesare stood at the window, staring outside. He sensed her eyes upon him and turned. "Good morning." There was an edge to his voice.

She stretched her arms high over her head. "Good morning."

"We should be going. It is a long walk back to the road."

She tilted her head to one side, a confused frown creasing her forehead. It was as though a wall had sprung between them overnight. "Caesare?"

He turned away from her. "Not now, Brianna."

"But—"

"I said not now," he told her sharply, opening the door and heading out. After a second of stunned silence, she leaped up from the bed and grabbed her sandals, hopping on one foot and then the other as she put them on and tried to run at the same time. He was already a good distance ahead. Even when she caught up, she had to skip every few steps to stay there.

"What's the matter?"

He kept walking.

"Caesare, please, don't turn on me like this without telling me why," she pleaded.

He stopped suddenly and turned. She stopped as well and struggled to catch her breath. "You have no business being out here."

"I said I was sorry about that . . ."

He lifted his hand in a dismissing gesture. "I am not talking about that . . . though your actions last night are just another in a long line of reasons why I am a fool to have even considered—" He cut himself off. "I should have sent you back to the United States the day you showed up. You have done nothing but turn my world upside down since you arrived."

"I've turned *your* world upside down!" she said incredulously. "So where do we go from here?"

"You are going back to Sonsonate."

"And you?"

"I have things to do here. When I get to Sonsonate tonight, we will talk. And then you will leave."

In silence, they walked to the road. A flatbed truck came roaring by, stopping ahead of them about fifty feet. Caesare grabbed her hand and ran up to it, talking to the man behind the wheel in Spanish. As she watched, they shook hands, and then Caesare turned to her. "This man will take you to my home. When you get there, pack your things. I will take you to the airport this evening." He put his hands on her waist and lifted her bodily onto the back of the truck.

She looked at him for a long moment, her heart shattering into a million pieces. She had certainly done it to herself this time.

Caesare yelled something to the driver, and the truck lurched. She grabbed the side to keep her balance. Her now-dirty white skirt billowed in front of her, and her hair blew in her face.

The Salvadoran stood watching, his long legs straddled, his hands in the pockets of his jeans. His carved face was solemn and taut.

As she watched, he turned and walked in the opposite direction. Her eyes burned with the tears that wouldn't come. She hurt too much to cry.

Hours later, the truck pulled in front of his house. She leaped off the back, and the man drove off immediately, not giving her a chance to thank him.

Kate met her at the door, horrified by her appearance. "What happened to you?"

Her throat was still constricted, making it difficult to talk. She walked past the older woman into the house and lifted her hand. "I'll talk to you later."

Kate frowned at her disappearing back. "I'll be in my studio!"

Brianna walked into her room and stripped, then stood under the shower. She was trying her best to blank out her mind, but she couldn't. How had she gotten herself into this mess? Of all the men in the world she could have fallen in love with, why Caesare de Alvarado? Why him?

After drying off, she put on jeans and a long, loose red blouse, tying it with a multi-colored sash low on her hips. Then she packed, carelessly tossing things into her suitcase.

Her mind still whirling, she lugged them to the front hall and went in search of Kate. She found her in her sunlit studio off the courtyard, sitting on a stool in her paint-smudged smock, her glasses down at the end of her nose. The only time she wore them was when she painted. She looked over the tops of them at Brianna when she walked in. "Well, hello again. Feel like talking now?"

Brianna sat down in a wicker chair and

pushed her hair tiredly out of her face. "Not really, but I owe you some kind of explanation."

Kate put down her brush and gave the girl her complete attention.

"First of all, about your car. As far as I know, it's all right, but I got a flat tire when I was on my way to San Miguel last night and had to abandon it. I imagine Caesare will take care of it."

"San Miguel?" Kate frowned at her. "What on earth were you doing there? I told you there was fighting in the area."

"I know. And that I was there, or why I was there, just isn't important right now. What's important is that I think Caesare is kicking me out of the country."

"You've lost me."

She smiled ironically. "No. I've lost *him*."

"Did he say that?"

"Not exactly."

"Then why are you trying to second-guess the man? Give him a chance."

"He told me to pack my things."

"Did he tell you to leave?"

"He told me he'd take me to the airport."

"Meaning that he intends to speak with you?"

"Not if I'm not here." She rubbed her forehead tiredly. "Kate, I don't think I can bear having him tell me to get out of his life."

The old woman walked over to her and shook her shoulder. "Then don't let him, girl! What's gotten into you? The Brianna Kendall who writes for *Newsview* magazine would tell him where to get off. Not the other way around. Stand up for yourself. Tell him what's on your mind. Be honest and don't hold anything back. You owe it to him, but most of all, you owe it to yourself."

She was right. Brianna knew it as well as she knew her name. She had spent her entire life being honest with people, and now, when she most needed to be, she shrank back in cowardice. It wasn't like her.

She rose to leave the studio but looked back at Kate. "This is going to be a very long day."

Kate just winked and went back to her painting. She had complete confidence in the common sense of both people involved. And if they couldn't see how much they belonged together despite everything— well, she'd give up.

It was indeed one of the longest days Brianna ever suffered through. Dinner was an ordeal; she tried to be friendly and chatty, while painfully aware that her luggage was standing by the front door.

After dinner, she went straight to Caesare's study and paced. And paced. She tried desperately to figure out what she was going to say to him but didn't have a single bright idea in four hours.

When he finally walked in and stood in the doorway, tired and unshaven, she was speechless.

He tossed his jacket over the back of a chair and sat on the corner of his desk, his eyes never leaving her. "I thought you might have gone without me."

"I—" She cleared her throat and tried again. "I couldn't do that. There are some things that need to be said."

"I agree."

She looked at him in surprise. "You do?"

"I do." He folded his arms across his chest. "You first."

She walked away from him and stood by the fireplace, drumming her fingers on the mantel. She was supposed to be a journalist. Where were the words when she needed them?

But suddenly they were there. She left the fireplace and came to stand within a foot of him. "All right," she agreed. "Me first. I think you're a fool, Caesare de Alvarado. I love you. I don't know how it happened. I don't know why, but it did. You're everything I've ever dreamed of in a man and then some."

A corner of his mouth lifted. "And yet I am a fool. Why?"

"Because you're letting me go," she said bluntly. "You're sending me away when you should be begging me to stay. I could make you happy if you'd let me. I would make you a wonderful wife. Or a wonderful mistress, if that's all you wanted me for. I would even be that for you."

"Are you finished?" he asked coolly.

Her eyes dropped. "Yes."

"Good." He pulled her into his arms, and his mouth came down on hers in a long, deliberate kiss that left her barely able to stand.

"What was that for?"

"Because everything you said is true. I want you to marry me."

She pulled back and looked at him in confusion. "But you told me to pack . . ."

"So I did. And I still intend driving you to the airport tonight."

"What are you saying?"

"That you are the most frustrating woman I have ever met. There are times when I want to shake you until your teeth rattle— and yet I know that I wouldn't love you as much if you were to change."

Her lips parted softly in wonder. "You want to marry me?"

He traced a path down her cheek. "God knows it isn't what I intended, but it happened. I knew you were going to be trouble from the moment we met."

"Why are you sending me away? Why can't I stay here with you?"

He kissed her lightly on the mouth again,

his arms still securely around her. "Because you, my Brianna, have a lot of thinking to do."

A frown creased her smooth brow.

"You haven't even begun to realize the enormous change marriage with me will mean in your life. You are an American. A brother you love lives in America. When you marry me, you will be living in El Salvador. You will have a husband who travels a lot and who just might not come home one night if he gets caught."

"I could help you."

"And if we have a family? You couldn't. I would never risk it."

She honestly hadn't thought about that, and it showed on her face. Caesare flicked her nose and looked at her with eyes filled with tender love. "You see? You have much to think about. And what of your career? You could not possibly live in El Salvador with me and keep up with your career at *Newsview* magazine. And if you tried to, it would be a constant source of friction between us."

"But I could do other kinds of writing."

"The question, Brianna, is would you want to? You have invested a lot of time and energy into building a reputation as a worthy journalist. You are used to the challenge and excitement of traveling to foreign countries and interviewing interesting peo-

ple. Could you give that up? Because you
would have to."

"Couldn't we work around it?" she suggested.

"No." He was firm. "I have limitations—
and that is one of them. I will not have my
wife—or the mother of my children—
risking her neck over some 'story' that no
one will even remember in twelve months.
So you see," he said warmly, "you have a lot
to think about. I cannot chance your decid-
ing after our marriage that life with me
isn't what you want, after all. What is mine
I keep. Never doubt that. Once you are
married to me, you will stay married to
me."

Oh, but she knew her heart well on that
one already. "And," she said softly, "if I tell
you that there is no question about what my
decision will be?"

"I will tell you to return to the United
States, anyway, for two months."

"Two months!" She couldn't believe her
ears.

"Two months," he said firmly. "You are
inclined to be impulsive. This is one time
when you must not be."

"And at the end of those interminable
two months?"

"I will call you for your decision." He
looked at his watch and got up. "We should
be going. I don't want you to miss your
plane."

Her liquid violet eyes looked up at him with all the love in her heart, and the man wavered in his resolve, pulling her into his arms and kissing her with a longing that told her in no uncertain terms how he felt. "Look at me like that again, and you might miss several planes."

She wrapped her arms around his neck and clung tightly, suddenly frightened. "Caesare, don't send me away. I have a feeling—a bad feeling about this. If I stay, everything will be fine, but if you send me away, I don't think we'll make it."

His hands cupped her face. "I don't want you to go. But we need to find out if there is an 'us' or if in truth there is just a 'you' and a 'me.'"

"But—"

He placed his finger over her lips. "Ssshhh. Come."

Chapter Ten

There was no question in Brianna's mind about what she wanted to do, but because Caesare had asked, she gave his reservations serious consideration. It wasn't a decision to be taken lightly, and there were parts of her life she was going to miss terribly. But that paled into insignificance when she tried to imagine what her life would be like without him.

As she sat at her desk nearly two weeks after her return to the United States, she tried to compose a letter of resignation. Max wasn't going to be pleased. He had done a lot to further her career and had taken some big chances in hiring her when he did.

At that moment, he walked quickly by her desk, rapping his knuckles on its surface. "In my office, Kendall. Now."

She followed him, wondering what was going on. "Close the door behind you," he ordered, sitting in his big swivel chair and eying her across his desk.

She did, and sat down.

He leaned back. "How serious were you last year when you said you wanted the permanent London assignment?"

"At the time, very. Why?"

"It's open. Henderson resigned, and we want you as his replacement."

She sat back in amazed silence. "Me?" It was the chance of a lifetime. Everyone wanted the London assignment.

"You. Henderson said he'll rent you the place he has outside London if you're interested. It's a good deal. The real estate prices in the city are out of sight. How soon can you be ready to go?"

She hadn't planned on telling him this way, but she couldn't avoid it now. "I can't, Max."

He held up his hand. "I know what you're going to say. You can't make up your mind that quickly. I understand. Think it over and get back to me by, say, Wednesday."

"You don't understand. I can't take the job. You'll have to find someone else."

A heavy frown creased his forehead as he

leaned forward and toyed with a pencil. "Why not?"

"My life seems to be taking another course. I'm going to be resigning from *Newsview* altogether shortly."

He angrily tossed the pencil onto the desk. "Damn." Then he looked back at her. "Who is he?"

A smile played at the corners of her mouth. "How do you know it's a he?"

"Because I know you. And I know nothing but something like that could make you give up this chance. So who is he?"

"Caesare de Alvarado."

He shook his head. There was something in the way she hugged his name when she spoke that told him argument would be useless. At least with regard to the marriage. "Is there some reason why you won't be able to continue with the magazine? I can understand why you won't be able to take the London assignment. I don't like it, but I can understand it. But why the resignation? There's no rule that says you can't stay on here in your current capacity."

"I won't be living in New York. I'll be in El Salvador."

He shrugged. "That's not a problem for me. There's no reason you have to live here. I can wire you your assignments."

"I'm sorry, Max. I can do occasional pieces, but nothing I'll need to travel for."

He shook his head sorrowfully. "You're throwing a lot away for him. He's a good man, I have to admit. I have a lot of respect for him. But you're throwing a lot away."

"It comes down to a very simple point, Max. I think I can be happy without this job. I know I'll never be happy without Caesare. I really have no choice."

He raised his hands. "Okay, no more argument. If that's what you want, then so be it." He looked at his watch. "How about a last lunch?"

Her eyes smiled at him. "I'd like that, Max. Thank you."

She worked at the magazine almost up to the day she expected to leave the country, clearing up a lot of little assignments, doing a few final interviews. All the while, she hoped Caesare would call her early to ask her to join him, but the call never came. The waiting was terrible.

On a Saturday morning, she began cleaning out her closets to get things ready for her move when the telephone rang. She picked it up, expecting it to be Annie. "Hello?"

"Brianna."

She gripped the phone tightly and closed her eyes. It was Caesare.

"Are you there?"

She nodded her ponytailed head. "I'm

here. I was just getting my clothes ready to pack . . ."

"No," he said harshly. Then, more quietly, he said, "No, Brianna. I don't want you here."

She pressed her hand to her mouth and held it there to stay the flood of questions and pleas that rushed to her mind. "Why?" she finally managed.

"There are reasons that I cannot go into over the telephone."

"Caesare, if there's a problem, perhaps I can help."

"If you showed up here, *you* would become the problem."

"I don't understand." But she was beginning to.

"I want you to stay where you are. Things have changed for me. I—I was a fool to think things could ever have worked out between us. Marriage is out of the question."

"Then don't marry me. I told you it was all right. But don't turn away from me." She was pleading with him, throwing her pride to the winds, but she didn't care.

"I can see that I shall have to be blunt with you. I do not love you, Brianna. I was attracted to you when you were here, but I have been attracted to many women. It's not enough to base an entire future on."

Brianna closed her eyes. She felt sick.

There was a pause at his end of the line, and then he said, "Good-by."

Caesare stood staring down at the telephone he had just hung up, his hand still on the receiver. His jaw was taut with the pain it had caused him to make that call, but it was something that had to be done.

At the knock on his apartment door, he straightened and took a deep breath before opening it. A uniformed man stood there unsmilingly, his gun drawn. *"Buenos dias,* colonel," Caesare said. "I have been expecting you."

Brianna put the receiver on its cradle and stood like a statue. She couldn't pull a coherent thought together. With deathlike calm, she walked into the kitchen and poured herself a cup of coffee, but when she tried to lift it to her mouth, her hand shook so badly that she couldn't hold on to it and it fell to the floor, smashed into a thousand pieces.

As she stared at the poor cup, the protective numbness began to fade. She wrapped her arms around her waist and doubled over in pain. Finally, the tears came and with them harsh, gasping sobs that shook her slender frame.

A year later, Brianna and a woman with whom she worked were in a fashionable London restaurant having lunch. Max had given her the job, after all, and she had settled into her new life nicely.

She and Robbin were laughing about something a man had said in one of Brianna's interviews. But her smile faded suddenly. Involuntarily, her head turned toward the door. Caesare stood there, his tawny eyes narrowed on her, an unfathomable expression in their depths. Her heart raced at the sight of him, but after her initial look of surprise, there was nothing in her face to tell of the turmoil within. But on the hand gripping the linen napkin, her knuckles were white.

Robbin leaned forward. "Who is that gorgeous creature staring at you?"

Brianna pulled her gaze from his. "Caesare de Alvarado." She looked at her watch. "I really have to be leaving if I'm going to get that write-up done by five o'clock."

"You can at least finish your lunch."

"No. I can't, really." She got to her feet, feeling a panicked need to get out. She still hurt too much to face him head-on. "I'll talk to you tomorrow."

"Wait!" Robbin caught her arm. "Who's that woman at the table he's approaching?"

Brianna watched as he made his way through the restaurant to a smiling woman who kissed him on the cheek in greeting. "I don't know her name, but she's an editor with Jamison Publishing."

"So he's a writer."

"He's a writer," she said quietly, thinking of how many more facets his personality had.

Without looking back, she drove to her quaint Tudor cottage on the outskirts of the city and, after changing clothes, went to work in the flower beds with a vengeance, digging and turning the soil around the colorful plants. She hadn't expected to see him. She wasn't ready to see him. There was still too much pain. There would probably always be pain where he was concerned. She had long since gotten over the anger—she thought.

But she was smarter now. She had been a fool.

A car went by, but she didn't think much about it and went on digging. Until she experienced the same feeling that had assailed her in the restaurant. She stopped digging and sat absolutely still. Slowly, she turned and looked up and into Caesare's tawny eyes. He was much closer to her than he had been in the restaurant, and she saw some changes. There was a whisper of gray at the sides of his thick, dark hair. He was a little thinner. And down one cheek was a long, thin scar. Strangely, it only made him more attractive.

"Hello, Brianna."

Feeling at a distinct disadvantage, she

rose. There was no running now. "What are you doing here?"

"In London or at your home?"

"Both."

"I came to see you."

She rubbed her forehead and left a streak of dirt behind. "You should have let me know. I could have saved you the trip."

"I would have come, anyway."

She forced herself to meet his gaze. "We have nothing to say to each other."

"On the contrary, Brianna." His gaze grew tender at the distress on her face, which she was trying so valiantly to hide from him. "We could talk for the rest of our lives and still not have enough time to say it all."

They stood there face to face. Her breathing quickened in helpless fury. "I loved you!" she finally blurted out. There was a world of accusation in those three words.

He reached out a hand to touch her cheek, but she flinched away. His hand fell to his side. "You still do. You always will. The two of us—we are in each other's blood, like a fever that can't be conquered."

"I will never let anyone hurt me the way you did. I've learned. I'm tougher."

"Do not get too tough, my Brianna." His eyes lingered warmly on her. "I am leaving for El Salvador in a few hours."

She swallowed hard at his words. "You're

leaving?" She should be glad. She wanted to be glad.

He inclined his dark head. "But be assured that this is not our final meeting. There are things to be settled between us."

"Not as far as I'm concerned." She turned away from him and began digging in her garden again.

She heard his car start moments later but didn't look up as he drove off. She dug for another fifteen minutes, jabbing furiously at the soil, determined to let nothing pierce the armor in which she had enclosed herself.

She threw the trowel angrily to the ground and pressed her hand tightly against her temple. Why couldn't he have left her alone? Seeing him again hurt so. . . .

Chapter Eleven

Brianna was browsing in a bookstore a few days later, as she often did. The middle-aged clerk smilingly approached her. "Good afternoon, Miss Kendall. I just this moment finished stocking some new books you might be interested in. They're by the front windows."

She smiled her thanks and wandered over. As she looked at the stacks of books, one stood out. It was by Caesare.

She reached for it automatically, then drew her hand back sharply. The clerk saw her interest and picked it up for her. "This is going to be one of my big sellers," she told her proudly. "It's the story of his months in a Salvadoran prison, what led up to his imprisonment, what has happened since.

There's a lot of historical detail about El Salvador—"

"He was in prison?" she interrupted urgently.

"Absolutely. And it sounds as though it was a very grim time for him." She turned the book over and showed her Caesare's picture, pointing at the scar Brianna had noticed. "He got this when a soldier slashed at him with a bayonette."

Brianna took the book and tenderly ran her fingers over the glossy black and white picture. "He never told me—"

"Do you know him?"

A sad smile curved her mouth. "Apparently not as well as I thought." She opened the front cover, and her name stepped off the page in the dedication. "To Brianna, the woman I love. The woman I will always love," it read simply.

She closed her eyes and hugged it to her breast. So many questions were answered now.

She bought it and raced home. She spent the next ten hours absorbing his words, sometimes with tears, sometimes with laughter. He was a wonderful writer. But when she got to the part about what they had done to him in prison, she could hardly bear to read it. It infuriated her that people could still be subjected to such horrible treatment. It tore her heart to know how he must have suffered. And while he was going through it, she had been in London sulking.

It was two o'clock in the morning when she finished, but she didn't care. She called Max and gave *Newsview* notice. And then she threw some clothes into a suitcase and raced to the airport to book a flight to El Salvador.

The guard at the gate of Caesare's home knew her and let her pass. She drove right up to the front door and walked in. Kate was in her studio and turned in surprise at Brianna's entrance. "Child, what on earth are you doing here?"

They embraced. "There are a few things that need straightening out. Do you know where Caesare is?"

"Riding his horse."

"Do you know where?"

"Not really. Any one of a dozen places around here."

She thought quickly. Chances were he was where he had taken her so many months before. "Kate, would you do me a favor?"

"If I can."

"Would you call the stables and tell whoever is there to saddle me a *very* gentle horse?"

She picked up the phone even as Brianna spoke. "It will be ready by the time you get there."

She tore through the house and outside

past the pool and into the gardens as fast as her feet would carry her.

Kate was right. By the time she got to the stables, José was just finishing saddling the little mare she had ridden before. He handed over the reins with a shy smile.

With more enthusiasm than skill, she climbed onto the horse and galloped, holding on for dear life.

Half an hour later, she spotted Caesare riding toward her, apparently on his way back to the stables. She slowed down. When he saw her, he stopped altogether and waited, both man and horse perfectly still. Her heart thrilled at the sight of him, but for the first time since she had started this mad romp over twenty-four hours earlier, she was afraid. Afraid he wouldn't want to see her. Afraid he wouldn't want her.

But it was too late to turn back now. And she wouldn't have if she could. The rest of her life hinged on that meeting.

The little mare stopped right next to the stallion. She and Caesare were facing one another, his expression enigmatic.

"I read your book," she told him. "Why didn't you tell me when you called that you were going to prison?"

"Because I know you," he said quietly. "And I knew that if you found out you would have foolishly shown up here in an attempt to set me free."

"Of course I would have!"

"And probably ended up behind bars yourself."

"They wouldn't dare."

He lifted an expressive dark brow. "Because you are a journalist? Because you are American? Don't kid yourself, Brianna. You are as vulnerable as anyone in El Salvador. Perhaps more so because of your association with me."

Silence fell between them. "Caesare—did you mean what you said in the front of your book?"

His eyes drank her in. "Yes."

She closed her eyes against the happiness that surged through her. "Why didn't you tell me that when you saw me in London?"

The stallion restlessly stamped a hoof. "I wanted to. That is why I drove to your home. But I knew you weren't ready to hear it. There was too much anger in you."

"It's gone now. Caesare . . . hold me."

Without hesitation, he dismounted and easily lifted her from her horse. His arms went around her slender form and held her close against him, as though he'd never let her go again. She buried her face in his neck, hardly able to believe that they were together."

He held her away from him, his hands on her shoulders as his eyes lingered on every feature. "From the first day I met you, I couldn't even look at another woman without wishing she were you. And when you came into my life again, I grew to love you so much that you became a part of me. Without you this past year, I have been an empty shell of a man. You breathe life into me."

"Don't ever send me away from you again. Please. I couldn't bear it."

"Nor could I." He kissed her softly parted lips.

She traced her finger down the thin scar on his cheek as her violet eyes shone with the love she felt for him. "I never wanted to fall in love with you," she confessed. "I fought so hard against it."

"You said that it would be the one great tragedy of your life. What did you mean?"

"It still might be. If anything ever happened to you, I don't think I could go on."

"Nothing is going to happen to me."

"That's what my mother thought about my father. She couldn't live without him. That's a beautiful, terrible kind of love."

He pushed her mussed raven hair behind her delicate ears. "For the first time in my life, I understand exactly how your mother felt," he told her. He kissed her again, and she wrapped her arms around his neck, pulling him as close to her as she could. The kiss deepened into unbearably sweet desire. Caesare groaned and held her away from him. "Marry me."

She thrilled to his words. "When?"

"Now. Tonight. We have been apart too long."

She looked at him steadily. "We don't have to be married to be together."

He tilted her chin with his finger and cherished her with his eyes. "We do. If our child is conceived tonight, I want it to be by my wife."

"A child." Her eyes filled with such tenderness that the man's heart caught. She wrapped her arms around his neck again. "Have I told you in the past two minutes how much I love you?"

"In a hundred different ways."

"I'll never stop, you know. You're stuck with me now."

"Then I shall have to make the best of it." He flashed her a lazy white smile that sent her pulse soaring. "And return that love with every fiber of my being."

The horses followed as, with their arms around each other's waists, they walked back to the house. Together, as they were meant to be.

IT'S YOUR OWN SPECIAL TIME
Contemporary romances for today's women.
*Each month, six very special love stories will be yours
from SILHOUETTE.*

$1.75 each

☐ 100 Stanford	☐ 127 Roberts	☐ 155 Hampson	☐ 182 Clay
☐ 101 Hardy	☐ 128 Hampson	☐ 156 Sawyer	☐ 183 Stanley
☐ 102 Hastings	☐ 129 Converse	☐ 157 Vitek	☐ 184 Hardy
☐ 103 Cork	☐ 130 Hardy	☐ 158 Reynolds	☐ 185 Hampson
☐ 104 Vitek	☐ 131 Stanford	☐ 159 Tracy	☐ 186 Howard
☐ 105 Eden	☐ 132 Wisdom	☐ 160 Hampson	☐ 187 Scott
☐ 106 Dailey	☐ 133 Rowe	☐ 161 Trent	☐ 188 Cork
☐ 107 Bright	☐ 134 Charles	☐ 162 Ashby	☐ 189 Stephens
☐ 108 Hampson	☐ 135 Logan	☐ 163 Roberts	☐ 190 Hampson
☐ 109 Vernon	☐ 136 Hampson	☐ 164 Browning	☐ 191 Browning
☐ 110 Trent	☐ 137 Hunter	☐ 165 Young	☐ 192 John
☐ 111 South	☐ 138 Wilson	☐ 166 Wisdom	☐ 193 Trent
☐ 112 Stanford	☐ 139 Vitek	☐ 167 Hunter	☐ 194 Barry
☐ 113 Browning	☐ 140 Erskine	☐ 168 Carr	☐ 195 Dailey
☐ 114 Michaels	☐ 142 Browning	☐ 169 Scott	☐ 196 Hampson
☐ 115 John	☐ 143 Roberts	☐ 170 Ripy	☐ 197 Summers
☐ 116 Lindley	☐ 144 Goforth	☐ 171 Hill	☐ 198 Hunter
☐ 117 Scott	☐ 145 Hope	☐ 172 Browning	☐ 199 Roberts
☐ 118 Dailey	☐ 146 Michaels	☐ 173 Camp	☐ 200 Lloyd
☐ 119 Hampson	☐ 147 Hampson	☐ 174 Sinclair	☐ 201 Starr
☐ 120 Carroll	☐ 148 Cork	☐ 175 Jarrett	☐ 202 Hampson
☐ 121 Langan	☐ 149 Saunders	☐ 176 Vitek	☐ 203 Browning
☐ 122 Scofield	☐ 150 Major	☐ 177 Dailey	☐ 204 Carroll
☐ 123 Sinclair	☐ 151 Hampson	☐ 178 Hampson	☐ 205 Maxam
☐ 124 Beckman	☐ 152 Halston	☐ 179 Beckman	☐ 206 Manning
☐ 125 Bright	☐ 153 Dailey	☐ 180 Roberts	☐ 207 Windham
☐ 126 St. George	☐ 154 Beckman	☐ 181 Terrill	

$1.95 each

☐ 208 Halston	☐ 212 Young	☐ 216 Saunders	☐ 220 Hampson
☐ 209 LaDame	☐ 213 Dailey	☐ 217 Vitek	☐ 221 Browning
☐ 210 Eden	☐ 214 Hampson	☐ 218 Hunter	☐ 222 Carroll
☐ 211 Walters	☐ 215 Roberts	☐ 219 Cork	☐ 223 Summers

IT'S YOUR OWN SPECIAL TIME

*Contemporary romances for today's women.
Each month, six very special love stories will be yours
from SILHOUETTE. Look for them wherever books are sold
or order now from the coupon below.*

$1.95 each

☐ 224 Langan	☐ 243 Saunders	☐ 262 John	☐ 281 Lovan
☐ 225 St. George	☐ 244 Sinclair	☐ 263 Wilson	☐ 282 Halldorson
☐ 226 Hamson	☐ 245 Trent	☐ 264 Vine	☐ 283 Payne
☐ 227 Beckman	☐ 246 Carroll	☐ 265 Adams	☐ 284 Young
☐ 228 King	☐ 247 Halldorson	☐ 266 Trent	☐ 285 Gray
☐ 229 Thornton	☐ 248 St. George	☐ 267 Chase	☐ 286 Cork
☐ 230 Stevens	☐ 249 Scofield	☐ 268 Hunter	☐ 287 Joyce
☐ 231 Dailey	☐ 250 Hampson	☐ 269 Smith	☐ 288 Smith
☐ 232 Hampson	☐ 251 Wilson	☐ 270 Camp	☐ 289 Saunders
☐ 233 Vernon	☐ 252 Roberts	☐ 271 Allison	☐ 290 Hunter
☐ 234 Smith	☐ 253 James	☐ 272 Forrest	☐ 291 McKay
☐ 235 James	☐ 254 Palmer	☐ 273 Beckman	☐ 292 Browning
☐ 236 Maxam	☐ 255 Smith	☐ 274 Roberts	☐ 293 Morgan
☐ 237 Wilson	☐ 256 Hampson	☐ 275 Browning	☐ 294 Cockcroft
☐ 238 Cork	☐ 257 Hunter	☐ 276 Vernon	☐ 295 Vernon
☐ 239 McKay	☐ 258 Ashby	☐ 277 Wilson	☐ 296 Paige
☐ 240 Hunter	☐ 259 English	☐ 278 Hunter	☐ 297 Young
☐ 241 Wisdom	☐ 260 Martin	☐ 279 Ashby	
☐ 242 Brooke	☐ 261 Saunders	☐ 280 Roberts	

SILHOUETTE BOOKS, Department SB/1

1230 Avenue of the Americas
New York, NY 10020

Please send me the books I have checked above. I am enclosing $_____
(please add 75¢ to cover postage and handling. NYS and NYC residents please
add appropriate sales tax). Send check or money order—no cash or C.O.D.'s
please. Allow six weeks for delivery.

NAME _____

ADDRESS _____

CITY _____ STATE/ZIP _____

Silhouette Romance

Coming Next Month

Song of Surrender by Elizabeth Hunter

A tempermental and exacting taskmaster, David Lloyd wanted Katy as his pupil. Katy knew this would advance her singing career, but could she resist the sweet insistence of his lovemaking?

Less of A Stranger by Nora Roberts

Megan and David clashed over his plans for the amusement park she ran. But Megan wanted the restless, roaming David, and at Joyland, dreams were supposed to come true.

The Felstead Collection by Kay Stephens

Jay was hired to determine whether the paintings in the priceless Felstead collection were real. But soon she was wondering if the love of dark, enigmatic Rhys Felstead was a true one.

Roomful of Roses by Diana Palmer

Only one thing stood in the way of Wynn's marriage—her legal guardian, McCabe Foxe. The tough war correspondent invaded her life again—and lay siege to her heart.

Best of Enemies by Joan Smith

Toni Ewell and Jack Beldon drew battle lines over the planned demolition of a town landmark. But sometimes the best of enemies can turn into something more than friends.

No Gentle Love by Ruth Langan

It took a man like Drew Carlson to recognize the sensuality beneath Kate Halloran's tailored suit. He hoped she'd find a love that wasn't forecast in the annual reports.

BEE-WARE!

Tom and his friends were having a difficult time traversing the lawn now that they were smaller than insects.

"Tom, duck!" Rick warned.

Tom swung around and was covered with a cloud of choking yellow pollen. The bee buzzing him pulled back at the last possible instant and hovered just above him, its stinger menacingly close.

"Get away, Tom!" Sandra ran forward, waving her arms to distract the honeybee. "If it stings you, you'll be dead."

The honeybee dived at Tom. As its wickedly barbed stinger moved forward to stab him, he could see a shining drop of deadly venom gleaming at the tip.

Books in the Tom Swift® Series

Available from ARCHWAY Paperbacks

TOM SWIFT 8

THE MICROBOTS

VICTOR APPLETON

AN ARCHWAY PAPERBACK
Published by POCKET BOOKS
New York London Toronto Sydney Tokyo Singapore

AN ARCHWAY PAPERBACK *Original*

An Archway Paperback published by
POCKET BOOKS, a division of Simon & Schuster Inc.
1230 Avenue of the Americas, New York, NY 10020

Produced by Byron Preiss Visual Publications, Inc.

ISBN: 0-671-75651-6

First Archway Paperback printing April 1992

10 9 8 7 6 5 4 3 2 1

Cover art by Romas Kukalis

Printed in the U.S.A.

IL 6+

THE MICROBOTS

"TOM, IT BROKE!" CAME ROB'S WARNING. UNSEEN death whipped through Tom Swift's underground laboratory. A workbench suddenly crashed, one leg entirely cut through by a ghostly knife. Then a long, thin gash appeared along one concrete wall with only a whisper of warning.

"I've lost contact on my sensors, Tom," Rob said. The seven-foot-tall silvery robot started across the lab and abruptly toppled to one side, his left leg cleanly severed. "Control has been lost in my lower limb," the robot repeated. "Short-circuiting is imminent."

"Don't move. Let me find the cable." Tom Swift strained to hear the almost invisible monofilament strand whistling past his head, but it wasn't likely that he would. The monofilament was too thin to create much sound as it lashed around like an angry rattlesnake.

Seconds earlier, a humming oscilloscope had shown just the right stress pattern on the wire. Now only a straight line burned in the green phosphor display. Tom's newest invention, a microthin wire made from a single crystal of steel, had broken loose and started slicing up everything in the lab. He had been stretching the wire to test its strength. When his laser detection system located the flailing cable, Tom's control console beeped frantically. He dived out of his desk chair just before it was cut in half like ice cream being sliced by a red-hot wire.

"Orb, help Rob!" the blond teenage inventor ordered. Rob's autonomous basketball-size memory and computational module—the superior brain of the pair—moved silently over the concrete floor to aid the fallen robot. Orb floated on an invisible cushion of magnetic repulsion provided by superconducting rails that lay hidden behind the lab's walls, floor, and ceiling.

For protection, Tom put on special gloves with palms made of woven diamond fibers, the strongest material on Earth—until now. He touched a control on his computer, and twin laser beams crisscrossed the room, quickly homing in on the unseen menace.

The laser beams locked on what looked like bare concrete floor, but they had located the single-crystal line, which had finally come to rest. Tom gingerly ran his glove along the floor, not seeing what he was touching.

"How close am I?" Tom asked Rob.

"It is at the tip of your index finger," the robot told him. Aided by the lasers' guidance, he had once more located the cable. Orb spun back and forth as it examined Rob's severed leg. Sensors glowed as Orb extended a tiny flexible probe that worked its way up inside Rob's leg to examine the damaged circuits.

Tom was extremely wary of the monofilament cable now cradled in his hand. He used the laser beams to keep it pinpointed as he carried the cable to his work table and saw what had gone wrong.

"I'm getting careless. You ought to have warned me, Rob. I didn't fasten the cable properly. When the monofilament broke free, it was under so much tension that it lashed across the room like a metallic whip."

"My programming does not permit me to nag, Tom. However, I did warn you of the general danger several times." Rob sat on the floor impassively as Orb continued to probe. Tom checked the two robots' progress and was relieved to see that Rob could repair himself quickly with Orb's help.

Tom reattached the end of the monofilament cable to a small ring of pure industrial diamond. He checked the other end, which was strung across the lab and still fastened to a thick steel I-beam. Then Tom stepped back, relaxing for the first time since the experiment began.

The lab was a shambles, with chairs and desks cut into pieces. But the equipment for his other important experiment hadn't been damaged. Tom started to examine the new experiment but paused when he heard voices. Three windows high on the basement lab's wall looked out onto a sunlit grassy lawn dotted with shrubs and trees. Under the windows, a low, long table with an acid-resistant black top was strewn with various pieces of equipment. This was a new lab, still under construction, and Tom hadn't settled in yet.

Tom pushed aside a direct-current power supply and climbed onto the table to look out one of the windows.

"Oh, no! I forgot I invited the guys over for a volleyball game." Tom saw that Rob and Orb had almost finished reattaching Rob's leg. The large robot would soon be whole again. Tom knew the monofilament experiment could wait for a while, and a break might help him be less careless when he got back to it. He grinned and jumped down from the table, turning to Rob and Orb.

"You two start work on the *new* experiment. And let me know if anything goes wrong."

"We shall," Rob said, testing his repaired leg.

Tom saw all was in order, then hurried outside to join his friends.

"There he is," yelled Rick Cantwell, Tom's

best friend. "I told you he wouldn't wimp out on us. Where were you? We looked in your lab, and you weren't there."

"He's in no hurry to get beat," drawled Julio Chavez, grinning at Tom. Julio was stocky, had long black hair pulled back into a ponytail, and gave the impression of being laid back. Tom knew that was deceptive.

Julio and Rick had teamed up early in the summer for two-man volleyball and made a powerful team. Julio's reflexes were lightning fast, making it hard for Tom to score a point against him at the net.

"I was working in my new lab," said Tom, indicating the building. "Sorry I'm late."

"I told them you would be here," said Alan Lee, Tom's partner in their summer-long volleyball tournament.

"Thanks for the vote of confidence," Tom said with a grin, not wanting to tell his partner how close he had come to forgetting this game. Alan was precise, determined, and almost as good as Tom with computers. He moved with a liquid grace and controlled power that showed why he had finished ninth in Central Hills's annual ten-kilometer run. "We've got to finish that program we started, when you get time," Tom said.

"I've been considering new algorithms—" Alan began.

Julio cut him off. "Are we going to play, or are we going to sit around talking about Algonquins?"

"Algorithms," Alan repeated. "They're—"

"We're going to play," Tom said, heading off what could be a long argument. Alan and Julio were friends, but they often argued because of the differences in their personalities. Julio was impulsive, Alan thoughtful; both were fierce competitors.

"What's it going to be, guys?" Rick asked. "You want us to beat you in just one game or do we have to humiliate you two out of three?"

"We've been at this all summer," Alan said. "You know as well as I do the score is dead even. That means a sudden-death game is called for."

"How about it? Just one last game?" Tom suggested. The others agreed quickly and moved to the volleyball net set up in the middle of the large expanse of lawn. Behind one team would be the gleaming glass-and-steel Swift Enterprises administration building. The other team had the new lab at its back. Seconds later the volleyball sailed over the net, angling down straight at Tom. He slid on his knees to get his forearms under it, saving the point. Alan returned the ball, and Julio spiked it at the net.

The game was on in earnest.

They played hard for almost fifteen minutes, until Alan called out, "Wait a sec. Time out. Please!" He sneezed hard.

"Hay fever?" Tom asked. "I'm sure the infirmary's got something to help." The medical technologies division was only a few hundred yards away. When Tom's father, Thomas Swift, Sr., had built Swift Enterprises, he had wanted only the finest in research facilities and scientists. The medical facilities were state-of-the-art.

"I just need a quick rest. We're only one point behind." Alan sat and fumbled a handkerchief from his pocket, blowing his nose loudly.

"Hey, what's going on?" came Rick's angry outburst. He had reached for a jug of water and wound up spilling it onto the grass. Julio was laughing so hard he fell down.

"What's wrong, Rick? Can't even drink from a bottle without drooling all over yourself?" Julio was finally able to say.

Rick turned to his volleyball partner, who was doubled over with laughter.

"Julio, you sneak! You put this inside." Rick fished out a circular plastic disk. "You turned my water bottle into a dribble glass." He tossed the plastic bottle at Julio, who ducked and darted as Rick chased him.

"Let them wear each other out," said Tom, kneeling by his friend, whose allergy had been getting worse all summer.

"This is a very dangerous situation," Alan said unexpectedly, bending over with his hands on his knees.

"What? Are you having trouble breathing?" Tom's mind flashed to CPR and other life-saving techniques that he might need.

"See? Down here. A line of ants. But they

aren't just common ants. These are fire ants and potentially deadly. You know, their toxin is similar to hemlock."

"What's that, Socrates?" called Julio, drenched with sweat and the water Rick had thrown on him. "You working up ways to forfeit this game?"

"No way!" Tom declared. He looked at Alan, who was crawling on hands and knees, hunting for the fire ants' hill. "Alan," he said, tapping his friend on the shoulder, "let's get back on the court and show them some real playing."

"The only way you'll see *real* play is if you're videotaping Julio and me," Rick shouted. He served and scored a quick point. Just as fast, Rick and Julio lost the serve, and Tom evened the score with his sizzling jump service.

Alan continued to sneeze but still played well. At the net, facing Julio, Alan called out, "Unfair tactics! Gas warfare!"

"That's my cologne," Julio said.

"It's strong enough to raise the dead."

"Good, then you ought to take a deep whiff. We're gonna bury you!" Julio made one of his patented quick moves and powered the ball past Alan. Tom dived for it and missed. The serve went back to Rick.

Tom saw his sister, Sandra, coming from the administration building. When she got close enough, she called to him. Tom was prepared for the small distraction, but Rick and Julio turned to see Sandra at the wrong instant. Tom spiked the ball and got back the serve.

"Hi, Sandra, you come to watch me beat those two?" asked Rick, ignoring the missed ball.

"Hey, we're a team," complained Julio. *"We* are beating them."

"That's not reflected in the score," said Alan. "We're tied."

The tempo of the game increased as Sandra watched. Rick and Julio dived for saves and slammed the ball through the best blocks Alan and Tom could put up. Tom was panting hard and starting to tire.

"Time out," Tom called.

"What's up, Tom?" Alan Lee bent over, hands on his knees, catching his breath.

"They aren't playing as a team at the moment," Tom observed. "We can beat them if *we* work together. Do you think we can get the points back?"

Both Rick and Julio were talking with Sandra. Alan took a deep breath and said, "We're down only three points. We can do it. Remember the plays we practiced at the beginning of the summer?"

"They haven't seen them lately," Tom said, nodding. He was glad that Alan's drive to win was overcoming his usual desire to do things on his own. "Let's show them how a *team* works."

They started play again, and Tom's observation proved accurate. Rick and Julio each wanted to impress Sandra and had started grand-standing, diving for impossible saves and racing from the side to make spikes instead of less flashy passes. Tom and Alan worked together, play after play. Their precise shots and good passing paid off. Point after point was shaved off Rick and Julio's lead until both teams were even.

"What are you doing?" complained Rick, shoving Julio. "You missed that shot!"

"If you'd been paying attention, I wouldn't have had to dive for it."

"Hey, guys, don't fight," Sandra said. "You're all doing just great. This is the best game I've seen this summer—"

She was cut off by the ear-splitting rise and fall of a nearby siren.

"That's an alarm," Tom shouted, "and it's coming from my lab!"

THE VOLLEYBALL GAME FORGOTTEN, TOM SWIFT
rushed into his new lab, expecting the worst.
The alarm almost deafened him as he shoved
open the heavy door leading into the lab and
looked around for the trouble. Orb hung from
the ceiling, trailing tiny jets of the liquid nitrogen vapor that cooled its superconducting magnetic levitation circuits. Rob stood at the black-
topped equipment bench. When the tall robot
saw Tom, he touched a control on his chest. The
siren died.

"Rob, what's wrong? Why did you sound a
warning?" Tom's eyes darted around the huge
room, trying to find the trouble.

"The EPROM programmer malfunctioned,"
Rob said. "Program failure is a class-four
emergency."

11

"This is only a data error," Orb said from its perch on the ceiling. It whirred and ran along a hidden track and down the wall until it was at Tom's eye level. "Equipment failure is a class four. Failure to program properly should be a lesser class-five condition," Orb said.

"Do they always argue like this?" asked Julio, pressing in close behind Tom.

"Orb was designed to be Rob's data module, but I've programmed artificial intelligence into both of them," Tom said.

"They're becoming more independent as they learn from experience," Alan explained. Julio frowned at this, and Alan explained, "If you're not learning, you're dead. Learning means dealing with unknown and new situations. For instance, take this spider." Alan reached out to a spot just under the open lab window and allowed a spider to crawl onto his hand.

"Kill it!" shouted Julio, moving away. "It— it might be a black widow, or something else poisonous."

"Don't be ridiculous," Alan said. "This is an *Argiope argentata*, a simple garden spider. It's clearly not a *Latrodectus mactans*, the black widow. See the—"

"Quit showing off," Rick said. "Ever since you won that science-fair prize for studying bugs, you've been making everyone's skin crawl."

"I won a scholarship with that project," Alan said with a small smile.

Rick turned to Tom and asked, "What happened to cause the alarm?"

Tom examined Rob's work on the table. He shrugged. "It was just a small glitch. Rob is supposed to use an ultraviolet light to erase this EPROM—that's an Electronically Programmed Read Only Memory chip—and then enter a new program. He got his error codes confused, that's all." Tom ran a quick diagnostic check of Rob's circuits to be sure the robot wasn't more seriously damaged than he'd thought by the monofilament wire. The shining giant checked out perfectly.

"Well, I'm glad it's nothing serious," said Sandra. "Dad has been upset lately at the way your experiments have been getting out of control."

"Not this time," Tom said. He pointed to six large insectlike machines on the worktable in front of Rob. "Now let me show you my latest."

"They look a little like bugs," Rick said.

"Why build robot insects when there are real ones all around?" asked Alan. He let the spider on his hand escape back to its web.

Julio let out a sigh of relief. The others looked at him, and he said defensively, "What's the big deal? I thought it was poisonous."

"Are these poisonous?" Rick asked. He poked at the mechanical insects on the table. Each stood about a foot high and stretched eighteen inches long. They were designed to be mobile. Wires and tiny motors powered six legs on each of them. Heads fitted with special lasers and sound sensors gave the models the look of a real insect's compound eyes.

"Not at all," Tom said. "Those are my microbots. They're electromechanical, remotely controlled robots—an experiment in nanotechnology," Tom said. "Machines can be made so small you hardly see them so that they can get into places larger ones can't. These look like insects because evolution has made such a good design that I figured I ought to copy it." Tom picked up a small box with buttons and neon indicator lights. "Here's my remote controller."

"Hey, does that turn on the VCR and run the microwave, too? I could go for some popcorn right about now," Rick joked.

"I could program it that way," Tom said, "but I need it for the microbots."

"But, Tom," protested Alan, "these are *big*. Nanotechnology machines are tiny."

Tom smiled and waved his arm with a flourish toward the other end of the worktable on which the microbots stood. "And this is another new invention." He rested his hand on a large gunmetal gray box fitted with a movable plastic cone. Through several slits in the cone gleamed highly polished lenses.

"It looks like the X-ray machine in the dentist's office," said Sandra.

"There *are* similarities," Tom said. "Two electromagnetic rays focus into a single beam. I've invented a way to reduce the physical size of any object in that single beam. I call it a molecular compressor." Tom switched on the device using his remote controller. A powerful hum filled the room.

"You build full-size robots and then use this gizmo to shrink them?" asked Rick. "Why bother?"

"Yes, Tom, why bother?" Alan cut in. "Nanotechnology microassemblers would seem to be a more reasonable approach."

"I've heard of those," Julio said. "Microscopic machines that can move individual molecules." Julio's dark eyes danced. "Think of the practical jokes you could play with something that small."

"As small as your brain?" Rick laughed. "Nothing's that small. But really, Tom, why not use regular nanotechnology if you want something small enough to push atoms around?" Rick bent over and examined the underside of a microbot fitted with mechanical wings resembling a housefly's organic ones.

"Nantoechnology assemblers and replicators aren't smart enough," Tom explained. "They can hold only a single computer chip. I need something that'll do a lot of things, not just one. My microbots have dozens of chips in them. That's why they have to be this size to begin with—to hold the chips. Rob was working on installing them when he set off the alarm. And I only intend to reduce them to the size of an ant, not something on an atomic scale."

"So the boy genius is creating itsy-bitsy genius robots, huh?" Rick held up a winged microbot and pretended to soar and dive with it, as if it were a model airplane.

"Why reduce your microbots at all?" Sandra asked.

"There are many applications for them," Tom said, warming to the topic. "Using the molecular compressor, I can shrink the microbots to any size I want. And there are a million uses. Think of sending thousands of tiny solar-powered bulldozer microbots to the moon. Unattended, they could level areas for more manned landings or extract minerals and leave them to be picked up. If one microbot broke down, thousands would still be working. Or they could be used to explore other planets. Instead of sending a lot of muscle, we'd be sending a lot of cheap brainpower and not risking any human lives."

"There would be advantages in undersea exploration, also," said Alan. "Pressure wouldn't be as important for such machines because of their small surface area."

"You just want to look a bug in the eye," accused Julio. He stared at a video monitor tuned to the winged microbot that Rick was playing with. The room, seen through the insect-shaped robot's visual sensors, surged and soared on the screen.

"Will it fly on its own?" asked Rick. "Let's see if I can make it glide." He turned and started across the huge room. Tom saw the potential danger to his friend instantly.

Rick was moving straight for the spot where the single crystal monofilament line was now strung. The strand could cut through steel without much effort. It would cut off Rick's head much more easily.

"Rick, don't! Stop!" Tom cried, but his friend thought he was joking.

"Come on, Tom, shoot me down!"

Tom put on a burst of speed and crossed the huge laboratory in record time. He dived and caught Rick in a perfect tackle, and they both went down in a pile.

"Hey, what's going on? You trying out for the football team?" Rick sat up, indignant.

"Fifteen-yard penalty for roughing the quarterback," Julio said. He played tight end on the Jefferson High School football team and spent much of his time on the field defending Rick, their starting quarterback, from opposing players.

"You almost ran into another experiment," Tom explained. "I've got a strand of monofilament cable strung across the laboratory."

"Where? In the laser beam?" Rick picked himself up and carefully placed the microbot on the table. He started to run his hand through the beam. Tom stopped him.

"Don't do that if you ever want to throw another pass. Watch." He picked up a steel rod and dropped it through the beam. The monofilament wire sliced the rod in half neatly. "I use the laser beams to show me where the cable is."

"I still can't see it." Rick stared at the cut bar.

"It's made of a single crystal of steel, incredibly strong and held by covalent bonds along the length. And the monofilament is only the size of the crystal lattice on the sides."

"I'll take your word for it," Rick said.

"Let me wrap it up," Tom said. "I don't want to keep worrying about you jokers shoving each other into it. Having two Ricks instead of one would be too much."

"I don't know about that," said Sandra. "Two might be twice as good." She smiled at Rick, and he winked broadly. They had been seeing each other for some time.

Tom put on his diamond-palmed glove and used a special fluorocarbon grease to coat the line, making it less likely to cut through anything it touched. He wrapped the cable around a special reel and distractedly stuck it in his pocket when he heard Alan complaining.

"It's not possible, Tom," Alan said, putting his hand on the base of the experimental molecular compressor. "You can't just shrink those robots down to the size of insects."

"Why not?" asked Julio. "Wouldn't they be a lot stronger? Ants can lift five hundred times their own weight. The microbots look spindly now, but when they're shrunk down—"

"This has nothing to do with size and strength,"

Alan insisted. "Mass. Remember your physics? If you keep the same mass and shrink these down small enough, they'd have a density greater than lead. They'd never be able to move."

"That's why you see only a fraction of the molecular compressor," Tom said. "This part sends out the shrinking rays, but its brain is a mainframe computer. I take a molecular 'picture' of what I'm shrinking and use Heisenberg's Uncertainty Principle."

"Wait, I'm getting a headache. First there was that monotonous filament stuff and now quantum mechanics," said Rick.

Patiently Tom explained. "You can never tell exactly where a molecule is and how fast it's moving—that's what the Uncertainty Principle says. I take advantage of that and allow only a small portion of the possible states to exist. The 'balance' is digitally stored in the computer and returned when I reverse the molecular compressor."

"It's like storing a package of cookies in a jar, but keeping out one or two to eat?" asked Rick.

"Is food all you ever think about?" asked Julio. "There are more important things." Julio smiled at Sandra, but she was looking at Tom's microbots and didn't see.

"That's one way of thinking about it," said Tom. "I could show you the math, but—"

"Give us a demonstration," Alan suggested. "I don't believe this will work."

"Well, why not?" Tom came to a quick decision. Rob had finished installing the last of the computer chips, and the microbots were ready to be shrunk. But Tom hesitated. The remote controller worked, but he needed more data before he risked exposing his insectlike robots to the compressor's ray.

"Shrink Rick down to size," suggested Julio. "His head's way too big."

"Orb, come here," Tom ordered. The spherical data module slid along the wall and stopped at his shoulder. Seeing Rick's surprise at the way Orb moved, Tom explained.

"Since this is a new lab, I fixed Orb with a transport system so he doesn't have to depend on Rob. Superconducting strips let him levitate and move wherever I've laid down the tracks. He's got an internal tank of liquid nitrogen to maintain the superconductors and—"

"Are you going to tell us about your robot or show us the molecular compressor?" asked Alan. "I don't think it'll work."

"If Tom says it works, I believe him," Rick said. "He knows what he's doing." Rick turned expectantly to Tom.

"I'll use Orb as my first experiment in molecular compression," Tom said. "Orb has an internal radio as well as speech devices and can report what happens."

"This device is untried, Tom," the silvery sphere said. "Please be careful. You know how unstable my circuits can be in unknown situations."

Julio laughed. "He's getting cold feet."

"He's always got cold feet, from the liquid nitrogen," said Rick. "He's getting an upset stomach."

Tom let his friends continue joking while he set up the table for the experiment. He positioned Orb at the focus of the molecular compressor. Using his controller, he turned on the machine. The hum coming from the device turned into a bone-shaking vibration Tom felt deep inside. Twin beams of red and green came together, leapt from the cone, and focused on Orb.

"Report via radio, Orb," Tom said, turning on data recorders. He fiddled with a receiver to get the robot's transmission, then turned up the volume for his friends to hear. Orb's words echoed from the speaker Tom had put next to the molecular compressor.

"I feel strange, as if my circuits are failing. However, internal checks show all is well."

Tom turned up the power. The red-and-green beam intensified, and Orb began to shimmer.

"Look at that! It's working!" cried Julio.

"Keep talking, Orb. Report everything."

"The sensation has gone away. Internal checks are within limits. The light coming to my sensors is changing in intensity and wavelength."

"He's getting smaller." Sandra crowded close to watch as Orb shrank visibly. Its basketball size turned into a softball, then a baseball. Bathed in the relentless beam, Orb became even smaller.

Then a loud burst of static over the speaker almost deafened Tom. He spun the dials on his receiver. "Orb, what's wrong? Orb!" Stricken, he turned to the others and said, "Orb's stopped sending a signal. We've lost him!"

3

"TOM, WHAT HAPPENED?" RICK CANTWELL STARED at the speaker as if he could look inside it to find what had gone wrong.

"I've lost radio contact," Tom said grimly. He used his remote controller to stop the molecular compressor. The red-and-green beam winked out of existence, but the damage was done. Orb had shrunk to the size of a pinhead.

Tom swung around and used his controller to turn on the laser beams he'd used to locate his monofilament line. The beams danced across the room and left hazy trails as the light scattered off dust in the air. Sweat beaded Tom's forehead as he worked to pinpoint Orb.

"There it is, Tom. I see Orb," said Julio, bending down and looking along the tabletop. "It's hardly as big as a dust speck."

With Julio's directions, Tom guided the laser beams to Orb. He used his controller again and restarted the machine. A blue-and-yellow beam flashed out this time, but nothing happened.

"Isn't it supposed to be getting bigger?" asked Alan.

"That wasn't Orb," Tom said, his heart sinking. He stepped back and looked at the table, his mind racing. What had gone wrong? Rick's staring at the speaker gave him the answer.

"Change the frequency! Rick, turn up the radio controls all the way. Get the highest frequency you can. Orb can receive into the high FM."

"Okay, but if Orb's radio isn't working on the usual circuit, why should this work?" Rick fell silent when the speaker squawked with static and Orb's precise words boomed forth.

"Thank you, Tom. I was beginning to feel very alone. Please tell me what happened."

"Tell us all," Alan said. "I don't understand."

"When Orb shrank, so did its receiving and transmitting antennas. It saw the normal radio waves as growing longer and longer, though *they* hadn't changed. It had."

"So you shifted to a frequency so high it could receive again?" asked Rick.

"Higher frequency, shorter wavelength, and more energy," said Tom. "I'll try to home in on Orb." He worked frantically, using both the radio signal and the laser beams. He suddenly stopped and stepped back, a smile on his lips.

"Did you find Orb?" asked Sandra.

"Let's try the molecular compressor again," said Tom. He turned on the machine, and the blue-and-yellow ray leapt out to a different spot on the table. In seconds Tom and his friends let out a cheer of joy. Orb was there, returning to its ordinary size.

"That was a close call," Tom said when the molecular compressor clicked off automatically, indicating Orb had been returned to full size.

"You needn't have worried, Tom. It was only a small risk," Orb said.

"Have you programmed it for making jokes?" asked Julio.

Amused, Tom shook his head. At times Orb, was a more independent thinker than even he realized. "Tell us what happened, Orb. Report in full."

"My complete data dump has already gone into Megatron's memory," Orb said, referring to the supercomputer that ran all Swift Enterprises' automatic equipment. Tom used the massive computer for his extensive computing needs.

"Give a summary, then," Tom said.

"All systems functioned perfectly. When radio contact was lost, I searched all possible frequencies until your request for information was received."

"Nothing went wrong? Nothing at all?" pressed Tom. He worried that there might have been something more than the change in size affecting communication.

"My self-test program reveals no damage," Orb said.

"That's a relief. I guess the molecular compressor works."

"It's a good thing I don't bet," said Alan. "I'd have lost this one. Congratulations, Tom. This is a major invention. You not only reduced your robot to the size of a pinhead, you brought it back to full size."

"Does that work on any pinhead?" asked Julio. "If it does, how about turning your contraption on Rick. The coach keeps telling him he's a pinhead for calling so many lousy plays."

"I'd show you who's a pinhead," retorted Rick, "but I'm too hungry. Let's celebrate Orb's return with some fast food." Rick rested his hand on the round robot. Orb released a tiny silver plume of cooling vapor in response.

"For once, he's right," Tom said. "I could go for lunch right now."

"Then it's settled," cried Rick. "Pizza, with triple everything. And it's Tom's treat!" He crossed the lab to the telephone on the wall and dialed Speedy Pizza Delivery's number from memory.

"How long before they get here?" asked Julio. "I want a head start. Otherwise, the black hole over there'll eat it all."

"Speedy's the best," said Rick. He made a big deal of checking his watch. "Fifteen minutes,

26

or the pizza's free," he said. "That leaves them thirteen minutes to deliver—they cook the pizza in the truck on the way. Let's wait for them at the gate," he said, looking at Sandra.

Rick and Sandra left after getting some money from Tom. Julio looked from where Tom and Alan huddled together, discussing intricate computer design, to Rick and Sandra. He hurried after them, leaving the two tech wizards to their debate.

"Hey, wait up, you two!" Julio called. He ran up the stairs after them. Rick and Sandra waited for Julio to catch up.

"Don't trust me to get the pizza all alone?" Rick taunted him.

"I know how you eat," Julio said, walking on Sandra's left side. "How do you put up with him?"

"I'm getting my license to drive a dump truck. All I have to do is fill it with food, back up, and dump it. Rick can eat his way out," Sandra replied with a laugh.

The trio went to the lawn outside the windows to Tom's underground lab and sat under a shade tree. Rick and Julio discussed strategy for how they'd win the tied volleyball game. They argued good-naturedly until Sandra pointed and said, "There's the delivery van."

Rick checked his watch and his face fell. "They *always* make it in time. I've never gotten a free pizza."

"That's why they're still in business," said Sandra.

"Back in a sec." Rick jumped to his feet and sprinted for the security gate. He skidded to a halt, then handed over the money and accepted two large boxes. Rick started back, opening the first box and inhaling deeply.

"He's going to suck it all in through his lungs before we even get a chance," Julio moaned. Sandra laughed at this. She had been thinking the same thing.

Rick closed the first box and opened the second, studying it harder than he did any of his textbooks. He started trotting back to the others. Halfway there he fumbled a bit, caught himself, and pushed open the lid again. "There's more than—"

Rick let out a yell of utter anguish as he fell forward. In the lab, Tom and Alan exchanged looks when they heard the outcry.

"Something happened!" cried Tom, looking up from the computer terminal where he and Alan were working. Tom swung around in his chair, jumped over the pieces of the other one that had been cut apart by the monofilament cable, and climbed back onto his worktable. He stuck his head through the open window, Alan crowding beside him to take a look.

Sandra and Julio ran over to where Rick lay facedown in the grass.

For a moment Tom thought Rick had been hideously disfigured. Then, despite himself, he had to laugh. Rick lifted himself up, pizza cheese and pepperoni dripping from his face.

"I tripped," Rick said through the thick, tasty mask. He scraped off a little and sampled it. "What a waste! This is the best pizza ever made!"

"Have you ever seen such moves?" Julio crowed. "No wonder he's our quarterback. Fast— and everything sticks to his hands!"

"Why don't you salvage what you can and bring it down to the lab?" Tom suggested.

"Sandra and I will do it," said Julio. "I don't trust Rick after this maneuver."

"So I tripped. What's so clever about that?" Rick asked, still pulling gooey cheese from his face.

"You got one entire pizza to yourself. Who wants to eat something you've rubbed your face in?" Julio and Sandra picked up what they could, left the rest, and Julio carried it down to Tom's lab. Rick followed, trying to clean himself the best he could.

"There's enough for a couple of pieces each," said Sandra, counting the slices. "But we get to start, Rick. You've already had your share."

"Not fair," Rick objected. "A lot of this has grass on it."

"It's good for you. Ask any cow," quipped Alan, picking up a slice.

Tom returned to his workbench with his slice. He took a large bite and then put it aside, his mind already wandering back to the experiment

29

he was planning. He stared at his equipment and knew he was set to take the next step. The microbots were programmed and ready. Orb had proved that the molecular compressor worked. Tom ran his thumb over the buttons on the remote controller.

"I'm going to proceed with the experiment," he said decisively. "There's no reason to hold back."

"Sure there is," said Rick, working on his second slice of pizza. "We're not done with lunch. Say, do you want the rest of your piece?"

"The reduction in size will take a while with the six microbots," Tom said, "and yes, I do want it."

"I've looked over Orb's data and see no reason to wait, Tom," said Alan. "Why not go on?"

The others agreed. Sandra and Julio pulled chairs closer to the table where the six microbots stood. Three were grasshopperlike six-legged mechanical gadgets, and three looked like immense silvery houseflies.

"I've made the adjustments in frequency so I can use the remote controller on them," Tom said. "And the laser receptors on their heads will be a good backup if I lose radio contact."

"Shrink away, maestro," urged Rick.

Tom turned his controller toward the molecular compressor and activated it. The red-and-green beam focused on the first microbot. Tom continued touching buttons on his controller until he was satisfied.

"It's going slower than before," observed Alan.

"I've changed the procedure slightly, limiting how far they will shrink," Tom said. "When one microbot is shrunk, the beam will automatically go to the next until all six are shrunk. Then we'll see how well my remote controller works."

The five watched as the first microbot shrank to the size of a large ant. They cheered. The beam then flashed to the next robot and started reducing it, just as a sudden crash and a loud hissing sound startled them.

"What happened?" demanded Rick.

"I don't know," said Tom. "Everything is going fine. Nothing seems to be wrong."

A second crash brought them around. Across the lab, Orb smashed repeatedly into a concrete wall, sending small pieces of its sensors flying.

"Orb, stop! You're denting yourself!" Tom cried. His only answer was another, even harder headlong crash into the wall. Orb was self-destructing.

4

T**OM GRABBED ORB BEFORE THE SMALL ROBOT** could damage itself further. The silvery sphere spun in his hand, though, and got in another good whack. Orb rang like a bell from a crash to the floor. Tom knelt to pick it up, then jerked back as Orb released a plume of icy liquid nitrogen, almost burning Tom's hand.

"Here, Tom." Rick handed his friend a fire blanket from the emergency cabinet. Tom threw it like a net over the errant robot. It took the combined strength of Tom, Rick, Julio, and Alan to hold down the blanket's corners as Sandra watched anxiously. Finally, Orb seemed to realize it was confined and stopped moving.

"Why did Orb do that?" asked Rick. "I've never seen it do anything self-destructive before."

"It's programmed to sacrifice itself if it can save a human from injury, but we weren't in danger," Tom said, puzzled at the silvery sphere's odd behavior. "The next level of programming tells Orb to preserve itself. It shouldn't have done this."

"Hook it into the circuit tester," said Alan. He wheeled the large device over from Tom's workbench. "Its self-test circuit must have been damaged."

Tom worried that Alan was right. Orb had reported being fine, but if the part of his circuitry that did the checking was damaged, it might have given a false analysis.

"Put Orb on the table," Tom said. "It'll be easier to check its circuits." Rick and Julio lifted Orb, only to have the robot surge away, skitter to the wall, roll up it, and race across the ceiling.

"Catch it!" yelled Tom. "It'll hurt itself." He tried to grab Orb, but the small robot suddenly stopped just above the workbench and then lost power. Like a metallic basketball, Orb plunged to the table, crashing into equipment and knocking Tom's remote controller to the floor.

To make matters worse, Orb tried to right itself and fell off the table and on top of the controller. By this time, Tom had cornered the wayward robot and held it down. Rick came to help lift Orb back onto the table.

"Rob!" Tom ordered. "Give full repair assistance to Orb."

The large robot had been standing silently at the side of the lab. He now came over and began working on the stricken sphere. Several minutes went by while Tom and Rob worked on Orb. Tom finally stepped back and shook his head.

"What is it, Tom? Is it serious? Can Orb be fixed?" asked Sandra, worried.

"Its higher order brain functions were interrupted, probably by something caused by the molecular compressor. I can't figure out what it was, but Rob's fixing it now."

Tom swallowed hard and felt a dizziness that made him grab the table for support. He took a deep breath, but the dizziness increased. He sat on the edge of the table, aware of a ringing in his ears.

"I'm getting woozy," he said. He worried that a construction gas leak or spilled chemicals might be causing his shaky legs and unsteady hands. A draft of fresh air blew in through the still open lab window and revived him a little.

"Tom, I feel strange," Sandra said.

"Me, too," chimed in Rick. "And you two don't look so good, either." Rick wobbled a little as he turned to face Alan and Julio. Julio was pale, and Alan looked as if he had eaten something that didn't agree with them.

"Must be the pizza," Tom said, but he doubted food poisoning felt like this. His blue eyes went wide when he looked over his shoulder and saw that the molecular compressor was still active—and its red-and-green beam was darting around the room.

"Down!" he shouted. "Everybody get down!" After Tom saw that the others had taken refuge behind his desk and a bank of equipment near the monofilament experiment, he followed his own advice and dropped to the floor, fumbling for his fallen remote controller. He pointed it at the molecular compressor in a vain attempt to turn it off. He gave up trying to make it work, stuck the remote in his pocket, and crawled under the table holding the molecular compressor.

"It's right above you, Tom," said Rick. "Need any help?"

"I can reach the power switch," Tom said. He had given the molecular compressor's computer a simple command to go from one object to the next. It had worked perfectly in reducing the microbots but hadn't turned off. The red-and-green reducing ray had swept the room searching for the next object to shrink. It had found Tom and his friends.

He chanced a quick look at the others. They were frightened, but none of them had been in the molecular compressor's rays long enough to start shrinking. Tom braced himself, then swung out from under the table and made a grab for the power switch.

"Tom, look out!" cried Sandra.

The machine's beam flashed past Tom's head.

He ducked out of the way, then dived for the switch and flipped it off. The deep hum from the molecular compressor died, and the red-and-green ray winked off.

"That was a close one, Tom," said Rick, breathing a sigh of relief. "I thought we were goners."

Tom stood on shaky legs, amazed that they had avoided the direct beams of the compressor. It wasn't like him to be so careless. He took the controller from his pocket and studied it.

"Orb damaged the remote when he fell on it," Tom said, shaking the small device. "That might have caused all the trouble."

"I felt rubbery in the knees," said Julio. "Sort of like the time I got my bell rung during the last game of the season."

"Sandra, Alan, Rick?" Tom looked from his sister to the others. "What did you feel?"

"Like I was walking on a bowl of gelatin," Rick said. "Lime gelatin, maybe with some whipped cream on it. And there was fruit underfoot, lumps of it that—"

"Very funny," Alan interrupted. "This is serious stuff. I got dizzy, but I feel fine now."

They all did. Tom dismissed their shared giddiness as coincidence or maybe just a result of the stress of seeing Orb bashing into the wall. Apparently none of them had been exposed long enough to the molecular compressor's rays to begin shrinking.

"Shrinking!" Tom shouted. "The microbots—

they've been reduced to insect size. Where are they?" He searched the workbench carefully but didn't find them.

"They can't have gone far, since they're so tiny," said Alan. "Will your controller work?"

Tom pulled it from his pocket again and began working frantically. He had made the necessary frequency adjustments so the microbots would receive his signal, but nothing worked. The more he fiddled with the remote controller, the less sure he was that anything was happening.

"There—there's one!" Sandra jumped up and pointed to the wall under the open window. She scrambled onto the workbench and snatched up the tiny robot. "What do I do with this one?"

Tom looked around, then pointed to a metal box. Opening the lid, he said, "Put it inside." After Sandra dropped the small microbot, he shut the lid so it couldn't escape.

"Hey, I've got another one," Alan shouted. "I trapped it as it flew around in the far corner of the lab." He held his cupped hands so he could add his flying microbot to the crawling one Sandra had captured.

But there was no sign of the other microbots. Tom knew a hit-or-miss hunt wouldn't do. He tried using the laser beams to seek out the tiny microbots, but he had the same trouble that he'd had locating Orb in its reduced state. There just was too much territory in the huge lab to cover quickly.

"Rob, find the microbots," he ordered. Tom began working on his remote controller. It looked as if it would be his only chance to regain command of the remaining four minuscule robots.

"Tom," reported Rob, "two have gone out the window, and the other two are following."

"Close the window. Slam it!"

Julio rushed to obey, but he collided with Alan. Tom tried focusing his laser beams on the open window to track the fleeing microbots. He saw nothing.

"Listen," said Rick. "Hear that? It's a humming sound, like a mosquito."

"A flying microbot," said Tom. "Catch it!"

They swatted and flailed around but found nothing in the air. Tom pried off the cover of his controller and worked feverishly to repair the damage inside. His work was makeshift at best, but it would have to do if he wanted to recover any of his microbots.

"Tom," Rob said, "both crawling microbots have left the lab, going after the two flying microbots."

"The window's still open. I thought you closed it," Julio said accusingly at Alan.

"You were going to do it," Alan snapped.

"There's no need to argue," Tom said dejectedly. "All four of the microbots have escaped out the window. We've got to find them fast. They're so tiny that they probably won't last ten minutes outside. A gust of wind, a maintenance robot making its rounds and crushing them—there's no telling what might happen."

"If they're in the grass, how can we find them?" asked Rick.

Tom wasted no time on further talk. He ran from the lab, motioning for the others to follow. They would have to find four moving needles in a vast green haystack.

5

TOM STOOD ON THE BROAD LAWN OUTSIDE HIS laboratory window and worried how to find the four microbots. The thick, grassy lawn could have been used for a football field, which was why he and his friends had chosen it for their volleyball games. Low shrubs and trees dotted the area and provided ample hiding places for any microbot.

"Can they move fast enough to get to the gate?" asked Rick.

"No, not in their reduced size," Tom said. "But if they're out long enough, there's no telling where they might end up. They're programmed to keep going until their batteries drain." He pushed the Recall button on his remote controller, but none of the microbots responded. The controller was still glitching from Orb's crash landing on it.

Alan came over and said, "I have done some calculations, Tom. It would take the crawling microbots almost an hour to reach the road, if they went directly for it. I made my assumptions about the microbots' speed based on insects of the same size."

"What about the flying ones?" asked Julio. "A bug can fly faster than it can crawl." He dropped to his knees and began searching.

"He's got a point, and it's not just on top of his head," said Rick. "We can't search the ground and the air. If the flying robots came out the lab window and flew straight up, they're long gone."

"The wind," muttered Tom, thinking out loud. "The wind might catch them. Insects float on the wind faster than they can fly."

"Don't forget big birds," Alan said. "They don't fly all the time. They soar on thermals and save energy that way."

"That means the flying microbots' batteries might not go dead as quickly as the two crawling along the ground," Sandra said.

"We'll worry about the flying microbots later," Tom said, coming to a quick decision. "Everybody check for the two on the ground. Be careful to look before taking a step. Rick, start at the window and work out in expanding circles. Julio's got his patch staked out already. Alan, go out as far as you think they might have gone and work your way back."

"But, Tom, what if he's wrong about how fast they can crawl?" asked Sandra. "Wouldn't it be smarter to start even farther away?"

"There's too much ground to cover now," said Tom. "We don't have much time." They had to find the microbots soon, before the tiny machines were lost or destroyed. He had put too much work into them to lose them now. Even when Alan began sneezing from his hay fever, Tom urged them on until they were out near the volleyball court.

"This isn't working, Tom," complained Rick after ten minutes of searching in vain for the microbots. "We've got to do more, and I don't know what."

Tom pulled the remote controller from his pocket and tried it again. No response rewarded his efforts. He had hoped it might recall the runaway robots.

"Maybe I can fix it, even if it takes a while," he said, fishing in his pocket for his all-purpose tool. The thick, four-inch-long device had a half dozen colored plastic buttons on the sides, tiny niches along the top, and small flexible tubes sticking out from the bottom.

"What's that gizmo?" asked Rick. "I've never seen it before."

"I needed a portable tool kit, but not just the usual screwdriver and corkscrew and scissors.

This is my electronic version of the Swiss army knife."

"A *Swift* army knife, huh?" Rick quipped, intrigued as Tom pressed buttons and unfolded slender extensions. One tip began to glow a cherry red.

"This one's a low-heat soldering iron. I've got a high-powered microlaser I can use, but it drains the battery too fast."

"You ought to make it solar powered," suggested Sandra.

Tom was working on the controller too intently to answer his sister. The luminous tip of the soldering iron touched a connection that might have broken when Orb fell on it. He switched to a micromanipulator to hold other hair-thin wires in place. He finished with a set of probes that measured voltage in the computer chips that formed the brain of his controller, getting readings on an LED display.

"Cross your fingers," he said. He tried the controller.

"I don't see anything," Rick said, "except this pesky fly." He swatted at something flying around his ear, blundering into an aluminum pole and causing the volleyball net to shake.

"Wait! Be careful, Rick. That might be a flying microbot! Try to catch it, not squash it."

"I'll try." Rick looked around for the source of his annoyance but didn't find it. Microbot or bug, it had flown away.

"Tom, I'm getting really tired," Alan said. "I feel as if I've just run a marathon."

"Me, too," Julio chimed in. This surprised Tom. Julio was the last to wear out in any physical contest. And crawling around on hands and knees wasn't that demanding, even if they had been at it for almost fifteen minutes.

"Now that you mention it, I'm getting tired, too," said Sandra.

"Strange," Tom said, working on his controller to recall his microbots. "Everybody, come over here."

The others abandoned their search and joined Tom at the south edge of the volleyball court. Alan sneezed harder and said, "You ought to get your maintenance robots to cut the grass more often. It's getting pretty high."

Tom looked across the spacious lawn and saw the low-slung, streamlined robots beginning their twice-a-week grass cutting. They tended the lawns and shrubs throughout Swift Enterprises' parklike four square miles. Tom worried they might run over his escaped microbots, then dismissed the idea. The tread-driven maintenance robots were an hour or more away. They moved slowly to keep the lawn in almost perfect condition. His father had even commented that the entire area could be turned into an immense putting green.

"How'd you get so tall?" asked Julio, staring at Rick. "You ought to try out for center on the basketball team instead of football quarterback."

"I'm the same size I always was. If you didn't slouch, you'd see that."

Rick ignored Julio and let out a yelp of joy. "Tom, it's back and buzzing me. It's got to be a microbot."

Rick started dancing around as if he had gone bonkers. He waved his arms and might have flown if he'd been a bird.

"Help me, you guys. I'm trying to herd it toward you. Get it!"

Tom tried to establish contact through his remote controller. Everything seemed to work perfectly now, but he didn't see the tiny green light come on to indicate he had linked with a microbot. He fiddled some more with his all-purpose tool, but the controller didn't have any more loose wires or chips popped out of their sockets.

"There it is. I see it!" Sandra jumped up and clapped her hands together, forming a trap around the flying mote. "I've got it."

The others crowded close to see. Tom looked over his sister's shoulder. He felt a little uneasy. Sandra seemed smaller than usual. His chin was high above the top of her head, far more than the few inches difference there should have been.

Sandra opened her cupped hands and displayed her catch. A collective sigh of disappointment went out. She had caught a large lady bug. Its orange shell dotted with black spots shimmered in the afternoon light.

"Let her go," Rick said. "Put her somewhere she can eat other bugs."

Tom watched as Sandra freed the surprisingly huge insect. He had been experiencing odd twitches in his arms and legs but had been too busy to notice. Now he did. And he took a good look at the others.

"Oh, no!" Tom cried. "It can't be!"

"What's that, Tom?" asked Rick.

"The molecular compressor's effect on us was only delayed. We're shrinking—just like the microbots!"

6

TOM SCREAMED AS HE SHRANK. THE PAIN HE HAD experienced earlier was gone, but he felt as though he had stepped into an elevator and found only an empty, endless shaft. He fell and fell and fell.

Twisting around, he tried to see the others. Vivid neon colors swirled around him in a wild kaleidoscope that made him dizzy. He was deafened by a loud roaring, as if an ocean storm pounded against a nearby shoreline. Worst of all was the sensation of being pulled and squeezed in a dozen directions all at once. He was sick to his stomach and curiously elated at the same time.

The dizziness subsided. Tom sat in the dirt, his few seconds of chaos having passed. A sharp pain in his hip made him roll over and see what was causing it. He worked hard to pry loose the roll of monofilament line he had stuck in his pocket. He just stared at it, not wanting to believe what he saw. The almost invisible thread had turned into a cord as thick as a rope.

Tom moaned as he realized what had happened. Huge green-barked trees surrounded him, and they were so closely spaced he'd have to squeeze between them if he wanted to move.

But they weren't trees. They were blades of grass, and they towered above him. A flash of silver made him look up. He swallowed hard when he saw an aluminum skyscraper—one of the poles for the volleyball net!

He remembered his words to Rick just seconds earlier and knew he had been right. The reducing beams had worked as well on the five humans as they had on the electromechanical microbots.

"Sandra!" he called. "Rick! Alan! Julio! Where are you?" His voice sounded normal, but it vibrated strangely in his throat. Tom tried to remember where the others had been standing when he had started shrinking. He had gotten turned around, and they might be in any direction.

Tom kept his cool, knowing that panic would only make matters worse. He pushed aside a few blades of grass in each direction, hoping to spot the others. All he saw was an endless stretch of more grass. Sitting down, he took inventory of what he had with him.

The roll of monofilament thread was a plus. He used it as a small table for everything he pulled from his pockets. His all-purpose tool still worked. That would be useful—it might save his life later. The remote controller had also shrunk.

Retrieving the microbots seemed less important now than finding his sister and friends and returning to normal size.

The only other piece of equipment that might be important was his pocket PC. The voice-activated computer was hardly larger than his all-purpose tool, but it could link with Megatron. Tom smiled as he realized that being shrunk was only a temporary condition. All he needed to do was connect with the Swift Enterprises computer and contact his father through Mr. Swift's pocket pager. It wouldn't take more than a few minutes for the older inventor to get them under the decompressing rays of Tom's invention.

"It looks like you've got an entire lab's worth of equipment," came a familiar voice. Tom swung around to see Rick forcing his way between two thick blades of grass. A long gash oozed blood on his friend's arm.

"What happened to your arm?"

"You know how you can cut your finger on a blade of grass? I cut my arm! Look at it. I had to use pressure to get it to stop bleeding, but it's all right now." Rick flexed his muscular arm to show that he wasn't hurt seriously. Blood streaked his T-shirt.

"We've got to find the others," said Tom. "I'll contact my dad, talk to him, and he can return us to normal in a few minutes."

"What are you going to do, creep up on his sleeve and yell at him?" asked Rick. "He might think you're an ant. Tom, we're *small*."

"We might be small but we've still got our brains—and I've got most of my equipment. It's a good thing I don't go anywhere without a lot of it."

"There they are!" came Sandra's joyous shout. She, Julio, and Alan struggled through the thick grass, coming from the opposite direction.

Tom stopped tinkering with his PC long enough to hug his sister and slap the others on the back. "I'm sorry, guys," Tom said. "I didn't realize the molecular compressor would affect us. When we didn't shrink right away, I thought we were immune."

"We were caught up in tracking down the microbots," Alan said, shrugging off Tom's apology. "And you're right. The robots were reduced in size immediately. Why did it take us almost a half hour to shrink?"

Tom thought hard, then said, "Metal is uniform in structure. The crystal lattices are regular and must be easier to shrink. Humans—and other organic objects—are far more complex, so it took longer."

"The only thing I felt was the dizziness back in the lab, and when I shrank everything weirded out," said Julio. "Otherwise, I feel great!" He bent and pried loose a large stone almost as big as he was. Grunting, he lifted it over his head like a miniature Atlas.

"The smaller we are, the stronger in proportion we get," said Alan. "That's why ants can carry so much. Julio's probably the strongest man in the world, if you consider only his mass compared to how much he can lift."

"I always wanted to be the strongest, and now I am," Julio bragged.

"Great, just great," Rick said in disgust. "We're in a real mess and you're showing off."

Sandra looked at her brother and asked, "We *are* in trouble, aren't we, Tom?"

The young inventor shook his head. "Not that much trouble. All I need to do is link with Megatron, get a message to Dad that way, and we're home free."

"You'd better do it fast," said Alan. "I hear the grass-cutting robots, and I think they're getting closer. The last thing I want to do is get caught in a lawn mower's blades."

"That *would* be the last thing you did," said Julio. "Don't worry. I can save you. I'll just run over to the robot and pick it up!"

"That won't be necessary," Tom said, smiling at his friend. Julio didn't realize the limits to his strength. "I'll tell Megatron to turn off the maintenance robots."

He picked up his pocket PC and spoke slowly into the speaker. The usual reply telling him the computer had understood didn't come. Tom spoke more clearly, louder, slower. He knew that voice-recognition equipment was often affected by emotion.

"What's wrong?" asked Rick.

"The pocket PC isn't picking up my voice commands. And it doesn't have a keyboard. I don't know why it isn't working. Orb didn't crash into it like he did my remote controller."

Then it hit him. Tom let out a sigh of relief and pried the back off the PC.

"The frequency problem," said Alan, reaching the same conclusion Tom had. "You've got to adjust it to recognize your voice now that its pitch is higher."

"Right. My vocal cords shrank, so I'm talking at a higher frequency," Tom said, using his all-purpose tool to make the small adjustment. "The PC shrank, too, but it might have been reduced further than us because it's made from metal."

"Why didn't that monofilament stuff shrink as much?" Julio asked, examining the roll of rope-size cable.

"It's a single crystal of steel. It shrank a little, but not as much, because it's already about as compact as it can get," Tom explained. He finished his adjustment and snapped the back onto his pocket PC.

He looked at his friends. The din of the lawn-mowing robots sounded louder now. He held the PC at just the right distance from his mouth and gave the commands.

"Megatron, turn off all robots engaged in cutting grass." Tom waited for a few seconds. The roar of the robots grew. He repeated his order.

"They're still coming," said Sandra, worried now. "What are we going to do? We can't run for it, not through this jungle!"

Tom repeated his command a third time—and the robots stopped. He heaved a sigh of relief.

"Why didn't Megatron respond instantly?" asked Rick, knowing the incredible speed of the parallel processor computer that oversaw all operations at Swift enterprises.

"The signal must be partially blocked," said Tom. "A line of sight to any of the roof-mounted receiving antennas will improve contact."

"How are we going to climb high enough to see anything through the grass?" asked Alan. "There's no way we can climb the volleyball-net pole."

"You've read all those stories about explorers in the jungle," said Tom. "This time you won't have to pretend to be hacking through the undergrowth—you'll have to do it. We'll hike until we find a line-of-sight opening in the grass."

Julio and Alan looked skeptical, but Rick laughed and dug in his pocket. He pulled out a tiny penknife and brandished it.

"Old Machete Cantwell to the rescue!" he

cried. "Which direction, genius boy? I'll take the point."

Tom parted the grass and got both volleyball poles in view, to his left and right. In one direction away from the pole was the lab. The other way led to the Swift Enterprises administration center. But he was turned around and wasn't certain which direction was which.

Then he remembered the path he'd heard the maintenance robots following. Lining up the poles and turning in the direction opposite the lawn mowers ought to give a bearing straight for the lab.

"That way," he said. "Lead on, O Mighty Jungle Lord!"

Rick began sawing and hacking at the thick blades of grass, the others trailing behind. Tom wondered if they were still shrinking, because his all-purpose tool and PC seemed smaller than before and the coil of monofilament larger. To carry the monofilament cable he took off his shirt and slipped it through the coil, tying the loops together. Then he slung it on his shoulder like a mountain climber's rope.

He trudged after Rick, noticing how fast he tired. Tom's stamina usually kept him going, but he was getting hungry and his eyelids kept drooping, as if he hadn't slept in a month.

"There it is, my faithful bearers," intoned Rick. "Our Mount Everest, our Kilimanjaro. We need only scale its majestic height, and we'll have line of sight with everything in Swift Enterprises." Rick pointed to a brass column towering above them.

Tom blinked at the sight. A lawn sprinkler looked entirely different from a bug's-eye point of view.

"Climbing that is going to be a chore," Alan said. "The sides are smooth and don't have any handholds."

"I can carve some into the metal," Tom said, taking out his all-purpose tool. "The laser attachment can melt tiny holes in the metal."

"Won't that use up the battery?" asked Sandra, remembering what Tom had said earlier when fixing his remote controller.

"When better to use it? We get to the top, talk to Dad, and he gets us back to our normal size." Tom pulled out the all-purpose tool and turned on the microlaser. An eye-searing spot appeared on the sprinkler's shaft and a hole appeared. Tom quickly moved up and to the left for the second. When the first few holes were cool, he started climbing, burning new foot- and handholds all the way to the flat sprinkler head.

Rick followed and helped push Tom onto the top. Tom leaned down and helped Rick and the others up. There was room for all of them.

"A great view," Julio said sarcastically. "It looks just like a prairie. There's hardly anything to see but the top of the lawn. Hey, wait, there's our volleyball net. It looks like it's a mile high!"

"There," Tom said, pointing toward the distant administration center's roof. "That's Megatron's receptor antenna. If I can see it, the PC can link with the computer and not have the signal fade."

"What about your all-purpose tool?" Sandra asked. "The laser was getting pretty weak."

"The battery will recharge itself a little bit if we don't use it. What does it matter, Sis? I can always put in a new battery when we get back to the lab."

Tom pulled out his PC and lined it up with the distant antenna. He hesitated when he noticed the metal under his feet beginning to tremble.

"Tom, it's an earthquake!" cried Julio.

"Worse than that!" Tom shouted, realizing with dread what was happening. Before he could warn the others, water bubbled around his feet, and then the sprinkler head popped up. The rush of water hitting them was stronger than any hurricane crashing into an unprotected shore. All five of them went sailing through the water-filled air!

7

FOR A SINGLE CRAZY SECOND, TOM THOUGHT HE was surfing. The flow of water around him, the incredible speed and sensation of flying combined in the same way as finding just the right wave and riding it to the beach. But the impact of hitting the ground took his breath away and ruined any enjoyment he might have gotten.

Tom landed in the middle of a large puddle and immediately fought to tread water. His kicking feet sloshed into mud, and his arms tangled with dead, soaked grass. He stopped struggling and just lay in the huge puddle. His friends were scattered around the base of the sprinkler and were also battling to sit up.

"Is everyone all right?" Tom called. He had to shout to make himself heard over the roar of the water. He had been in heavy rains, but this was the worst downpour he'd ever endured.

"Right as rain," joked Rick, wiping water from his eyes. "How'd we survive that fall in one piece? One second we were on top of the world, and the next it was like parachuting through a thunderstorm."

"We are smaller and stronger in proportion," said Alan. "We can fall from many times our own height without being hurt." He stared up at the sprinkler through the downpour and got a heavy blast of water that knocked him flat on the soggy ground.

"I'll help you," said Julio, but he was bowled over by the rush of water, too.

"We have to get to shelter," Sandra cried over the roar of the water. "We're going to drown if we stay here."

"Maybe not drown," Rick told her, "but we're definitely going to get hammered into the ground real soon." He stood almost waist deep in water. As he spoke, a new watery assault struck Rick and spun him around. He landed facedown in the puddle, splashing to keep from being submerged.

Tom fought through the clinging mud to reach his friend and help him up.

"Sandra's right. We have to get out of this." Tom looked up and marveled at the sight. The spraying water from the sprinkler caught the sunlight and turned it into a thousand miniature rainbows. As beautiful as the water was, it was proving increasingly dangerous for them.

"How? Where?" demanded Julio. "There's nothing but matted grass and mud. And the water's rising fast." He sputtered as if to prove his point.

There wasn't any need for him to fake it. Tom was having a hard time keeping his feet—and the water was rising as it puddled under the sprinkler. He wiped water from his eyes and finally pointed.

"There, over there. We can make it." The small rise with a huge dandelion growing at its summit looked like a desert island rising from the ocean. Tom helped his sister, protecting her as much as he could from the hammering water. Together, they sloshed to the base of the island and waited for the others.

Rick and Alan struggled up, and finally Julio pulled free of the last bit of clinging mud and joined them.

Alan sneezed when they reached the top of the hill and crouched behind the dandelion, momentarily out of the artificial rainstorm pounding at them. He looked up and sneezed again.

"Even being small doesn't help my hay fever," he complained.

"Pollen grains are micron size," Tom said. "We're still huge in comparison."

"I'd hate to be so small that a grain of pollen was bigger than me," Alan said. He shuddered and wiped his nose.

"Now what do we do?" asked Julio.

"I have a good enough line of sight to use the PC again," Tom said. "I got Megatron to turn off the robots mowing the grass. I can get it to stop the sprinklers."

Tom spoke quietly to the PC, but nothing happened. He turned a little, making sure he was facing the right direction. Again he gave the command to turn off the sprinklers and nothing happened. The water was rising rapidly, the sprinklers pumping out more and more water.

"We're going to have to swim for it if you don't hurry," Rick said. "The ground is turning to mud and we're sliding off the hill." He grabbed hold of a dandelion leaf and clung to it as a new wall of water washed over their sanctuary. Julio and Sandra helped Rick stay on the hill. Alan rejected their offer of aid, preferring to huddle behind the dandelion by himself.

"The water's shorted out a chip," Tom said, opening the PC's case and peering inside. "I can see the chip—it's an EPROM. I'll have to reprogram it."

"You mean like Rob was doing during our volleyball game?" asked Alan. "He had an ultraviolet light source and all the equipment in your lab. There's no way we can redo a chip now!"

"Don't worry about it," Rick assured him. "Tom's going to do it, aren't you, Tom?"

For once Tom Swift didn't have an answer.

His mind raced. He could reprogram the chip, but he had to be sure it was completely erased first. Where would he find an ultraviolet light source?

He saw the air filled with rainbows from sunlight diffracting through the water drops. He jumped to his feet and cried, "That's it. We can use a water drop as a prism!"

"How?" asked Julio. "I know light is spread out in a spectrum—that's why we see rainbows. But how can that help?"

"The intensity of the light is a lot less than I use in the lab, but we don't need as much of it. A single pass of ultraviolet light across the open EPROM port will do. I know it!" Tom staggered as more water cascaded down on him. Rick and Sandra helped him stay on his feet.

"Sounds impossible," said Alan. "I don't think it will work."

"It will!" Sandra cried. "We pull down a drop, hold it just right, and get the purple light shining where Tom can use it, then let him reprogram. Right, Tom?"

Tom nodded. "Use a stick or a blade of grass to catch a drop. Let it roll down. Two of you can move a single droplet around, if you're careful. Surface tension will hold the water on the blade in a tight sphere." Tom worked to pull the shield off the EPROM's programming port. He had to be ready when they got the spectrum.

Alan scoffed at Rick and Julio as they pulled up long blades of grass, hunkering down against the water. They waved the blades around wildly until Rick settled down and talked with Julio.

"We've got to do this together. You swing your blade around and catch a drop. I'll try to guide it."

Tom saw that Julio didn't like Rick giving the orders but did as his friend suggested. With a huge leap worthy of any defender at a volleyball net, he jumped up and swatted at a droplet. Like a jai-alai player, he swung the grass blade around and trapped the water. Rick rushed to help him. The surface tension of the water held it in a huge shimmering globe.

"Move it around, there, yes!" cried Tom. Using two blades of grass, his friends got the water drop in the right position to catch the light. A fan of brightly colored light spread out in a spectrum. Tom pushed his PC to the violet ray and pulled off the EPROM's shield to let in the light.

"Is it working?" Rick asked anxiously. It seemed impossible, but the sprinklers were spraying even more water than ever. The friends were partially protected by the dandelion stalk, but the puddle around their islet was turning into an ocean. They had less than five paces of space left—and it was shrinking by the second.

"Got it!" Tom exclaimed. "The EPROM is blank. Let me give it a new set of instructions. The chip controls transmission—without it there's no hope of getting through to Mega tron."

Tom spoke quickly into the computer's microphone to give the chip new instructions. Water lapped around his ankles, and the others huddled close to the dandelion stem. Tom noticed that Alan sneezed occasionally but looked more worried about the turbulent sea they'd have to cross than his allergy.

"Ready," Tom said, holding up the PC. "Megatron, turn off the sprinklers. Do not water the lawn anywhere in Swift Enterprises."

"The water's coming down as hard as ever," Julio said, peering around the dandelion stalk. "You didn't get the chip programmed right."

"That's possible," Tom admitted, "but I don't think so. I'll try it again." Over and over he sent the command to the mainframe computer to shut down the sprinklers. Just as the water reached his ankles, a sudden silence descended on the five adventurers.

"Am I deaf?" Alan asked hesitantly. "No, I can hear you. What—"

They cheered when they saw that the sprinklers had turned off. Tom sagged a little. He had been under a lot of pressure to get through to Megatron. And he'd done it.

"I'm sorry I doubted you, Tom," Alan said, wiping away the water from his eyes.

"Yeah, Tom, good going," Rick congratulated him. "What do we do now?"

"I don't know about you guys, but I'm exhausted. And hungry, too. We haven't been shrunk very long, but it seems like days."

"I've got an idea about that, Tom," Alan said. "It's not that time moves any faster. I can still see the sun, and it hasn't been an hour since we were reduced in size, but being smaller makes time *feel* as if it goes faster."

"You mean we burn up more energy and get hungrier faster?" asked Rick.

Sandra sniffed at this notion. "You'll take any excuse to eat. Being small like this hasn't changed anything about you."

"We burn calories faster," insisted Alan. "Julio can pick up those 'boulders' weighing a hundred times his weight, but it costs him a lot of energy. Small bodies radiate heat faster, so we do need more food. And sleep."

"He's right," Tom said. "In proportion, elephants eat a lot less than birds."

"And cats and dogs sleep a lot more than we do," said Sandra. "It's not because they're lazy, either."

"So I can eat more and sleep longer? Hey, I like being small." Rick laughed. He curled up on the muddy slope and rested his head on his arm. In seconds he was snoring softly.

Alan, Julio, and Sandra were soon sleeping, too. Tom could barely keep his eyes open, but he had to see if the water level was going down around them. Finally satisfied that it was, he slipped into deep sleep, only to awaken twenty minutes later according to his wristwatch—which still worked properly because it was electronic.

Tom stretched and felt as rested as if he'd slept all night. He checked his PC again and decided his major problem hadn't changed. He had to get a better line of sight to be sure of a reliable communications link with Megatron, so that through the computer he could talk with his father.

"Julio, you're awake, too," Tom said, seeing his friend sitting up and rubbing his eyes. "I'm going back to the top of the sprinkler or find some other point higher than this hill. I have to get in touch with my dad."

"We should stay together," Julio said, still half asleep. "Let me come with you."

"I won't be gone long. Tell the others where I went when they wake up. They need their rest."

Julio yawned again. Tom hefted his equipment and slipped down the muddy slope and across the drying grass. He knew where the sprinkler head was and could climb it again to make contact. With any luck, he would be back with good news before the others awoke.

Tom trudged along in knee-deep mud, surprised at how quickly the water had gone out. He found the sprinkler and looked up the tall spire. Climbing it this time would be easier, even if he felt anxious. The last time he had reached the top, he had been blown off by the blast of water. Tom climbed, telling himself that wasn't possible now. He had successfully ordered Megatron to turn off the lawn sprinklers. When he reached the top, he would contact his father, talk to him, and they'd be out of this mess in nothing flat.

Tom reached the summit of the sprinkler and looked down the four inches to the ground. It seemed half a mile away. The bright California sun had already evaporated much of the water. Most of the rest had soaked into a thirsty lawn. Tom sighted the antenna on top of the main building and aimed his PC in that direction.

"Dad, this is Tom. I need help," he said. No response. He worked on the PC, fiddling with its tiny controls. Again he tried, and once more he got no reply. More frantic now, he tried to link with Megatron.

Only crackling static greeted him. He had lost contact!

RICK CANTWELL YAWNED WIDELY AND STRETCHED his aching muscles. He looked around and noticed that Tom was missing.

"Where's Tom?" he asked.

Alan shook his head. Sandra was still asleep. Julio stood, wiped some of the mud off his pants, and said, "Tom woke up before you guys. He took off to contact his father."

"Alone?" protested Alan. "That's crazy. He might get hurt."

"He's not afraid of his own shadow," Julio retorted. "Like some people."

"I know how to take care of myself," Alan shot back. "I've spent time in the wilderness, unlike some of us." He took a step toward Julio.

"Hey, he didn't mean anything by it," Rick

said, putting a hand on Alan's shoulder to hold him back.

Sandra stirred and sat up, awakened by the loud voices. "What's going on?" she asked.

"Tom's taken off to get in touch with your dad," Rick told her. "That leaves us on our own."

"What's that noise?" Sandra asked. "It sounds like a jet engine."

"I hear it, too," said Rick. "Oh, no, look out!" Rick dived and tackled Alan, driving him backward into the mud. Alan sputtered and fought, not seeing the danger.

Rick tried to pin Alan to keep him down, but the hum got louder, and he had to turn to fight off a flying canary-size monster with what looked like a spear sticking from its head.

"A gnat!" cried Alan, shifting under Rick.

The gnat hummed closer, its wings moving too fast to see. Rick let out a yelp when the gnat darted forward and nipped his chest.

"They're bloodsuckers. Stay back," cautioned Alan, moving away.

"No way!" Rick jumped and grabbed the gnat in his hands. The insect hummed louder and fought—and then the sky darkened with hundreds of the blood-drinking creatures.

"Killed it," Rick gasped, staring at his gore-drenched hands. His victory was cut short. Dozens of gnats homed in on him.

"Burrow!" he called to Julio and Sandra.

"Dig! We have to get away. We can't fight them off!"

The trio began digging furiously, the gnats biting ferociously at them. The soft mud gave way and soon the three were mostly buried. Rick turned enough to stick his nose out of the mud to breathe, wondering if the danger had passed. After what seemed an eternity, he poked his head up and saw the gnats had left.

"It's okay, guys. All clear," he said, sitting up. Mud caked over his wounds, which burned like fire. Beside him Julio and Sandra wiped mud from their faces. Both were bloody from gnat bites.

"Where's Alan?" asked Sandra.

"There he is," Julio said, his face dark with anger. "He ran off and left us."

Alan pushed through the grass at the base of the small island, dirty but unhurt.

"Where'd you go?" Rick demanded hotly.

"If you don't look out for yourself, no one else will," Alan said. "I dived into a puddle, and the gnats left me alone."

"This wouldn't have happened if Tom had been here," Rick said. "He'd have been prepared for anything."

"Yeah," Alan snapped. "Too bad he went off and left us."

"Hey, is anyone as hungry as I am?" Sandra cut in, trying to avoid a fight. "I could eat a horse."

"Let's forage!" cried Julio, splashing through

a small patch of mud. "I'll get you something great, Sandra. You just be ready for the best meal you ever had."

"I think he's got the right idea," Rick said. "There's nothing to eat here, unless you have a yen for fillet of gnat." With distaste he eyed the gnat he'd killed.

"We have to eat, though," Alan said. "Our bodies are burning up calories at an incredible rate. I calculate that, at this size, we're living the equivalent of a *day* for every hour that passes," he added after noting the position of the sun. Then he looked around. "Dandelion greens are edible."

"No wonder I'm famished!" Rick said. "It's been more than an hour since I ate—that's a full day! You eat weeds. I'll get some good stuff." He followed Julio's path down the side of the small hill, then pushed through the grass in a different direction.

Sandra yelled, "Rick, wait!" Rick turned around and waved, a smile on his face. Sandra frowned, turned back to Alan and said, "Sometimes Rick can be so bullheaded I want to scream."

"He's right," Alan said, watching Rick leave. "We're all hungry, and sitting here isn't filling our stomachs. I'll show them how to find real food."

"Not you, too, Alan," protested Sandra. "I think we should stay here and wait for Tom. It would be awful if he came back and didn't find anyone."

70

"He can take care of himself," Alan said. "After all, *he* left *us*, not the other way around." He turned to go.

Sandra didn't feel like arguing. She sat on the hill and pulled up her knees, resting her chin on them.

A cry stopped Alan and spun Sandra around. Tom had bogged down in a mud puddle and was fighting against suction to pull his feet free. Sandra hurried to help him, Alan hanging behind a bit.

"Did you get through to Dad?" Sandra asked anxiously, tugging on Tom's arm to get him out of the mud. Alan stood back as if not sure he ought to help.

Tom dropped down on the hillside and wiped off some of the grime. "Afraid not. I got to the top of the sprinkler, but the PC didn't work. I'm sure the EPROM was reprogrammed correctly or Megatron wouldn't have shut off the sprinkler."

"This is a voice-controlled unit, Tom," Alan said with a touch of annoyance. "That's a delicate and complicated circuit. Maybe you can get around it and just send a simpler message."

"Yes, that's it, Alan! I don't need to talk directly to Dad. It's a lot easier reaching his electronic mailbox and leaving a note than getting a voice message through to his pocket pager."

"What if he doesn't read his e-mail until later?" asked Sandra.

"He's due in the office any time now. He always checks his e-mail." Tom looked around and saw that the three of them were alone.

"Where are Rick and Julio?" he asked.

"Gone to get food," Sandra said. "I told them they ought to wait for you to get back."

Tom cut back an angry response, then realized he hadn't handled matters very well. He had to do better. "Come on, Alan," Tom said, "help me switch the circuits in the PC."

Tom took out his all-purpose tool. The battery was weak but held enough power to use the soldering iron. The laser was completely dead.

"You drained the battery using the laser to cut the footholds in the sprinkler," Sandra said. "I worried about that. Now nothing works."

"Not quite everything's dead. If I don't use it for a while, the battery will recharge a little." Tom knew that the battery would never completely recharge, but if he resisted using it too much now, later he might be able to operate the laser on low power.

Alan and Tom worked on the pocket PC until finally Tom looked up and said, "I think this will do. Computers only know on and off like a light switch."

"It's really zero and one," said Alan. "Long strings of binary numbers give the computer all its capability."

"I've disabled the analog circuits—the voice recognition—and turned the PC into a pure digital machine. Do you have the message ready, Alan?"

"Ready," his friend said. Alan gripped the simple on-off switch he had installed.

"This won't be a long message. It takes a lot of zeroes and ones to make up a single letter in ASCII," said Tom, referring to the binary language he'd have to use. He turned on the PC, and Alan began flipping the switch, giving the computer their digital message.

Ten minutes later, they had sent the message. Tom rocked back on his heels and looked in the direction of the Swift Enterprises administration building. Tom knew that Mr. Swift always read his e-mail when he came into the office after working in his lab all morning. Tom hoped that day wouldn't be an exception and that he and Alan had remembered the ASCII codes for the alphabet.

"I'm worried about Rick and Julio," said Sandra. "They aren't back yet. Also, I'm getting really hungry."

"Well, don't worry about Julio. *I* found us some food," said Rick, who showed up struggling up with a huge brown chunk.

"What is that?" Sandra shuddered as she stared at Rick's trophy.

"Don't you recognize a candy bar? The brown stuff's chocolate, and the big chunks are peanuts. I found it stuck to the wrapper I dropped just before the volleyball game."

"I can't eat that. It's got dirt all over it." Sandra shivered at the thought of even sampling it.

"It's not so bad," said Rick, ripping off a

chunk and eating it with gusto. "The caramel's a bit chewy, though."

"We can find something else," said Alan. "It's a matter of being methodical. A grub would provide better nutrition, if properly prepared."

"Sorry, man, we're fresh out of steak sauce," said Rick. He broke off a piece of crumbly chocolate for Sandra, who reluctantly took it.

"Julio's still out there. You two shouldn't have gone off like that, Rick," chided Tom. "We have to stick together."

"Like you did when you went off to who knows where? We didn't know if you'd been eaten by the gnats or what."

"Gnats?" Tom asked.

"You think all this is a Halloween costume?" Rick indicated his T-shirt. Through the grime Tom saw the streaks of dried blood.

Rick looked at the PC. "Did you get through to your dad?"

"I don't know. I left a message for him, but it might be a little jumbled. He's due back any time, so we'll just have to wait."

"How long, Tom?" Alan asked. "How long do we wait before we *do* something? Time moves faster for us." He tore off a piece of Rick's candy bar and gnawed on it. "This will do for now, but what about later?"

Tom yawned. He was tired again. And hungry. He worked on a piece of peanut at the edge of the candy bar.

"You're right, Alan. Dad might be delayed

getting back. Or the message might not have been received. I think it got through, but I don't know since I didn't get back any verification. I wish Julio hadn't rushed off," Tom continued. "Everybody shout. Maybe he'll hear us and come back."

They shouted and shouted, but Julio had strayed too far away to hear.

Julio was pushing through the tall grass, hunting for food. He'd show Sandra what he could do. But everywhere he went in the green-bladed forest, things looked the same. He had a feeling he was getting turned around. Julio stopped for a moment, then realized what had to be done.

Every five steps he bent a blade of grass until it broke, making a trail back. It wasn't much of a way of marking his path, but it would have to do.

Julio let out a cry of victory when he saw a pizza crumb on the ground. He almost didn't recognize it. Crumbs had become boulders at his current size. He rushed forward and picked up the fist-size piece of crust. His hands slipped on the greasy tomato sauce, but he didn't stop until he had devoured it.

Then he regretted his impulsive meal. He had nothing to take back to Sandra and the others. The only thing he could do was keep hunting and find more.

"So tired," Julio murmured. He remembered

what Alan had said about time seeming different, but he hadn't really believed it until then. "Just a catnap, then I'll find some more and take it back," he told himself. Julio curled up on the ground and was asleep in seconds. He never heard the distant clamor his friends made.

"It's no use, Tom," Alan said. "He's either ignoring us or too far away to hear."

"Something might have happened to him," said Rick.

"You're right," Tom said. "Julio might be hurt, but we have to help ourselves. Relying on Dad to bail us out might take too long."

"So what do we do? Send smoke signals?" asked Rick.

"Microbots," Tom said. "Listen. Do you hear that sound?"

"More gnats?" Rick started looking for a new place to burrow. Then he turned and squinted into the sky. "No, maybe not. It sounds different from a bug."

"It sounds mechanical!" Alan cried. "How are we going to contact it?"

"I still have my remote controller," said Tom. "If one is near enough, I might be able to summon it."

"There it is! Up there!" Rick jumped up and pointed at a silvery speck above them.

Tom signaled with his remote controller and was rewarded by a suddenly glowing contact

light. The controller worked. The flying microbot began a slow downward spiral and landed
clumsily a few inches away. It was twice as tall
as Tom now.

"It looked strange before we shrank," Sandra
said. "Now it looks positively freaky." She went
to the robot and examined the ornithopter
wings and sleek body.

"Could we ride it?" Alan asked. "Aerial recon-
naissance would help us find Julio in a few
minutes."

"Too risky," Tom decided. "If we get back to
the lab, I can use the remote controller to return
us to normal size. Finding Julio will be a lot
easier then."

Alan looked uncertain about Tom's decision.

"I sure don't want to stay this size any longer
than I have to," said Sandra.

"I guess not," Alan said, staring out into the
jungle of grass.

Tom began uncoiling the monofilament line
he had been lugging around. "Attach this to the
microbot," he told Rick. "I'll use the controller
to fly it in stages toward the lab window. Then
we can use the cable as a guide through the
grass. There's no sense in us getting lost, too."

"Sounds like a good plan," said Rick, cinch-
ing the line securely around the microbot's rear
section, clear of its wings. "Let 'er rip!"

Tom turned on the controller and started the
microbot's wings flapping. It struggled a few
seconds to get airborne with the new burden of

the trailing cable, but Tom found controlling the robot wasn't much different from playing a video game.

"Here we go," he said, spiraling the microbot up to a good altitude before guiding it for the lab building.

"I can't wait to get some real food," Sandra said. "And take a bath. I'm caked with mud. And—"

Suddenly Tom was fighting the microbot's controls. He tried to steer it left and it dived. He barely brought it out of its plunge when it veered right. The remote controller wasn't correcting the microbot's flight fast enough—or with the proper signals.

"I'm losing control," Tom said. "It's not doing what I want!"

They watched in horror as the microbot looped and took a nosedive straight for a shrub off to the right of the microbot's intended flight path. Tom righted it, but the monofilament line came loose and fell. Then he lost all power over the flying microbot.

"At least it didn't crash," Rick said. "You can tinker with that gadget and get it back."

"If we have a chance," Alan said in a choked voice, standing on tiptoe. "The end of the line fell into a spiderweb."

"So?" asked Rick.

"So look what's coming our way along the cable."

A hairy-legged, monstrous spider came into

view. Its wickedly sharp mandibles gleamed with freshly killed insect juices. The eight-legged horror worked its way down the mono-filament cable toward them, intent on adding them to the cocooned food already swinging in its glistening web.

9

"STOP IT, TOM! DON'T LET IT COME ALL THE WAY down the line!" Sandra shrieked. She tugged at his arm as he tried to jerk the monofilament line free.

"The line is stuck in the spider's web," Tom replied. His eyes were glued to the spider as it bobbed and rolled from side to side, walking the single crystal line as if it were part of its own web. "This end is still tied around the roll. There's nothing I can do to get the other end free!"

"Everybody shake the line," Alan said. "That might dislodge it."

"I don't think so," Rick said, visibly shaken by the size of the spider. "It's walking that line like a circus high-wire walker."

"We can only try," said Tom. "Be careful, though. The line is greased with a special lubricant, but it's still dangerous."

They grabbed the line and worked in unison to send ripples down the cable. The spider was used to such disturbances. The struggles of flies and other insects caught in its web sent out similar waves.

"Run for it," Tom cried. He knew they couldn't fight a spider five times their size. The vicious mandibles opening and closing in front of the arachnid's mouth told him this was a formidable opponent—and one they couldn't fight with bare hands.

"Where? It moves faster than we do!" Sandra edged back and looked for something to throw. The pebble she picked up and hurled bounced harmlessly off the spider's thorax.

"You'll only make it mad," Alan said, sliding away. "We have to outsmart it."

"You're the expert on bugs," Rick told him. "What do you suggest we do?"

Alan had no answer. Only a choked cry came from his lips when the spider pounced. It leapt off the slender cable and dropped directly in front of Rick.

Tom dived forward and tackled a hairy back leg. The spider twitched powerfully and sent him sailing. It had zeroed in on Rick and wasn't going to be driven away from its dinner.

"Take this!" Rick shouted, picking up a small twig and swinging it like a baseball bat. He hammered at the spider, to no avail. From the creature's abdomen came a whirring sound, and silk shot out, wrapping around Rick's leg.

"Break it, Rick. Get away! That's how the spider cocoons its prey!" Alan started forward to help, but Tom held him back. What Alan had said was right. They had to outsmart the spider, not outfight it. His mind raced. How could he ever save Rick?

"Tom, help!" Rick Cantwell cried in anguish as the spider jumped back onto the monofilament line. Rick dangled upside down, frantically clutching at grass blades and anything else he could find to try to stop the spider. But the huge arachnid was too powerful and carried him back toward its web.

"After it," Tom urged. "I know how to stop it!" Tom raced ahead of Sandra and Alan, trying to keep up with the rapidly moving spider. The monofilament line gave it an aerial highway he lacked, but he kept fighting through the grass until he came to a damp patch just under the web high in the shrub.

Tom swallowed hard when he saw the dried husks of insects hanging in the web. Here and there dangled dozens of cocoons—the spider's future meals. And it wanted to add Rick to that larder!

"There they are!" Sandra pointed to the lower edge of the web where the spider was lashing two new strands around Rick's leg. Rick tried to keep his hands off the sticky web, but not being able to fight against his bonds worked against him. He bounced against a dismembered insect leg stuck nearby. Some bug had escaped with its life, but at the expense of a limb.

The spider was too efficient at spinning more entrappping silk for Rick to ever escape.

"Not all the web is sticky, Rick!" shouted Alan. "Grab the vertical lines. The spider uses those to go back and forth."

Rick swung hard and grabbed a strand just beyond the sticky one he was glued to. The spider worked methodically on Rick's legs, but he had both hands on a safe strand and tried to pull himself away.

"Keep fighting, Rick. I'm coming up."

"No, Tom, don't. It'll get you, too!"

Tom dropped everything but his pocket PC. He pried the back panel off it and fiddled inside for a few seconds, then began the hazardous climb up the shrub. Branches dangled low and gave a precarious path up to the web. Using leaves and twigs like a rock climber, Tom got to the bottom of the web, two feet above the ground. The spider was only inches away, but the distance might as well have been a light year.

"It's got my knees, Tom. I'm losing feeling in them. The silk webbing is cutting off my circulation," howled Rick. "I can't even get to my pocketknife. The sticky silk's wrapped around my waist."

"Just another second, Rick. I'm coming." Tom looked at the web, found two safe strands and used them. He brushed a sticky one, ripping part of his pants leg off, but he reached the spider. For the first time, the arachnid took notice of him.

"You're shaking the web, Tom, and it knows you're there!" Alan shouted from the ground.

Tom saw the danger. The spider stopped spinning its cocoon for a moment to turn agilely on its web. As it did, Tom thrust out his PC. Two battery leads touched the spider on either side of a hairy, groping leg.

Tom winced as a flash blinded him and the smell of burned flesh filled his nostrils. The spider recoiled so fast it almost fell from its web. As it recovered, Tom got into better position to attack again. He used the battery leads, this time burning the side of the spider's head. The mandibles clacked menacingly, but the arachnid had taken enough punishment.

It abandoned Rick and raced up its web to the far side, huddling there fearfully. The web shook wildly, forcing Tom to grab tightly on the nearest strand to keep from being thrown to the ground.

"The battery doesn't carry much juice," Tom said, less than an inch from Rick. "But for a creature that small even a few millivolts is quite a shock."

"Get me down!" wailed Rick. He slipped off the safe strand and plunged headfirst toward the ground, only to be stopped by the silk around his legs. He swung to and fro like a human pendulum.

In spite of his friend's plight, Tom had to laugh. And from below Sandra called up, "How much for that cuckoo clock? The one that looks like Rick?"

"Very funny! Get me down before that hairy house-size horror comes back."

"Break off a piece of the web near your legs," suggested Sandra. "That will drop you down a foot or so, and we can reach you then."

Try as he might, Rick wasn't strong enough to rip the web. Sweat pouring down his face, he had to give up.

"Spider silk is stronger than steel," Alan said. "Maybe not Tom's monofilament line, but most steel. There's no way Rick can break it with his bare hands—and there's no way we can get him free, either. That glue the spider uses is *strong* stuff."

"Catch," Tom said, dropping his PC to Alan. "Throw up my all-purpose tool. If the battery's recharged just a little, we might use the laser to cut the web."

"Good luck," Alan said, rummaging through everything Tom had dropped before starting his climb. "It doesn't look charged enough to me. You've got to do something fast, Tom. That spider is looking awfully hungry."

Tom's heart sank. Alan was right. Then it hit him. "I'll burn the web! The soldering iron doesn't take much current at all. Get ready, Rick."

"I'm a born gymnast." The words were hardly out of his mouth when Tom touched the hot soldering iron to the web and set fire to a strand. It parted with a pop, and Rick went tumbling down two feet to the base of the shrub.

If Sandra and Alan hadn't broken his fall, he'd have fallen on his head. "See, I told you I was good. And only the best are smart enough to have catchers under them!"

Tom saw the fire spreading in the web and felt sorry for the spider. It had only been looking for food. He hoped the spider wouldn't be injured and could rebuild quickly. He also hoped that they would be far enough away by then. And with luck, his father would see the e-mail message and rescue them soon.

"You didn't need the pants legs, anyway," said Sandra. "You've got nice legs."

Rick used his pocketknife to cut at the spider cocoon wrapping his ankles. "I'm just thankful I've got any legs left at all. That stuff burns wherever it touched my skin. Let's get out of here."

"We need to roll up the monofilament line first," Tom said, "and get to a safe camp. I'm getting tired and hungry again."

"Forget the line," Alan said. "It got us into this mess. We still have got forty feet or more to cross to get to the lab."

"We take the line," Tom said calmly, but inside he was annoyed. It wasn't like Alan to complain like this.

"I wonder how Julio's making out," Sandra said. "We should try to find him."

"He'll have to get back to the lab on his own," said Alan. "He's the one who left." As if realizing how this sounded, he added, "He'll be fine. He's smart enough to keep out of trouble."

Tom wasn't so sure—and he was certain now that he'd made a bad decision in trying to reach the lab and leaving Julio outside. They had to stick together or they'd each end up in a mess like Rick.

"Let's make camp," Tom suggested. "Away from the shrub." He looked up and saw the spider high in the foliage. "After we rest, we can decide what to do."

Julio Chavez wasn't feeling particularly smart at that moment. He had foraged long and hard, slept little, and hated returning to Sandra and the others without something to eat. But he had to admit defeat.

His only problem was losing his way. The bent blades of grass would help him retrace his steps, but only up to the spot where he had begun the marking. He could see the towering silver poles holding the volleyball net, but the angle looked unfamiliar.

His stomach complaining about lack of food and his feet leaden with fatigue, Julio stumbled into a small field. Muddy spots had dried rapidly in the bright sun, but he hardly noticed that.

"Food! Lots of food!" he cried. Julio's fatigue evaporated like the water around him, and he ran for the piece of pepperoni on the ground. Rick's tumble with the pizzas would save them yet.

Julio dropped to his knees beside the remnant from the pizza and ripped off a tiny piece. He couldn't remember tasting anything as good. He stuffed a second chunk into his mouth and chewed happily. Looking around, he realized that he wasn't in a small field at all but a trampled down area made by a footprint.

He wasn't sure what alerted him, but Julio suddenly looked over his shoulder—and screamed. A large red ant stood at the edge of the muddy flats not six inches away, antennas waving. As if it had radar, it turned this way and that and finally homed in on him. And behind it came a line of a dozen or more ants, all trotting straight for him!

10

TOM WORKED ON HIS REMOTE CONTROLLER, TRY-
ing to find why he had lost control as he had.
Contacting the wayward microbots still looked
like the best way of getting back to his lab,
where he could use the molecular compressor
to reverse the shrinking.

"Still at it?" Rick asked, stirring from his
heavy sleep. "Boy, I really conked out." Rick
looked around, and Tom knew he was hunting
for the spider. They had camped a foot from
the shrub, retracing their route. Tom had hoped
they'd get a glimpse of Julio but hadn't seen
any trace of him.

"Don't wake the others," Tom cautioned. "Let
them sleep as long as they can. We're going to
need all the energy we've got to get through
this."

"Don't be such a spoilsport," Rick said, always looking on the bright side. "I got away from the spider, didn't I?"

Tom didn't bother pointing out that he had rescued his friend. He only shrugged. "I just don't know, Rick. It was my mistake that caused us to be shrunk."

"Don't feel so bad, Tom," said Rick. "You'll get us out of it." He slapped Tom on the back.

Tom shook his head, not so sure. "It's up to me to get all of us back to normal size quickly—and safely. And Julio's off on his own, maybe hurt."

"Julio can take care of himself," Rick said. Tom heard a note of bitterness enter his friend's voice when he added, "Ask Alan. He's always saying we need to go more on our own initiatives."

Tom frowned but didn't respond. He looked to where the lab building rose up like some unscalable mountain. The forty-foot distance to it looked like forty miles.

"Your controller working?" asked Rick.

"I thought it was, but I'm not so sure after I lost control of the flying microbot. I've turned up the gain and adjusted the frequency to better match changes caused by differences in size."

"So give it a try, why don't you? I'm so hungry I'm thinking what a great Thanksgiving feast that spider would make."

"What do you mean?" asked Alan, rubbing sleep from his eyes and sitting up.

"Think of having eight drumsticks all to yourself!"

They turned when they heard a loud cry of fear.

"It's coming from back the way we came!" Rick cried. "It must be Julio!"

"Wait," Tom cautioned, holding his friend back. "It's better to call out to him and let him come here. Otherwise we'll all get separated."

Calling to their friend woke Sandra. She quickly joined Tom, Alan, and Rick in shouting. In less than a minute, Julio burst through the thick curtain of grass, not six inches away. His eyes were wide, and he was panting heavily.

"It's good to see you," Tom said in relief. "We thought you were lost."

"Ants," Julio gasped out. "Huge ants. Red ants. Dozens of them, bigger than I am. I found part of the pizza and ate it, and they came up and they're chasing me. I don't know how I stayed ahead. They're *fast!*"

"Not red ants," Alan said in a whisper, his voice choked. "*Fire* ants. I warned you about them earlier. We're in big trouble, unless we can get away."

"Hemlock," muttered Rick. "You said their venom was like hemlock poisoning."

"It's similar, and since we're so tiny now, it'll be even faster acting," Alan said. "A fire ant can down a full-grown man. Think what it might do to us!"

"Get moving, don't stand around talking,"

Julio said, struggling to get his breath back. "You can't imagine how horrible they are. They're like sci-fi movie monsters come alive."

Sandra let out a gasp. Tom saw the reason. A large red head with wiggling antennae poked through the curtain of grass behind Julio. The ants had found them.

"This way," Tom called, pointing to a gap in the grass on their right. "Run! We can dodge and get away from them."

Alan contradicted him. "Not that way. Follow me. Go straight for the lab."

Tom didn't argue over Alan taking charge like this. Staying alive was more important. And he had to admit they were less likely to start moving in a circle if they kept their goal in sight as much as possible through the tall grass.

They ran until they were winded. Rick had quickly given up using his small knife to hack through the grass. Pushing the thick blades aside took more effort but less time, and they all knew the ants were close.

"We're not getting away. It's like they know where we are," cried Sandra.

"How do they do it?" gasped out Rick. "They can't see us through the grass. If we try hiding—"

"No!" shouted Alan. "We don't dare try that. Ants track by pheromones. They're sniffing us out."

"Their antennae," Tom said, remembering now that ants followed one another by scent.

One ant might find food. Others followed his exploratory route by odor, then retraced their path to their nest using the same scent as a road map.

He picked up a rock. He took a deep breath and then threw the rock with impressive accuracy. The stone hit the nearest ant's antenna and broke off the top portion.

"That's as good as driving a dirt clod up its nose," Alan said. He picked up a rock and took three shots to duplicate Tom's throw. The leading ant backed away.

Sandra cheered, but the joy was short-lived. A second ant assumed the lead.

"We can't fight them," Alan said. "If they get close enough to bite, we're dead."

"The pepperoni," Tom said, looking at Julio. "You've still got some. They're after that. Drop it!"

"But we need food," Julio protested. He swallowed hard when he saw more ants moving toward them. Quickly changing his mind about how hungry he was, Julio dropped the small pieces of pepperoni he had stuffed into his pockets.

"Now let's make for the tall grass and let them eat," Tom said.

The five friends crowded together and watched as the leading ant stopped for a moment and wiggled its antennae at the pepperoni. Then it turned and started for them. Dodge as they might through the tall grass, the ant homed in on them like a smart bomb following a laser beam to its target.

"What are we going to do?" asked Rick, looking to Tom for advice.

"Split up. Everyone for himself," said Alan.

"No! If we split up, the ants will, too, and there are a lot more of them than us." Tom wished Alan would stop giving orders. He needed time to think and wasn't getting it.

"So what do we do?" demanded Alan.

"I don't know what to do," Tom said, bending over, hands on his knees as he tried to catch his breath.

"Julio," Alan said slowly. "Your cologne."

"Will you stop complaining about it, already?" Julio looked back apprehensively. "This isn't some dumb volleyball game."

"Your cologne is drawing the ants," Alan said. "It's so strong they can sniff it out. No matter how much we run, they'll follow it."

"Mud!" Tom shouted, an idea hitting him. "Find a muddy patch."

"Tom's right," Alan said. "We find mud and burrow in it. The ants won't be able to smell us then."

The ants continued to narrow the distance between them until Tom found a large, slippery mud puddle. He didn't break stride as he splashed into it. Alan and Rick followed, but Julio and Sandra hung back.

"Are you sure this is going to work?" Sandra asked. She saw Tom's expression and knew he wasn't playing a practical joke. She plunged in, slipping and falling heavily. No one helped her up.

"Come on in, Julio, the water's fine!" Rick laughed. He threw a blob of mud at Julio, hitting his friend in the face. Julio blundered forward and fell in beside Sandra. Rick and Alan took special glee in smearing Julio all over with mud.

"This'll repay you for all the dirty tricks you've played on us," Rick said. He fell silent when a pair of antennae came through the grass at the far edge of the mud puddle. "Can they hear us?" he asked in a whisper.

"I don't think so," said Alan, "but there's no reason to take any chances."

Tom helped his sister sit up, mud dripping through her blond hair. Julio burrowed deeper in the mud, staying under the filthy surface of the puddle as much as he could. Alan and Rick watched in rapt silence.

"It worked!" cried Alan as the ant wiggled its head back and forth, then trotted along the edge of the puddle, never turning in their direction. The other fire ants followed, obediently trailing their leader. Within a minute that seemed to last forever, the deadly fire ants vanished.

"Safe." Tom sighed, wiping mud off his face. Then he looked at his friends and knew he was a sight, too. He broke out laughing.

"Safe and dirty. What would your mother say?" wondered Rick.

"Are you hungry?" said Julio. "I left all the pepperoni back there for the ants. I'm *hungry*."

"The ants will come back this way," Alan said, "following their own pheromone trail. Let's make for the far bank, as far away as possible from them. Then I'll show you all how to get food."

"Lead on, fearless one," said Rick. "I really like the part about food." Alan responded to Rick's comment with a wicked laugh. Rick shot Tom a puzzled look. Tom just shrugged and began to follow Alan's lead.

They found a small patch of bare dry earth, not too far from the start of another stretch of lawn. Sandra sat down, wiping off mud. Julio hung back, not sure if he ought to clean himself. Alan waved to Rick and said, "This way to dinner." The two left the others and returned a few minutes later dragging a large white grub.

"That's dinner?" Sandra groaned. "I remember one camping trip where we had to eat roots and other yucky stuff. But a grub? No way!"

"Don't worry. It'll be great the way I fix it," Alan said confidently. "You'll never notice the icky stuff oozing down the outside, and the guts inside will taste good. Well," he said, smiling his wicked smile, "maybe not good. The innards really ought to be baked for the best result, and we're short an oven or two."

He fumbled out a magnifying glass from his pocket and quickly built a small fire in a patch of dry dead grass to roast the white-skinned grub. The five were so hungry they didn't even quibble about what they were eating. Alan used Rick's pocketknife to slice off thin strips, which he held over the small fire. Juices popped and sizzled.

"Who wants the brain?" Alan asked, holding up a tiny yellow piece. "This is the best part."

"Oh, gross," groaned Sandra. "You eat it." She closed her eyes when Alan did just that, apparently with gusto. He even licked the juice from his fingers.

Tom finished his share of the roast grub and went to work on his remote controller and pocket PC. He put the controller aside for the moment. It was possible to reach the microbots, even if his control of them was weak. But what he really wanted was to send another message to his father using his PC.

He pried open the back panel to expose the bare leads to the battery. His fast thinking, using the current to shock the spider, had saved Rick's life. Now he had to face the consequences of that bravery.

The circuits in the PC were completely ruined. There was no way to reach his father. The five adventurers were entirely on their own, no contact possible now with the full-size world.

TOM SNEEZED AND ROLLED OVER, SINKING DEEP into gooey mud. He thrashed around until he got his bearings. The small area they had staked out for their camp had turned into a mud flat, the sun drying much of the water. He checked his PC once more, before the others awoke, to be sure he was right.

Nothing had changed. It hadn't miraculously fixed itself while he'd slept. They were cut off from Megatron—and everything else at Swift Enterprises. The only chance they had was to return to the lab and the molecular compressor. As interesting as it was to Tom to see the world from an ant's point of view, it was far too dangerous to explore without preparation.

"Everybody up," Tom called, waking his friends.

"We've got to hike today." He tried to think of it having only been a few hours since they had been shrunk, but he couldn't. They had gone through microdays and micronights, even if the sun didn't agree.

"Breakfast time already?" asked Rick. He stared at the pieces of uneaten half-burned grub left from dinner and made a face. "I hate leftovers."

"Eat as much as you can," Tom said. "We'll pack up the rest, and then it's a hard hike for the lab. It's too dangerous staying out here any longer."

The others grumbled at being rushed, but none of them wanted to stay microsize a second longer than necessary. In only minutes, Tom had them marching in the direction of the lab building, trying to keep on a straight path.

After less than ten minutes trooping through the tall grass, Julio began complaining. "I need to rest. There's no reason to kill ourselves."

"I'm bushed, too," said Alan. "Julio's right. Why get blisters getting to the lab when your father's going to read his e-mail any time now?"

Tom started to prod them back into walking, then stopped. It wasn't fair to keep anything from the others. They were all in this jam together.

"I don't know if he got the e-mail message," he admitted. "Sandra's right when she said he might not bother reading his mail today. Or maybe he was held up and won't go to his office until later—or tomorrow."

"There's more, isn't there, Tom?" said Rick, who knew him well.

"I'm afraid so. The PC is shot. Even with the equipment in my lab, it would be easier to start with a new one than try to fix it."

"So you're out of touch with both Dad and Megatron?" asked Sandra. She shivered and looked around.

"That's the way it looks," Tom said. "We're on our own, with no help from anybody else. I'm afraid if Dad hasn't helped us by now, he's not going to. The message might not have gotten through."

"Or it might have been garbled," Alan said. "I've been wondering if I correctly remembered the ASCII codes for the various letters. I might have gotten a few mixed up."

"You mean all that work might have been for nothing? Great! And I thought you two were geniuses. You're nothing but a pair of—" Julio sputtered when he couldn't think of a name sufficiently vile.

"They're doing the best they can," Sandra said.

"It's not enough. Maybe somebody else ought to take over." Julio stood with his fists clenched.

"Like you?" Rick demanded, squaring off.

"Maybe," said Julio. "I can't do much worse."

Tom saw that he had to break up the potential fight between Julio and Rick. He stepped between them and said, "We can make better time after we rest and eat. We're all getting stressed out. We have to keep our cool." Tom realized that he couldn't push them as hard as he wanted. Rick and Julio backed off, but Tom saw that nothing had been resolved.

"I'll be glad when it's gone," Sandra said, taking a piece of the greasy grub meat with distaste from Alan.

"That's the last of it," said Alan. "We'll have to find something else if we're out another day or two."

"Back to hiking," Tom said, still anxious to reach his lab. He fingered his controller, hoping it would still work on the molecular compressor. He had done all he could to fine-tune it to reach his microbots, but contact was still weak.

"Tom, duck!" warned Rick.

Tom swung around to see what caused the outburst and was covered with a cloud of choking yellow pollen. The bee buzzing him pulled back at the last possible instant and hovered just above him, its stinger menacingly close.

"Get away from it, Tom. Get back!" Sandra ran forward, waving her arms to distract the honeybee. The insect worked its wings harder and lifted a few inches above their heads but remained within striking distance.

"It's frightened," Alan said. "If it attacks and loses its stinger, it'll die, so it's being careful."

"If it stings one of us, he—or she—will be dead," protested Julio.

"Here it comes again," Alan warned. "Scatter! Don't stay together so it can get us all at once!"

The group split apart and ran, Alan diving through a small opening in the wall of grass leading back onto the lawn toward the volleyball court. Seemingly from nowhere, a second bee appeared overhead. Alan put his head down and pulled his way through the grass, turning and twisting to evade the flying monster coming after him.

Tom had little better luck with his attacker. No matter how he ducked and weaved, the bee stayed directly over him. Whatever he had done to attract it, the honeybee wasn't going away.

"How do we scare it off?" Rick asked Tom. Rick picked up a small pebble and started to fling it at the bee. Tom held him back.

"Not like that. You'll just make it mad."

"So what do we do?" demanded Rick. "You're running everything. Tell me!"

Tom couldn't answer. The honeybee dived at him, its wickedly barbed stinger moving forward to stab him. A shining drop of deadly venom gleamed at the tip. Tom waited until the last possible instant, then dived and rolled in the direction opposite to Rick. He was stopped by a thick thatch of grass. But the bee didn't give up.

"Distract it, just for a second," Tom called. "We might be saved! Do you hear it, too?"

"All I hear are the bee's wings humming,"

Julio said from his vantage more than a foot away. He backed off even more and looked into the azure sky. "No, wait. There's something else. Another bee! We're being attacked by an entire hive of them!"

"It's a microbot! I recognize the distinctive mechanical buzz," insisted Tom, pulling out his remote controller. He worked frantically to make contact with the errant robot. Stooping to avoid another dive-bombing by the bee, he stabbed down hard on the button designed to summon the microbots.

Just as he was sure the remote controller had quit on him, the buzz of mechanical wings got louder. The microbot surged past, creating a gust of wind that almost knocked over the adventurers. The sudden rush of an opponent had the effect of drawing the honeybee's attention.

"Go get 'em!" cheered Julio, hurrying to rejoin Tom. "Knock them out of the sky!"

Tom had a few seconds to get better control of the flying microbot. The machine banked sharply and dived on the bee. The second bee flew off, not wanting to do battle with this strange intruder. The first bee was going to fight, until Tom directed the microbot to ram it squarely with its metal snout.

The bee crashed to the ground, beat its wings and finally got airborne again, flying frantically to escape.

"Look at it go," Rick gloated. "He sure is moving!"

"That was close," Tom said, playing his microbot with all the skill of a fighter pilot. He brought the ungainly robot to the ground a few inches away. Only then did he look around.

"Where's Sandra? And Alan?" he asked, worried at their absence.

"Here I am, Tom," came Sandra's voice. She crawled out from a narrow tube. Tom blinked when he saw that it was the end of a discarded soda straw, blown there by the wind. "Alan ran back into the grass. I didn't see what direction he took."

"Shout, tell him it's safe to come back," Tom said, distracted by the tiny neon indicator lights flashing on his remote controller.

"What's wrong?" asked Julio, staring at the controller. "What do the lights mean?"

"The other microbots!" Tom exclaimed. "I'm getting recognition signals from all of them. We finally got into their range." He looked around. They were still almost thirty feet away from the lab. The initial search for the microbots had taken them beyond the small robots.

Tom began working furiously to regain mastery of his flying and crawling creations.

"There comes Alan," Sandra said. But when the grass parted, a huge mechanical contraption lumbered through instead, its six legs pumping in a complex gait.

"A crawling microbot," Tom said. "And there's the second one." Not three inches away lumbered the other wayward microbot. The two machines were twice Tom's shrunken height and were ominous in the way they crunched and clattered, but he had regained complete control.

"I'll land the other flying microbot," Tom said, idling the three he had already corralled and concentrating on the last one.

"Maybe you can use it to find Alan," suggested Rick. "I'm not up for blazing a trail through the lawn again."

"I want to land it and check for damage first," Tom said, bringing in the last of the returning microbots. "Alan is probably on his way back, now that the bees have gone."

The bee that had been diving toward Alan had veered away at the last minute, leaving him shaken on the ground. Alan stood up and looked around. All he saw was grass. He couldn't even find the path he had taken to get to this point. The blades had snapped back upright high above his head, hiding the trail. Alan jumped up and down, trying to figure out where Tom and the others were.

He failed. He started to panic, then calmed himself. Letting his emotions run wild would only get him in more trouble. He tried shouting, then listening. Nothing. He was too far away, having been chased by the bee in a zigzag he couldn't hope to retrace.

"There's nothing to do but find some high ground and get to the building, then find the window to Tom's lab," Alan said aloud to himself. He had his magnifying glass and knew he'd be all right. His wilderness training would serve him well, maybe better now that he was on his own and didn't have to argue with the others.

He'd show them all by beating them back to Tom's lab. Alan started walking.

12

"WHAT ARE YOU DOING, ROB?" MR. SWIFT ASKED. The inventor stopped in the corridor outside his laboratory and faced his son's robotic assistant.

"A dangerous device is being removed, sir," Rob said. The seven-foot-tall robot carried Tom's molecular compressor easily in his strong arms.

Mr. Swift frowned. He had completed an experiment of his own and was on his way to his office to check his e-mail.

"Why didn't Tom deal with this himself? Or did he order you to remove this gadget?" He studied the molecular compressor but couldn't identify what it did.

"Orb issued the warning. This device malfunctioned during a test."

107

"Tom's all right, isn't he?" Mr. Swift asked, concerned. His son managed to get into some real jams. Although he had confidence in Tom, Mr. Swift still worried. He turned toward his son's lab at the far end of the corridor but stopped when the robot answered.

"He is unharmed, sir," Rob said, after processing his answer for several seconds. "Orb has deemed this device dangerous. Dismantling the compressor for later study by Swift Enterprises engineers is an acceptable solution to a confounding series of unknowns."

"Oh, yes, good," Mr. Swift said, distracted. "Let the engineering staff dismantle it and fix whatever's wrong." He watched as Rob walked off, clutching the molecular compressor to its shining chest. Mr. Swift shook his head, making a mental note to ask Tom what had gone wrong. If Orb had ordered Rob to take the machine to the engineering lab, then somebody there must be able to fix the problem.

Mr. Swift took his private elevator up to his office, intending to call Tom. Even as he sat at his desk and tried in vain to contact his son, Tom was trying to find Alan.

"Keep shouting," Tom urged. "He'll hear if he's close."

"I'm going hoarse, Tom," said Rick. "I don't think our voices carry too far. The grass muffles sound."

"I don't feel like I'm projecting, either," said Sandra.

"I should have realized it. Our lungs are smaller, and so are our vocal cords," said Tom. "Our voices are higher pitched, and high frequencies travel shorter distances and die out faster."

"The microbots," urged Sandra. "Get one of the flyers into the air. Alan's bound to see it."

"I guess that's all we can do," Tom said. "Searching for him on foot will only get us all lost again." He started one microbot flying. Its wings flapped harder and harder and finally the artificial insect blasted into the air. Tom flew it like a remote-controlled airplane up to an altitude of several feet, then started it flying in a slow, expanding spiral, trying to make sure he flew it over Alan.

"I hope this doesn't take too long," Tom said, worried. "We have to get back to the lab."

"Don't be such a downer, Tom," said Rick, slapping his friend on the back. "We've got everything under control. We'll make it. What could go wrong now?"

The words were hardly out of his mouth when they heard a distant roaring like an approaching train. It grew louder and the ground under their feet began to quake ominously.

"What's happening?" cried Julio. "No, it can't be!"

Tom ducked as the sprinklers turned on again,

sending hurricane force water crashing down on them.

"You ordered Megatron to turn *off* the sprinklers. What went wrong?" demanded Rick.

Tom's heart sank. His PC had glitched earlier than he had thought. The sprinklers must have turned off on their automatic cycle before. Now he and his friends were doomed to a long drenching—and worse. He remembered how the water had risen before, forcing them to practically swim for their lives. This time would be even more dangerous, since it was the afternoon soaking cycle. Somehow, they had to survive a half hour of watering.

The sound of the sprinklers turning on distracted Mr. Swift. He turned off the autopager, since Tom wasn't answering. He'd have to track his son down later. Turning to his desk monitor, Mr. Swift made a quick check of Megatron's performance and saw nothing out of the ordinary. In spite of Tom's assurance that the massive parallel processor computer could successfully run everything within Swift Enterprises, Mr. Swift didn't quite trust it. Eight million lines of code might have a glitch in it somewhere, no matter how carefully Tom had written the program.

"Note," he said to thin air. An automatic secretary clicked on at the sound of his voice to record his message. "See if we can't invent a silencer for the sprinkler, something to make watering sound more like a gentle spring rain." He turned to his monitor and popped up his schedule, on which two items were blinking in bright red. He had an important meeting with a government research agency later.

Mr. Swift swung around in his chair, then stopped. The second item might be as critical. He used his mouse to run the cursor to the insistent item and tapped a key.

"Just what I need," Mr. Swift said, disgusted. Somebody had marked a practical joke message as top priority. Garbled words scrolled up in his e-mail file. He started to erase it, then stopped. Frowning, he studied the message more carefully. When he finished, he ran it again, finally making sense of the misspellings.

"Oh, no!" Mr. Swift's fingers blurred as they moved over the keyboard. In a few moments he had accessed Megatron. It took only seconds more to turn off the sprinklers.

Tom and the others huddled together as sheets of water blasted down on them, knocking them to their knees and sending them into a mud puddle.

"How do we get out of this?" asked Julio. "We can't stand more of this water torture."

"I wish it were as easy as saying 'Stop!' but it—" Tom broke off in midsentence and just stared at the sky. The sheets of water were gone as suddenly as they had begun.

"You're good, Tom," said Rick. "Why didn't

you just tell it to stop earlier? This is positively ruining my clothes." Rick stood and wiped sticky mud from his tattered, bloodied T-shirt and pants.

"I don't know what happened," Tom admitted. "It came at a good time, though." He checked his controller and found it still worked. The flying microbot circled aloft, away from the effects of the sprinkler. He activated the other three microbots and sighed with relief when they all responded.

"Why don't we ride?" suggested Sandra. "My feet are killing me."

"Why not?" agreed Tom trusting that the two crawling microbots would support their weight. Riding seemed a lot better than walking the remaining thirty feet to the lab, and it would give them a chance to search more territory looking for Alan.

"Sandra and I will take Champion," Rick said, helping Sandra onto one microbot's back. "You and Julio can ride on Trigger."

"These aren't going to be saddle-trained mounts," Tom warned. "The six-legged gait is uneven, so hang on tight."

"Anything beats slogging through the mud," Sandra said with feeling. She settled down, Rick's arms around her waist.

"Forward ho!" Tom cried, using his controller to start the microbots crawling. He was almost unseated by the sudden lurch as his started. Julio braced him until he regained his balance.

"Keep an eye peeled for Alan," Tom told Julio. "Keeping the robots moving together is going to take all my concentration."

Even as Tom and the other three were looking for Alan, he was trying to find them. He had the uneasy feeling he was going in circles and, when the sprinklers had started, he got even more turned around. He weathered the brief soaking, and the first thing he saw when the water turned off was the tall, spiny weed poking up through the grass.

"It's not the Sears Tower, but it'll do," he said, struggling through mud to reach the base of the weed. Alan sneezed, his hay fever intensifying the nearer he got to the plant. He wiped his nose and started climbing. To his relief, he had to climb only four inches before spotting the lab building almost twenty feet away. Just to be sure, he twisted around and saw the twin aluminum poles of the volleyball net supports behind him. He had his bearings again.

In his haste to get down, he cut himself on a spine. Alan tumbled to the ground, his arm burning like napalm. He sat up, but dizziness hit him like a baseball bat. Wobbling, his vision blurred, Alan stood and stumbled toward the lab.

Not three feet away, Rick whooped and hollered like a cowboy riding a bronco. "This is the way to travel. Glad you invented these ole paints, pardner!"

Tom worked hard using his remote controller to move the grasshopperlike microbots in unison. Suddenly he looked up and saw something that made him laugh.

"I need an invention that'll make you less clumsy," he called to Rick. Tom pointed to a piece of pizza Rick had dropped earlier that afternoon. It seemed like weeks ago. They had been scavenging small tidbits, and here was an entire piece out in the hot sun.

"I wish we could get some of it," Rick said. "I'm hungry again. And am I sleepy!"

Tom saw that they had to give the slice of pizza a wide berth. Large black ants worked industriously to haul off the meat and vegetables, leaving behind the cheese. Some worked on the crust and left a small trail of crumbs as they returned with their treasure trove to their hill.

"We'll be back in the lab soon," Tom said. The building's wall was less than ten feet in front of them, and riding atop the two microbots made travel much easier. It wouldn't take them long, once they reached the wall, to find the window to his lab.

He fiddled some more with the flying microbot, swinging it in circles, hoping that Alan would see it. But he held out little hope this would work.

"You're flying the microbot too low, Tom," said Julio. "I can hear its wings. It—" Julio recoiled in horror, his arm shooting up to protect his face. He bumped Tom's hand and sent the remote controller flying off into the pizza.

"What's the big idea?" Tom looked from Julio to what his friend was reacting to. A monster-size bird flapped down toward them, its immense beak opening wide.

Tom cried out involuntarily. The bird wanted them for lunch!

13

TOM SWUNG AROUND TOO FAST AND SLID OFF THE slick metal back of the microbot. He crashed hard to the ground, landing half on damp dirt and half on a sticky piece of cheese from the pizza. Struggling to stand, Tom only got himself more stuck in the cheese, which had melted and turned gooey like paving asphalt on a hot summer day.

"The bird! Watch out for the starling!" cried Julio. He tried to wave his arms and distract the feathered monster, but the bird was too intent on Tom.

"Use the controller," called Sandra. "It's under the microbot!"

Tom saw the remote controller but couldn't reach it, not with the starling flapping hard to reach him. Tom barely missed being jabbed by a savage peck. The bird turned a feathered head to the side and raked at him with the side of its beak, then flapped back and tried to grab him with its claws.

The cheese held him like glue, making a fight impossible. All he could do was twist and turn to avoid the ferocious jabs of the hungry starling. The beak finally found a target, puncturing Tom's leg. Pain shot through him and he sagged.

"The microbot's running off," called Julio. "How can I stop it?" The microbot ran out of control now that Tom was no longer guiding it.

"You can't," said Rick. "I'll get the controller and help Tom!" Rick slid off his microbot and fell to the ground, landing on hands and knees. Nothing worth flinging at the starling was within reach, and shouting and waving his arms did nothing to distract it.

Rick dived like a quarterback sneaking for the goal line and rolled, coming up next to the controller. He held it up.

"I've got it! Now what do I do with it?" He punched futilely at the buttons. Lights flared red and amber on the small box but nothing happened.

"Let me have it," shouted Sandra. "I can use it."

Rick looked at the distance between them, then made a quick decision.

"Catch!" He reared back and made the best

pass a quarterback could hope for. The controller arced up, flashed silver against the sky, and came down in Sandra's arms. She fumbled and almost dropped it, then got a good grip on it.

"Take this, you lousy starling!" she cried, working furiously at the buttons. The red lights winked out and green ones appeared.

A whistling sound drowned out the bird's angry chirps. From above plummeted a flying microbot, wings tucked back for a power dive. The starling gave up its attack and let out a frightened squawk, but Sandra wasn't letting it off that easily. She kept the flying microbot after the bird.

"Help! I can't get off. I'm caught!" Julio fought to get off his wandering microbot but couldn't.

"Let's get Julio before he's out of sight," said Rick, vaulting back onto the microbot behind Sandra. "Just like in the movies where the cowboy plucks off the victim of the runaway horse."

"That won't be necessary," Sandra said, mad at Rick's clowning around. She touched a button and brought Julio's robot to a halt, then started the one she and Rick rode until they came up beside it.

"I'll get you off it," Rick said, leaning over to help Julio. His friend's leg had gotten caught in the wires just behind the microbot's head, pinning him securely.

"Thanks," said Julio, slipping free and sitting

behind Rick and Sandra. "That was great, the way you chased off the bird."

"It was nothing," Sandra said. "If you hang out with Tom you start picking up how to run all his gadgets."

"Tom!" cried Rick. "Where is he?"

The three turned and looked back to the gob of pizza and saw Tom struggling to free himself. The cheese held him like epoxy—and now he had company. An enormous black ant, attracted by the pizza, was heading straight for him.

Tom stopped trying to jerk free of the cheese and applied slow, even pressure. The cheese began stretching like a strong rubber band. He got his feet free just as the black ant loomed high in front of him.

"Help him, Sandra," Julio said. "Send a microbot to help Tom!"

Tom saw his sister turning the crawling microbot around to come to his aid, but he had to stay alive until it got to him. The ant's mandibles clacked in front of his face. He smelled the pungent formic acid ants used to dissolve their food and knew even a light touch of its serrated claws would burn him.

In spite of the cheese stuck to his shoes, Tom got to his feet and reached into his pocket for his all-purpose tool.

"Run for it," Sandra begged. "The microbot'll get to you in a few seconds."

Tom knew he couldn't outrun the large ant. He whipped out the tool and opened it to the soldering iron. Turning it on, he backed away, brandishing it like a torch. The ant reared back and used a front leg to swipe at him. The all-purpose tool went sailing.

Having no choice, Tom ran for it—and found himself getting bogged down fast. He had run across another patch of pizza cheese. Each step was harder than the last. Like a mastodon in a tar pit, he was being trapped. The ant closed in.

"Duck, get low. Let the microbot handle the ant!" Sandra called.

Tom looked over his shoulder and saw the crawling microbot smash into the ant. The insect appeared confused. Then there was no question at all. The microbot moved forward, crushing the ant under it. Twist and flail as it might, the huge black ant couldn't budge the robot.

In her haste, Sandra overcompensated and gave the ant the chance to get out from under. Using its incredible strength, the black ant lifted the microbot's front legs off the ground. This tactic might have worked for an organic foe, but it had never fought a microbot before.

"That's it, Sandra, keep after the ant!" Tom cried.

Applying full power, Sandra drove the microbot forward and bowled over the ant. It tried to fight on, but the robot was too much for it. Sandra backed the microbot off a bit, and the ant limped away, two of its legs twisted and useless.

"Get me out of here!" Tom said, trying to sit up. The springy cheese held him firmly.

"I'll walk the microbot over to get you," Sandra told her brother.

"No, don't do that. This gunk will bog it down. Can you bring the flying microbot down low enough so I can grab on?"

"I'll see," Sandra said, as she worked at the controller. Finally she got the hang of the aerial robot and brought it swooping down. "How's that?"

The microbot fluttered just inches above Tom. He pried off some of the cheese and sat up. Struggling hard, he got to his feet, though he was buried knee-deep in the cheese. Tom strained and his fingers brushed the bottom of the hovering robot.

"Again, Tom. You almost got it." Julio cheered him on. "Jump!"

"Jump, he says. I can't even take a step." Tom gritted his teeth and stretched as Sandra brought the microbot lower. Getting a firm grip on the dangling undercarriage, Tom yelled for Sandra to lift him out.

The flying microbot's wings sped up. Tom clung on as tightly as he could. Slowly at first, then with increasing speed, he was pulled out of the cheese. When he came free, the microbot surged high into the air.

"You did it!" Rick roared. "You got Tom out of the pizza prison."

"But I can't control the microbot. It's not responding!" Sandra worked frantically at the remote controller to regain command.

Tom fought to keep from being thrown off. Although he could survive a fall many times his current height because of his new small size, he knew better than to let loose when he was five feet off the ground. From this dizzying height, he got a good look at the lawn.

Spots of water glistened in the afternoon sun like small lakes. The grass didn't look like an impenetrable jungle from this altitude, but Tom still wished he was on the ground. His hands cramped as he swung under the microbot. The robot flew farther away from the building, but Tom saw the underground lab window they needed to reach less than ten feet away.

He heard a change in the pitch of the robot's flapping wings as Sandra brought it under control. He enjoyed the view from aloft, even if it was a little scary.

The flying robot banked and began a slow downward spiral as Sandra recalled it, using the controller. Tom hung on and enjoyed the trip.

He never saw Alan down below, flapping his arms frantically and calling out. And Tom never saw his friend sink to his knees, too dazed by the toxin from the dandelion spine to continue waving.

Tom savored the slow spiral downward
until he felt a gust of wind blast by him. The
added lift made the microbot's snout rise
abruptly. Then it stalled out and plunged down.

At this speed, dropping off the microbot was
out of the question. Tom would splatter himself
all over the lawn, no matter how small he was.
But clinging blindly to the falling microbot
didn't seem like a good idea. Crash or drop.
Those were his only options.

Tom closed his eyes and tried to come up
with a solution to this life-and-death problem.
Just when he knew there wasn't one, he felt
power flood into the microbot again. The
wings beat harder and started braking—but not
enough. Tom Swift and microbot crashed, and

the next thing he knew, he was underwater. Tom clawed his way frantically through the muddy liquid and finally broke the surface with his lungs burning from the strain. He took a huge gasp of air, paddled feebly to the edge of the mud puddle, and passed out.

"I'll help you, Tom," he heard a distant voice say. Tom tried to focus his eyes. The world still swung in wild circles. He remembered the flying microbot becoming a permanently land-bound robot.

"The puddle," he said, trying to piece it all together. "I crashed in a puddle."

Strong hands lifted him out of the water. He turned and saw the microbot half-buried in the mud. Parts of the fuselage had bent, hinting at extensive internal damage. The robot might be more electronic than mechanical, but it could still be damaged beyond his ability to repair it.

"I need my all-purpose tool," he said, still dazed.

"Don't worry about that," said Rick. "Are you okay? That was an awesome spill. You were totally OOC."

"OOC? What's that?" Tom asked, shaking off his aches and pains.

"Out of control," Rick told him.

Tom looked around and saw Sandra on the crawling microbot. Julio and Rick supported him, and the second microbot lumbered along to join them like an obedient dog. Tom took a step, wobbled, then took a second, stronger one. His strength returned rapidly.

"That *was* some fall," he said, staring up.

"By the time you hit, you must have been traveling at a speed relative to our size of about thirty miles an hour," Sandra said from her robotic perch.

"There's one good thing that came of it," Rick said, grinning. "You lost all the cheese on your shoes."

"It's not a method I'd recommend," Tom said, laughing. "And I'd hate to see what you'd do to remove chewing gum."

"We're about bushed, Tom. What do you say we find a place to camp, get something to eat, and rest?" asked Julio.

"I should fix the microbot. It's bent, but I might be able to repair it enough to fly." He started for the wrecked robot. Rick held him back.

"Tom, it's a pile of junk. We'd do better looking for Alan. We still don't know where he is."

"I'd forgotten about him. Or maybe I just had it knocked out of my skull." Tom tapped the side of his head, as if listening for loose bolts inside. "The other flying microbot still works, doesn't it?"

"Yes, Tom, it does. Want me to start it hunting for Alan?" Sandra asked.

"Go on, though I'm not sure what good it will do. We need some way of getting a signal to the microbot and back, if it finds anything. Otherwise, it'll fly right over him and we'll never know."

"You said it had a sound-activated sensor on it, didn't you?" Rick went to the crashed microbot and poked at it. "Why not program the working flying microbot to respond to a cry for help?"

"That's it!" Tom said, slapping his forehead and immediately regretting it. Pain lanced through his head. "How could I have overlooked something that simple? And I can use the laser in my all-purpose tool as a homing device." Tom looked around, patting his pockets.

"Julio's got it," said Sandra. "The ant knocked it out of your hand."

"The battery might not have much juice, but by now it might be enough for a weak signal. When we get back to the lab, I can set up a real beacon."

"Why not salvage the crashed microbot's battery?" Sandra suggested. "You can use it in the Swift army knife."

"A good idea," Tom said, realizing he had missed such an obvious solution to his problem. The fall had shaken him up more than he wanted to admit. It was a good thing the others were alert to answers he had missed. As he had hoped, they worked well together. He just wished Alan was back with them to complete the team.

"I've got the flying microbot in the air," said

Sandra. "Why don't we prowl around on the ground hunting for Alan? He couldn't have gone too far."

Tom wasn't so sure of that. He hoped Alan could see the building and go for it on his own.

"Let me use the remote controller a minute," he said, programming in the audio response needed to summon the microbot. Finished, he sent the microbot upward in a climb, then leveled it off a foot above the grass. It had to fly low enough to "hear" Alan and yet far enough above the ground to avoid running into anything unexpected. For all the fancy electronics Tom had built into the robot, he hadn't put in terrain-following radar.

"Off we go," he said, watching the flying microbot vanish from sight.

Even as the microbot disappeared from Tom's view, it hummed into Alan's. Staggering, Alan waved weakly. The toxin from the weed was taking its toll on him and making him weaker by the minute. He had pushed himself hard, summoning up every bit of strength and determination he had. But Alan wasn't sure he could keep going much longer. Not without help.

"No," he moaned as the microbot flew past. "Come back. Please, don't go." Alan sagged down, falling to his knees. The microbot had missed him.

Alan started sneezing hard, his hay fever

worse than ever. He tried to stop, to save his strength for the walk to Tom's lab, but he couldn't. Tears ran down his cheeks, and his stomach knotted from the strain.

And then he heard it. The microbot had returned! His sneezing had been loud enough to attract its attention.

"I've never seen anything more beautiful," Alan said, straining to get to his feet. He stumbled and threw out his arms, catching the microbot around its mechanical neck. Unsteady but refusing to quit, he pulled himself onto the robot's back.

Nothing happened. It sat and hummed with power but didn't take off. Alan laid his head on the microbot's and clung weakly, wondering how to order the microbot to return to the others.

"Tom," Rick called, riding on the microbot with Sandra, "see any sign of Alan?"

"Nothing," Tom shouted back. The clanking of his crawling microbot was louder than he had expected. Some design changes would be needed to reduce the noise and improve its movement. "I've lost contact with the flying microbot."

"Can't you recall it?" asked Julio, riding in front of Tom like a maharajah on an elephant. He gripped the robot's frame just behind its head, as if steering it.

"I've tried. The controller's power level is

okay, so there must be some other trouble." Tom started to turn up the gain when Sandra let out a shriek that made him jump.

"What's that?" Julio stared ahead at whatever had frightened Sandra. "I've never seen anything like it."

"It's a worm," Tom said. "A common earthworm."

He had slowed Rick and Sandra's microbot and pulled even with it.

"What are we going to do?" asked Rick. "It's not going to let us keep going this way." He shuddered. "I think it wants revenge for all the times we went fishing and used its cousins as bait."

The incredibly long, slimy brown body wiggled and slipped past, as tall as they were. Tom was glad they were riding the microbots. The worm was harmless enough, but it might have hurt them simply by twisting around and crawling over them.

"Get rid of it, Tom," urged Sandra, tightly clutching Rick.

"Yeah, Tom, get rid of it," Rick said, clearly enjoying this now that it was obvious there wasn't any real danger.

"No need. It's starting to burrow again." Even as he spoke, Tom saw the warm diving down into the soft earth like a dolphin diving hard in the ocean. The worm's tail eventually vanished into the hole, leaving behind no sign that it had ever been on the surface.

Tom knew that finding Alan was important, but the encounter with the worm warned him that returning to the lab was even more vital. The longer they stayed small, the more dangers they would face. Their resources were dwindling as the batteries went dead.

It was a tough decision but he had to make it.

Tom took a quick inventory of what he carried. The PC was useless, and his all-purpose tool now had the crashed microbot's battery in it. Tom thought it might generate enough laser energy to be useful. His only real worry was the remote controller, and how much they had used it. Sooner or later its battery would begin to fade in power. Without the controller, he'd lose control of the microbots—and be unable to turn on the molecular compressor once they got back to the lab.

That would doom them to remain forever small.

"We go straight for the lab, while the microbots are still in good working condition," he told the others. He hesitated to use the remote controller more than he had to, but he had no other choice.

He sent the signal recalling the flying microbot, thinking he could send it out again when they had been returned to their normal size. He had lost touch with it, but maybe a signal would get through.

* * *

The signal caused the microbot to shiver and its wings to begin flapping. Alan was shaken out of his daze enough to cling harder to the robot. When it took off, he didn't even notice it was flying in lazy circles, unable to home in on Tom's signal.

TOM ALMOST FELL OFF THE MICROBOT AS IT crashed into the wall of the building. He jerked awake, not realizing he had been dozing. He grabbed for his controller and halted the microbot, then looked around and saw Rick and Sandra frantically waving to him from a foot away, signaling that their microbot was mired down. It had blundered through another patch of pizza cheese and had tangled its feet.

Stopping their microbot took only a second. Tom let out a huge sigh of relief. He had been more tired than he thought. In spite of being reduced in size for most of the afternoon, he still had trouble realizing time flowed differently. He and the others had lived days, not hours, in their pint-size world.

"There it is, Tom. We did it!" shouted Rick. He slid off his microbot and helped Sandra down.

The cheese wasn't too thick here, and they were able to slog their way through it. On impulse, Rick turned back, pulled a hunk of cheese off the ground and slung it over his shoulder. Seeing this, Sandra laughed. Rick simply shrugged and said, "You never know when a snack attack is going to hit." They turned and continued walking over to where Tom and Julio waited. Along the wall, not more than a foot away, stood the open window to Tom's underground lab.

"No open window's ever looked better to me." Sandra sighed. "I can get a bath soon and be regular size again."

Tom had to shake Julio awake. Although the impact of the robot into the wall had brought Tom around, Julio still slept heavily.

"What? We're there? Already?" Julio's face broke into a huge grin. "We're going to be full-size again?"

Tom fingered his remote controller, hoping it had enough juice left to turn on the molecular compressor. He didn't share his worry with his friends.

"It'll be a few minutes, but we're almost there. Help get the equipment to the window."

Tom and Julio dragged the mostly useless equipment the twelve inches to the lab window. Tom put the PC and his all-purpose tool to one side and dumped the roll of monofilament cable to the ground.

"It's a lo-o-ong way down there," said Rick, peering over the edge of the window. "I haven't been rock climbing in a while. I hope I remember enough not to kill myself."

"Easy for you to say," said Sandra. "I've never been rock climbing. What are we going to do, Tom?"

"We could fly down, if we had the other flying microbot," he said. He thought for a second about Alan and hoped the microbot had located him, but he couldn't tell since it hadn't responded the last time he'd tried to contact it.

"We might hang glide down, if we had a sail," said Julio.

"Or we can rappel down," Tom said, unrolling the monofilament line. "This is still dangerous, being only one crystal thick, but we only have to use it for a few feet."

"It must be seven feet to the floor," said Rick, looking again.

"We only have to go to the table where the molecular compressor is," Tom pointed out. "We've got enough line for that. We protect our hands and slide down to the table, I use the remote controller to turn on the molecular compressor, and we're back to full-scale size again."

"You make it sound easy," Sandra said skeptically.

"Really, Sandra, don't worry. I'll go first and catch you," Rick said.

"Or I can go first," Julio said.

"Let Rick," said Tom. "Then Sandra, then you, and I'll go last." He looked back across the lawn, hoping for some sign of the flying microbot.

"Alan will be okay, won't he?" asked Sandra.

"I'm going to set up my all-purpose tool laser as a beacon. That might give the microbot a homing signal. But there's no way to know if it's found Alan." Tom quickly dug a small hole to hold the device, aimed the laser outward toward the distant volleyball court, and worked on the all-purpose tool. Theoretically, a weak signal was all it would take to contact the microbot and bring it homing in.

Rick dropped the hunk of cheese he was toting and took off his tattered T-shirt.

"I'll use my T-shirt to protect my hands," he said, looking down the monofilament cable. "What are you going to use, Sandra?"

She looked down at her pants. "The jeans are ruined anyway. I might as well turn them into cut-offs." She found a small tear and began ripping at the denim. It took a couple minutes for her to get the cloth wrapped securely around her hands.

She nodded to Tom that she was ready.

"Hey, want a snack before you go?" called Julio, bringing back a huge gob of cheese from where Rick and Sandra's microbot had gotten bogged down.

"I never want to see another pizza as long as I live," said Sandra.

"Over the side. Be careful, you two," warned Tom.

"It's the deep six for this pirate," Rick said, grabbing the monofilament line and swinging into space. He slid down rapidly, jumping the last six inches onto the table. He waved that he'd made it.

"Me next," Sandra said, obviously not looking forward to the drop. She went slower than Rick had and stopped three-quarters of the way down.

"What's wrong?' called Tom. "Go on."

"Tom, the line's slipping. It's coming loose!"

Tom made a wild grab for the end of the monofilament line he had fastened on the window sill. The knot was coming untied.

"Look out, Sandra!" Tom cried, but the warning came too late. The line slipped free, sending her plunging to the table, falling twice as far as Rick had.

Tom and Julio looked over the edge, concerned at what they might see. Tom cheered when he saw that Rick had been true to his word and had caught Sandra as she fell. They sat on the table, shaken but unharmed.

"What are we going to do, Tom?" asked Julio. "The line's down there, and we're up here."

Tom held the remote controller and considered dropping it to Rick. The sure-handed quarterback wouldn't fumble it—but if he did, the

controller might be ruined. And he wasn't sure
Sandra knew the right combinations to use for
the molecular compressor, since they were so
different from running the microbots.

"I'll go get it," he said, an idea coming to
him.

"How? You can't troop around through the
door, down the stairs and into the lab," protested Julio. "That'd take forever!"

Tom pulled at the pizza cheese that Rick had
dropped before climbing down.

"You aren't thinking of using that as a rope?"
Julio said, astounded. "It stretches! What if it
breaks?"

"All I need is one quick trip down." Tom
began fashioning the cheese into a thick line.
He fastened one end at the windowsill, coiled
the cheese rope, and fastened the other end
around his ankles.

"But, Tom, it won't reach. There's not enough."

"Get ready to pull me up. I'm only going to
get one try at this. You know about bungee-cord
jumping. This time I'm going down and coming
back with the monofilament line so we can both
get down into the lab."

"I don't know," Julio said skeptically. Then
he nodded. "Go on. You can count on me."

"I am," said Tom. He called down to Rick
what he was planning, and saw his sister and
best friend holding up the end of the monofilament cable as high as they could for him to
grab.

Tom checked to see that Julio was next to the springy rope of pizza cheese he had fastened to the windowsill, then looked into the chasm. Tom jumped.

"Here, Tom, here it is!" Rick and Sandra shoved the cable up. As he hit the bottom of the rope, he felt the jerk as it tried to return to its original length. Tom's finger closed on the monofilament cable.

"Got it!" he exclaimed. He bobbed down, then didn't go any lower. The cheese had stretched to its limit. It was up to Julio to pull him back up.

But Julio wasn't watching Tom. He stood with his back against the wall, mouth dry with fear. A large spider was walking by. Julio remembered Alan saying only half of all spiders spun webs. The rest were hunters, going after their prey on foot.

"Julio, pull me up. Hurry! The cheese is giving way!" called Tom. He hung upside down, clinging to the monofilament line. The cheese rope started stretching slightly. If it broke, Tom would be dropped on his head.

"I—" Julio couldn't talk. Fear made his heart hammer.

"Julio, I'm slipping. Don't let me fall!"

Tom's voice cut through Julio's fear. He stared at the spider, which moved closer. He saw its furry legs, vicious pincers beaded with droplets of shining fluid, the way it bobbed closer and closer. He wanted to run, to scream and run and run.

Julio screamed, but he also dropped to his knees and grabbed a double handful of dirt and flung it at the spider. The arachnid backed off. Julio charged, waving his arms and kicking up as much dirt as he could.

The spider jumped, caught the wall beside Julio, and scuttled off. It could find something for supper that acted as proper food should.

Julio wiped sweat from his eyes, then spun and dropped to his stomach. "I've got you, Tom. Here goes!"

He pulled hard, gathering up the ropy cheese until Tom wiggled over the windowsill with the monofilament line. Tom lay flat for a moment, then looked up.

"What happened?"

"Nothing, Tom," his friend said, looking up the wall after the fleeing spider. "I thought I'd lost it, but I was wrong. I was bitten by a spider when I was a little kid."

"Was it bad?" asked Tom, seeing the spider high on the wall and knowing the panic that Julio must have just gone through.

"They had to take me to the hospital." Julio looked up, but the spider was long gone. "I never thought I'd have to look a spider square in the eye like this."

"But you did, and you got me out of a tight fix. Thanks," Tom said as he fastened the mono-filament cable again, tugged once to be sure it was secure, then let Julio go down. Tom pulled the last of cheese rope from his ankles, tasted it and made a face, then followed Julio down the line to the table.

He dropped the last foot and landed hard, but he protected the remote controller. Tom got to his feet and found the others clustered together. Sandra was crying, and Rick and Julio looked grim.

"What's wrong?" he asked. "We made it!"

"Tom," Rick said, "the molecular compressor's gone. We can't get unshrunk!"

16

WHAT ARE WE GOING TO DO?" SANDRA WAILED. "Without the molecular compressor, we can't ever get back to normal size!"

Tom stared at the empty spot on the table where his molecular compressor had been. To the side sat Orb. If any source of information could tell him what had happened, Tom knew it had to be the silvery sphere.

"I've got to talk to Orb," he said, walking toward the basketball-size robot.

"Your voice won't be pitched right, Tom," Rick cautioned. "Remember what happened before. You only adjusted Orb to pick up high frequency *radio* signals."

Tom had forgotten that, but he had other routes open to him. He started walking until

141

the round robot towered high above him. Tom hurried to one of the small ports he used for programming Orb. It took him several seconds to pop the lid, exposing Orb's internal circuits.

"Wait, Tom, you can't go inside," protested Sandra.

"Yes, I can. It's the only way to find out what happened to the molecular compressor. And Rob is missing, too. I'll be all right." Tom peered into the dark interior and hoped he could pull off what he intended.

The others crowded the small opening as he worked his way past soldered connections. All he had to do was reset the frequency-recognition circuit, but he started worrying. The heavy smell of solder made him woozy, and a misstep caused him to jump back with a hot foot. He'd stepped on a live connection. Orb's internal voltage was low, but Tom had to keep reminding himself he couldn't take even a milli-amp of Orb's operating current.

Tom reached the potentiometer controlling the audio-reception circuit. The small knob looked immense to him. Tom put his shoulder to it and started turning. He had to get Orb to recognize the most high-pitched squeaks—now his normal speech.

As he worked, Tom felt colder and colder. He turned from the knob and saw white vapor rolling in like dense fog around him.

"Oh, no!" Tom exclaimed. Orb's liquid-nitrogen dewar had sprung a leak. The vaporous nitrogen wasn't dangerous, except that it replaced all the oxygen—and it was cold! Tom had done experiments dropping rubber balls into liquid nitrogen and had been delighted when they shattered like glass when dropped on a table. That could happen to him!

Tom strained to get the knob turned to its limit. His legs were getting increasingly numb from the nitrogen cloud boiling over him. When he started worrying about frostbite in his toes, the knob reached its limit. He had reset Orb's voice recognition circuit.

Teeth chattering from the cold, Tom retraced his path on hands and knees and dropped to the table beside Rick. He rubbed himself until he warmed up enough to talk.

"I did it," he said, turning to Orb's sensor. In a loud voice, he asked the robot, "Where is the molecular compressor, Orb? What happened to Rob?"

"There is danger, Tom," came Orb's immediate answer. "My inner circuits are not working properly. I tried to tell Rob, but he thought I meant the molecular compressor had malfunctioned."

"What did he do with it?" demanded Rick.

"Hello, Rick," Orb responded. "Rob took the device to the engineering lab to be dismantled."

"Recall him immediately. Get him back here with the molecular compressor!" Tom tried to keep from shouting. If the Swift Enterprises engineers tore the machine apart, it might never get put back together right.

"It is done, Tom. Rob informs me he is returning."

Tom wanted to question Orb further but held back. He had to see if the molecular compressor was undamaged, and if the battery in the remote controller was strong enough to turn it on. Tom ran his fingers over the controller, wanting to try it but holding back. He might get only one chance.

"There's Rob," said Julio. "And he's got the gizmo with him!"

Tom watched apprehensively as the tall robot carried the molecular compressor in his arms. He worried that a single misstep might cause Rob to drop their hope for returning to normal size. He didn't have to worry. Rob's repaired leg functioned perfectly, and the robot's gait was smooth.

"Set it on the table, Rob," ordered Tom. The immense robot did not obey. Tom remembered to relay all instructions through Orb.

The molecular compressor's projection cone pointed at a spot on the table. Tom herded the others to the focal point, then stared up at the machine. It had to work. His finger stabbed down on the remote controller's button.

Nothing happened.

"It's broken!" moaned Rick. "We're stuck at this size forever."

"Wait, maybe not. Listen," said Tom. "The

compressor is resetting. It's working, but it will take time." A moment later, Tom saw a blue-and-yellow beam spring from the compressor and focus on Sandra. Tom jumped when his sister yelped and began to twitch—and grow. He wanted to reach out to reassure her but knew better than to interfere with the resizing process. When she was full size, the machine switched off automatically.

"Julio, go next," Tom said, but he couldn't get his remote controller to work. The batteries had died.

"Orb," Tom barked out. "Tell Sandra how to operate the molecular compressor. Explain that the controller's battery is dead." Tom knew that trying to talk to Sandra himself wouldn't work. At best, he would sound like a droning insect to her.

Orb gave Sandra instructions on how to program the proper settings on the molecular compressor. In short order, first Julio was returned to normal, then Rick, and finally Tom. Dizziness hit him, and the kaleidoscope of weird neon colors whirled around him like water going down a drain. The next thing he knew, he sat on the table, his long legs dangling over the side. He could hardly believe he was back to full size.

"This feels good," Tom said, wiggling his fingers.

"You can say that again," said Rick.

Tom saw that his remote controller had been returned to normal, also. He wasted no time replacing the battery with a fresh one. He touched one button after another until green lights winked at him from the top of the controller.

"What're you doing?" asked Sandra.

"Calling in the microbots," he said. "I'm going to decompress them and repair them."

"But Alan is still out there! You can't abandon him."

Tom hadn't forgotten Alan. If anything, this would aid in getting him back. "I'm recalling them, including the flying microbot. Repaired, they can do a better job of finding him."

"There they are, Tom," said Rick, squinting hard. Shiny flashes of sunlight bounced off the returning microbots. "They're both on the wall under the window. They look so small!"

Tom guided the first one to the focus of the yellow-and-blue beam and restored it. Julio moved the foot-long robot to make room for the next one. The beam flashed out, but something went wrong.

"It's taking too long. Look at the power surge," Tom said, tapping a meter on the molecular compressor's instrument panel. "This isn't—"

"Alan!" the others cried. Their friend hung on to the restored flying microbot as if he were bulldogging it. Then the microbot stopped growing, having returned to full size. Alan continued to grow until he crushed the microbot. For several seconds Alan just stared, then he let out a yelp of glee and jumped up on the table, leaving behind the wreckage of the flying micro-bot that had saved him.

"I made it!" Alan cried. "*We* made it! You guys rescued me! I'd never have made it on my own."

"How'd this happen?" asked Rick. "Not that I'm complaining, mind you."

"The all-purpose tool laser must have hit the flying microbot's sensor. I thought this was the second crawling microbot," said Tom.

"The other microbot is probably still stuck in the pizza cheese," said Julio. "We'll have to go get it."

"Later," Tom said. "I can build more micro-bots. I haven't figured out how to build another friend."

"Indeed, is that so, Tom?" came Orb's mea-sured tones. "Rob and I are offended."

"You two are excluded from that," Tom said. He was too happy that they had all made it back to full size to argue.

"Tom, what's going on?" came a deep voice. Tom turned to see his father at the lab door. "I got this jumbled message in my e-mail telling me to cut off the sprinklers." He frowned and pointed at the molecular compressor. "I thought you wanted that thing dismantled."

"Unfortunately, Mr. Swift, the engineering staff refused to work on it without written or-ders from Tom," said Rob. Tom and his friends looked wide-eyed at one another, realizing how close they'd come to being insect-size forever.

"I had Orb get Rob to bring it back," was all that Tom would say.

"This is getting confusing. You'd better have a good explanation for being so filthy, too." He looked at their cuts and ragged, dirty clothes and shook his head.

"Nothing to worry about, Dad. I'll tell you everything later."

"Very well. I'm ten minutes overdue for the last half of a meeting with a Department of Energy representative. Tell me about all this at dinner. And don't be late."

"I won't, Dad. You wouldn't believe how hungry I am." Tom smiled and the others laughed. Mr. Swift eyed them suspiciously.

"Not even a tiny bit late," he added for emphasis, then hurried off.

Tom and Sandra looked at each other and burst out laughing.

"Here, Tom, here's the other crawling microbot," Julio said. He had crawled halfway through the high window and snared the robot stuck in the gooey cheese. It took only a few minutes to restore it.

"That's all of them," Sandra said.

"No, no it's not," said Alan. "There's another flying microbot, isn't there?"

"It was damaged and won't return, no matter how strong the recall signal," Tom explained.

"Wait, Tom, wait! There! Hear it?" Rick swung around, head cocked to one side. "It's buzzing me. The other microbot made it back!"

Like a madman, he darted here and there across the huge lab and finally made a wild grab, his hands cupped together. From the prison made by his palms came an angry buzzing.

"Put it under the molecular compressor's beams," Tom said. "This is getting to be routine."

"Hurry, it's feeling freaky." Rick held his cupped hands under the yellow-and-blue beam, but nothing happened. Then he let out a yelp.

"That's not a microbot, that's a mosquito. And it's draining my blood!" Rick smashed his hand down on the table to squash the thirsty insect. "Why do I listen to you about your dumb inventions?"

Tom looked at the bite and smiled. "Are you going to wimp out or do you want to finish the volleyball game? It's still tied."

"Not for long," Rick declared. "And the loser's got to buy dinner." He smiled broadly and added, "As long as it's not pizza!"

Tom's next adventure:

Wheels of fire are spinning out of control, and Tom and his sister, Sandra, are feeling the heat. He's developed a jet-powered cycle, she's designed a near-perfect flame-reflective suit, which renders its wearer invisible . . . and now both inventions have fallen into the wrong hands!

Someone calling himself Captain Invisible has stolen the devices in order to mete out vigilante justice in the streets. But he is unaware of the side effects—and of the grave risk he faces. Worse yet, if the inventions end up on the wrong side of the law, they could be used to unleash a criminal firestorm of disastrous proportions . . . in Tom Swift #9, *Fire Biker*.